# AGENT ZERO: THE REGION TWO SERIES

## TWO SERIES

### BOOK ONE

JANET WALDEN-WEST

JANET L. WALDEN-WEST

Agent Zero: The Region Two Series Book One

Copyright © 2021 by Janet Walden-West

All rights reserved.

Cover by Black Bird Book Covers

Editor Jenny Lane

ISBN 978-1-7372190-0-2 (ebook)

ISBN 978-1-7372190-1-9 (paperback)

Contact Information: janetwaldenwest@gmail.com

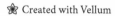 Created with Vellum

# CONTENTS

# CHAPTER 1

## BRUCE

ive-inch height disadvantage or not, Bruce stared the taller restaurant owner down. "My kitchen means my fucking kitchen. You do not fuck with my prep line, my stations, my sous, or my plating. You definitely don't. Fuck. With. My. Menu."

The asshole readjusted his hundred-dollar tie. Probably an attempt to impress upon Bruce that a tie equaled all-powerful owner, while food-spattered coat and tattoos equaled subordinate chef. "After opening four restaurants, I can assure you the menu is always open to change."

"That mindset is why your restaurant needed me." Bruce crossed his arms, blocking the kitchen's swinging door and daring the guy to move one inch further into Bruce's territory.

The line cooks and the sous darted glances his way. They also kept cooking, smarter than their boss.

Sensing a losing battle, the guy took a different tact, angling in to Bruce and lowering his voice. "With the Food and Drink editor doing me a favor and letting slip that she would be here this evening, everyone who fancies themselves a foodie is in our dining room tonight."

Bruce snorted. "Your crowd is here thanks to me."

"Either way, there's enough money and influence out there to buy and sell Scottsdale several times over. All I'm asking is for you to accommodate two diners, with a few minor alterations to their meal."

"You. Get over here." Bruce pointed at the waiter who had brought in the contested order minutes earlier. "Repeat the table's *minor alterations*."

The waiter kept a healthy distance, adams-apple bobbing, but recited back the order. "The gentleman at the table requires you to sub out for jalapeños on his second course. The lady specified crema instead of the featured sauce, and double the amount."

"That's reasona—"

"It's bullshit. Replacing heirloom Cochiti chili with fucking jalapeño? Drowning a delicate jicama and roe under trash cheese? If they want shit commercial food, send them to a drive through."

The owner's eyelid twitched. "That's the mayor and her guest, and I'm sure they're tired of waiting. Make the changes."

The kitchen went still, line cooks stopped mid-sauté, dishwashers frozen. The pop of hot oil carried in the charged silence.

Bruce took his glasses off, polished them on his jacket sleeve, and replaced them. The closest cook took a long step back, but the owner only glared. "You want jalapeños and cheese?"

"Yes."

Bruce turned and swept his arm down the plating station, china flying and shattering, his volume rising with every word. "Then cook it yourself, you hack."

He rolled up his knife case, and stomped over the shards on his way past the open-mouthed owner.

The asshole recovered enough to hiss, "The door is behind you."

Bruce flipped him off, shoving past him and marching through the dining room. Ignoring the diner who half-rose and his, "Could I get a selfie?" Leaving startled silence then the frantic buzz of conversation in his wake.

The dry, early-evening desert air washed over him. He stood his ground on the sidewalk and a crowd of Saturday night revelers shot him annoyed looks but separated and flowed around him.

He rolled his shoulders and stepped out of the restaurant's shadow, his irritation dropping away. The owner had promised Bruce free rein and the autonomy to completely overhaul the concept and menu. Instead, the guy had whined and second-guessed, pushing back against all of Bruce's changes.

Now, plans and possibilities swirled in his head as he crossed the street to the parking complex. Too restless from the fresh ideas spinning themselves into existence like silk from a cocoon, he unlocked his car. He tossed his chef's coat in, then carefully tucked his case underneath, and relocked the car with a soft beep of the fob. Not in the mood to fight crowds for a restaurant table, he cut through the empty garage, aiming for the other side of the neighborhood.

A *scree-shriek* like metal against concrete split the air.

He put his back to the closest car and scanned the parking deck. He also wasn't in the mood for drunk assholes. The weak overhead lighting didn't penetrate the pools of shadow in the corners. He waited a beat. Then another. His phone buzzed and he let it go to voice mail. The shortsighted restaurateur could stew in the mess of his own making.

When nothing moved and the noise didn't repeat, he

stepped out of the structure. Stray cats and those damned bold coyotes were all over this area. Historic iron lampposts and adobe gave way to plain lights and neon. Gentrification hadn't made inroads here yet, leaving a pocket of mom-and-pop owned businesses.

He aimed for a decent sized bar across the street. Shoving its front door open, he almost turned away. Karaoke, shitty vocals, and the impossible to banish ghost of cigarettes long-banned assaulted him. But the well-populated tables and happy vibe promised decent service.

"Fuck it." He cut right, to the long bar. The bartender looked his way. "Bottle of Tipsy Roadrunner." The local brew was the one highlight of this Arizona gig.

His drink arrived at the same time as a commotion on the raised stage. He spared a glance over his shoulder. A guy who resembled the duke in some new historical romance flick his sister wouldn't stop drooling over whistled. The smaller, curly-haired woman with him thumped the surface of their hightop, and clapped.

What had to be the other half of their group hopped onto the platform. Vintage Lady G poured out and he winced. While the brunette on the right wasn't much of a singer, when the one on the left opened up... Shit, she should've been arrested for the way she slaughtered the song.

He still found himself turning, elbows on the bar behind him and watching the performance. As a limelight hog, he recognized the trait when it was stealing the spotlight right in front of him.

Both singers were into their performance. The one brutalizing vocals though—she was in another league. Brown arms lifted high, watch-me pink skirt swirling around toned legs, she moved like the music was part of her. Like she didn't give a shit about anyone's opinion.

His phone buzzed again and he ignored it. The same as he

ignored the woman who sidled close, brushing against his side. He frowned, scrubbing a hand over his arm to wipe away the itch from whatever faux-snakeskin fabric her dress was made of. He sidestepped to keep his singer in view. Hopefully, whoever it was got the message that he wasn't interested as the pair launched straight into another song, murdering Lizzo with the same glee.

The lead singer flipped her hair in synch with the lyrics, laughing and swiping strands out of her eyes, oblivious to how her amber-dark waves fell, as long as they didn't interfere with her performance.

His phone came to life again. The dumbass owner wouldn't dare text after having calls ignored, but Bruce's family certainly would. He pulled the phone out, confirming his guess. He swore as he scrolled, one missed call from the guy, two missed calls from his sister, who had stooped to having his niece text, complete with a five-year-old's spelling errors and a photo with cartoon puppy ears and nose over hers. Like the little shit needed any help being adorable.

If he didn't call, he'd probably O.D. from whatever next-level cuteness the kid came up with. He dropped a twenty on the bar and anchored it with his sweaty beer bottle. Giving the stage a last glance, he forgot what he was doing for an instant. The singer pivoted like she felt his gaze. Her eyes locked with his, humor and intensity shining.

It felt as if she was reaching out and physically touching him. Touching something under his skin, real and alive. Like with no effort, he could reach back, completing the weird connection between them.

His phoned danced in his hand, reminding him of his obligations. More bodies had packed the front of the bar. He aimed for the closest quiet spot, usually behind a restaurant or bar where employees ducked out to smoke or bitch about their boss. He spotted the exit sign and let himself out.

The door opened onto a side street and a strip of businesses. A boot shop, the real deal instead of the trendy stuff tourists gobbled up, took up most of the space. The rest was divided between a tiny jewelry store and a florist, their signs in Spanish. All were closed for the evening.

He hit redial, pacing back and forth through the alternating strips of light and shadow.

"It took you *forever* to call me," greeted him, his niece as impatient as ever.

He couldn't help grinning at the aggrieved, high-pitched complaint. "Since when is, let me check…oh, yeah. Since when is four minutes forever?"

"You're old and don't remember but minutes are looong."

His laugh bounced back to him from the shop fronts. "I'll keep that in mind, Miss Sass-Mouth. What are you and Sass-Mouth Junior up to?"

"A time out. I only told the baby sitter that her frappe was full of chemicals and growth hormones and she probably wouldn't make cheer squad if she kept drinking it."

"You were right."

"I know. Here, tell mom, okay? Loveyoubyeee."

The last sentence ran together. A five-year-old had just played him.

"Love you more," he raised his voice over the static of the phone getting passed off to its rightful owner.

"She's going to rule the world." He tried for stern as his sister took the phone but the amusement leaked into his voice.

"Assuming she can stay out of timeouts long enough," came Marissa's tart reply. "Your niece is also leading her younger sister down the same path. They were literally tag-teaming the sitter. What four-year-old asks if the coffee is free-trade?"

"The kid was right. No teenager, hell, no sentient

6

anything, should drink that fructose-laden, factory dairy shit. Mandy was educating this unqualified nanny on responsible consumption. Give the kid a letter of pardon so she can get on with planning her eventual run for president."

"Does going on to tell this poor teen that her frappe was also definitely the reason she had acne and didn't make homecoming court educational? She sounded exactly like you."

Since he didn't see any damn problem with that, he changed topics. "Did they like the care package?"

"We need to discuss why you think a snowboard is appropriate for a child."

"She asked for one."

"She already has a set of skies for this winter."

"Skiing is boring. Snowboarding isn't."

"Is that really Chloe Kim's signature on the board?"

"Yes."

"How in the world did you manage that from Oregon?"

Shit. "It was from Vail, where she has the training camp. She came in with her coaches for my tasting menu." Aaand, in three, two, one—

"Vail? You were in Portland."

"Yeah, well."

He gritted his teeth at her disappointed sigh, and stayed quiet, juggling the phone to pull off his glasses and clean them on his shirt in an effort to get rid of the smudgy halo around everything. Probably a gift of stale cigarette smoke from the bar, fucking the lenses up.

His sister caved first. "Fine. Mandy found something for you. Send me your Vail address."

"Give me a week or so, and I will as soon as I have a new address."

There was a beat of silence and then, "You were fired *again*? You can't have been there four months yet."

Two months in Vail, one here, and sure as hell no need to give his sister that ammunition. "Chefs move from position to position. I was there to revamp a failing menu, I did, and I left."

He couldn't get her, or his brother and parents, to understand he wasn't some line cook at Applebees, or that he was rarely fired since he was the one doing the firing or quitting. "I go where I can be creative."

"You have got to take your future more seriously, Robert. Skipping from job to job looks terrible on a resume, and what about insurance? Your 401K—"

Jesus Fucking Christ. Not again. "Look, I have to go. Friends are waiting," he lied. "I only called to give one of my three favorite nieces a quick hello. I'll text you my next address."

His sister blew out a breath, possibly as weary of the same argument and the same pointless lecture as he was. "All right. Mom expects you home for her and Dad's anniversary, and I expect you home for at least part of Passover. We love you, troublemaker."

"Yeah you do. Tell Dad his team sucks—I saw them first-hand in Colorado." He tapped the screen, squinting to make sure he'd hit end call, the icons difficult to make out.

After two attempts, he got his phone into his pocket. When he tried to focus, the displays in the store windows blurred and bled together. He blinked hard and aimed for the club door and the brighter lighting.

His feet tripped over non-existent obstacles and he got a hand out in time to catch himself, splinters from the wall puncturing his palm.

Fuck, but had he been roofied? He breathed in, held it, let it out. Getting oxygen to his fritzing brain. Trying to remember when he'd taken his eyes off his drink between the bartender opening it and him drinking.

8

A *scuff-thump* came from behind him. He more fell than twisted, but got his back to the bar wall. He blinked, making out a female-ish shape coming down the street. Except, the only door into or out of the bar was beside him, and the only entrance to the street was off to his left, and damn, he wasn't *that* messed up.

"Hey, can you call 91—" That was as far as he got. The woman...melted. Ran together like a too-warm panna cotta melting. Then reformed and where there had been an ugly snakeskin dress, there were now scales. Her fingernails flashed in the light. The longest nails he'd ever seen, appearing sharp as knives. Gleaming bright as polished mother of pearl.

An impact hit his back. Like getting nailed by a pissed football player. Sending him stumbling, fighting to keep contact with the wall and stay erect. His pulse jacked up until he felt it in his temples.

As his knees gave, the melty person-thing in front leaped on spring loaded legs. Leaving him caught between a wall and lethal knife-nails arcing toward his face.

# CHAPTER 2

## VEE

*I* heaved against the employee exit, fighting whatever was blocking the door from the outside. It finally gave, opening on the guy about to become a ghoul's snack. My momentum propelled him out of my way but the change from bright stage lights to near dark blinded me.

Going off the shadowy outline in front of me, I shucked the silver and chem-coated wire that passed for a lariat necklace. Then whipped it out, in a vicious whirl, wrapping around the cryptid's outstretched hand.

I snapped my arm hard to the side.

Instead of burning through cryptid flesh and bone and neatly severing the hand, the wire caught.

The ghoul jerked back and despite the teardrop emblem that served as handle, scoured a line of fire along my palm. Forcing me to turn loose or lose fingers.

The ghoul reared, putting itself squarely in the weak pool of light, and hissed.

My ghoul wasn't a ghoul. Nor any cryptid I'd ever seen.

A forked tongue flicked, testing the air, then curled back in, between short, serrated teeth instead of double rows of fangs. The cruddy light over the exit sign bounced off of a glimmering dress that overlapped in an intricate pattern. The skirt moved like it was a second skin or—

Okay, not a skirt. Reptilian scales.

"Fuck me," echoed from behind me.

The not-a-ghoul's head whipped from me to the civilian I'd shoved.

Impressive thigh muscles, clearly outlined underneath the scales, bunched. Preparing to launch at the man. In a crackle of Velcro separating, I jerked the small KelTec from my bellyband.

Sighted and fired.

The cryptid screamed, red-green blood ribboning along its chest. It flipped and twisted, spine too flexible, and leaped. Right at the wall over us. In a physics-defying landing, its hands and feet suctioned on. It raced up the side of the building in a sinuous dance, and disappeared onto the roof.

"Holy fucking shit."

I kinda agreed with the civie, but, not the time. "Quiet. Stay put."

I sprinted down the street, craning my neck to scan rooftops, grabbing my phone from in my bra and hitting the shortcut on the screen. Even amid the increasingly inexplicable cryptid weirdness, this was professional-grade weird.

"Did you wisely reconsider your pro-pineapple vote?" My sister and lieutenant's voice came through.

"Emergency patrol. Skyline, headed east." Right in their direction, toward the twenty-four-hour pizza place the rest of the team was hitting for our post-singing takeout while I'd settled our bar bill.

"Ghoul or vampire?" Liv's tone went hard and clinical.

"Unknown cryptid, Level Two fast. Civil on scene, possibly injured. Report in ten." I cut the call and doubled back.

The guy was more or less being held up by the bar wall. And he was still swearing. I took a second to admire both his range and volume. He was more accomplished than our favorite sniper trainer, and every third word from her was a four letter one.

Aside from using the wall for balance, he seemed fine. Adrenaline often masked pain though.

"Are you injured? Does anything hurt?" Despite knowing it hadn't been a ghoul or vampire, I caught his thick right arm, rolling it to check the light skin for bites, then the same for his left. The tattoos I'd glimpsed when he walked into the bar like he owned it formed colorful sleeves, starting at his wrists and disappearing under his shirt. I caught his chin, his short blondish beard scratchy, and turned his head to check his throat.

He blinked and some of the intensity and intelligence I'd seen while he watched us sing eclipsed his bleary-eyed stupor. He hadn't seemed drunk earlier, but he definitely was now.

"What?"

"Are you hurt?" He let me turn his head from side to side, the skin unblemished except for a hint of green ink curling up at the neck of his tee. I ran my hands down his sides, then knelt and repeated the search along his legs.

"No."

"No, you're not hurt?"

"Right. Quit."

"I'm sorry, but I need to confirm. There. All done." I rose and faced him. "All good except for the drunk off your butt part."

He scowled and straightened, the strong jaw I'd felt under the facial hair setting into a stubborn line. "I'm not drunk." His tone was fierce and for a moment, his words sharp and clear.

"Then what did you take? How long ago was it?" Crap. If he'd taken something after he came out here, it worked fast, meaning the drug was possibly as dangerous as the escaped cryptid. I caught his wrist again, pressing two fingers against the underside and monitoring his pulse.

"I'm not high and I sure as hell don't abuse drugs," he snapped, his frown lopsided. "Something must have been slipped into my drink."

Maybe, maybe not, but his pulse was strong and only as elevated as confronting a large predator would account for. "Any friends inside waiting for you?"

"No. Told that shithead Lewis to piss off." His gaze lost focus.

"Sounds like you've had an eventful day—ahh, here we go." I opened the wallet I'd palmed during his exam. "Mister Kantor."

"How'd—"

I flipped through the rest of its contents. The Colorado address on his license didn't help me out, nor was there a keycard to a local hotel inside. His phone was equally unhelpful, password protected, and the code wasn't 1234. Kimi, my other sister and teammate, could crack it in under sixty seconds, but since she was occupied searching for our mystery cryptid, I was on my own.

"Hey! Put that fucking back."

I complied, tucking it into his pocket, but kept the key fob I discovered. "I hope this serves as a life lesson about not getting wasted and following sketchy women into alleys to make out." I glossed over the part about it not being a woman he'd followed.

"I wasn't fucking following her, damn it. And I told you I'm not drunk."

"Gotcha. Hey, where's your car?"

"In the parking garage. Where else would it be?" He listed sideways, belying the not-wasted assertion.

"We're off to the parking garage, then." I fit my shoulder under his arm, realizing he was only an inch or two taller than me.

He made a go at focusing but his gaze kept drifting off-center. "Why should I? You told me not to trust sketchy women in alleys."

I bit the inside of my cheek, keeping my laugh in. "That would be a valid point if I wasn't the woman who just rescued your drunk butt."

"I'm not drunk, damn it."

I steered us down the street. "You argue a lot."

"The fuck I do."

My laugh popped out. So much for not antagonizing him. We garnered a sympathetic eye roll from a couple crossing the road, probably assuming we were another couple out for some fun, and now I was stuck hauling my inebriated partner home.

He was leaning hard by the time we entered the garage. At least when I hit the fob, headlights blinked on the first level and only feet away.

I tapped the unlock button then maneuvered my load into the passenger seat, hand on top of his head to protect his skull.

"In you go. What are the odds you can tell me where you're staying?" I asked as I buckled him in.

He flicked a wobbly finger at the dash. "GPS. House rental."

"You seriously need GPS while sober in order to find your place?"

He shrugged, sliding lower in the seat. "Why bother learning? I'll be leaving again anyway."

I pulled up directions and enjoyed the novelty of being in

a car instead of the SUV or Liv's jacked up truck. The GPS took us a few miles out, into an area of gated communities and exclusive views. I wasn't especially familiar with this section since it wasn't a cryptid hotspot, thus we only patrolled it sporadically.

"Last house."

I glanced over, surprised my passenger wasn't passed out. He'd sunk down in the comfy seat, his head turned to watch me. The streetlights here were bright enough to see his hair was brown, not the dark blond it had appeared in the bar.

I drove to the end of the small enclave, pulling into a short driveway with a two-story glass and steel house. "Garage?"

When I didn't get a reply, I checked in. His eyes were finally closed. I played with compartments and screens on the dash until the garage door rose, lights coming on as we entered and the door silently lowering.

I let myself into the house, gun out, did a fast sweep of the house, then repeated it on the deck circling the west side. Using the rail as a boost, I pulled myself to the roof, the memory of the creature shimmying up walls fresh. All I got for my effort was a great view, desert on one side, city on the other, a patchwork of light and neon under the stars.

The guy was still out when I opened the car, a dead weight as I finally managed to get him out. "We should discuss the merits of single-story homes and gym member-ships, mister," I muttered, hefting him up one slow step at a time on the free-floating staircase. Which wasn't really fair. The chest against me was solid, a muscled arm draped over my shoulders.

But our night out, the first in weeks thanks to what felt like non-stop mission call-outs, was shot. Whatever the crea-ture turned out to be, it wasn't part of Arizona's natural cryptid biome. The mystery of the novel cryptid and what it was capable of nagged at me. Plus, we wouldn't even get pizza, and after my winning the draw and getting to choose toppings for once.

None of which was the fault of the person I'd finally gotten to the top of the stairs. I sorta-lowered, sorta-dropped his top half onto the bed then lifted the bottom part. As apology for snarking, I removed his shoes and emptied his pockets. I wrestled the blanket over him, then hesitated. Rolling over with glasses on sounded uncomfortable. Gingerly, I eased his off.

My face was inches from his when his eyes opened, deep mahogany and momentarily clear and focused.

"You're home for the night," I improvised, hoping he went back to sleep. This was a nice neighborhood, houses close enough together that if neighbors heard a resident screaming about home invaders, the police response time would be snappy. On a normal mission, Liv would've called our regional HQ, who would've used whatever official contact or agent we had planted in the local emergency services or law enforcement to keep our path unobstructed. But, nothing about this evening was normal. "It's all good."

He grunted what I decided to take as agreement, then blinked again. "You okay, Karaoke Girl? Godzilla didn't get you?"

For a second, I was at a loss, my training not covering this possibility. There had been lots of saves and lots of civilians, but none had ever asked if I was injured.

"I'm fine," I whispered respecting the intimate cocoon of soft darkness and quiet.

"Are you lying? Your hand." He managed to lift his in demonstration.

"No, I promise."

He grunted again and snuggled deeper into the blanket. "Good."

I gave it a minute but he stayed out this time. Checking for any meds that might not interact well with whatever he'd taken or drank, I went through his nightstand and bath, then repeated the search downstairs.

Satisfied on that front, I texted Liv.

*Status?*

Her answer came immediately.

*Patrol complete. No sign of the objective or additional vics.*

Not what I was hoping for. I texted her my location and got a *20 minutes out* reply.

It was probably rude by non-Company standards but, twenty minutes to kill. So I snooped.

We rarely got to see where and how vics—any civilians—lived. Especially one who lived in such a modern place. I had no idea about cost since all our needs were taken care of from birth but this house was nice which had to mean expensive.

Taking my time, I opened cabinets and drawers. The kitchen was sleek brushed steel and granite. A fancy coffee maker like those in the HQ Office wings took up a quarter of the counter. A fridge capable of holding a month's worth of our stuff, with compartments top and bottom, occupied one wall. Except ours wasn't full of leafy green things and weird vegetables, and what I figured out were five kinds of cheese but with heavy paper labels. Ditto for the cooler built in beside the fridge with unfamiliar wine labels.

I hadn't found meds but the kitchen was stocked with vitamins and herbs that didn't seem meant for cooking. Probably the source of the fresh-grass scent that hung in the cool air like a fading ghost. I wandered into the living area, winding around minimalist furniture that looked more like artwork, nothing worn, mismatched, or overstuffed like ours.

I excused my going back upstairs by checking on my vic,

still bundled under the cover. Putting Company stealth to a not-exactly-Company purpose, I browsed. He had more products than Josh, Kimi, Liv, and I combined. Mostly bottles with exclusive looking labels and tags stamped or marked *small batch* and *certified organic*. Even his toothpaste was different, charcoal and mint, and in a pot.

The closet was equally full, thin sweaters folded on one shelf, polos on another, a couple of suits hanging at the end. Button down shirts were arranged by color, light to dark, with pants and jeans folded over hangers. Multiple winter coats, which were mostly out of place here. A dozen jackets, all the same style, half in white, half in black, finished out his organized arrangement.

The jackets seemed familiar and I took one out, holding it closer. It was the kind worn on one of the cooking competitions queued up on my streaming service list.

Shoes stood in an orderly row underneath the clothes, arranged from athletic to polished leather, right by several wheeled suitcases.

The whole place was exact and precise, from the food in the fridge to the products grouped in the bathroom.

My fingers itched to open drawers and discover their mysteries. Behind me, fabric swished against fabric. I turned and the guy was pushed up on one elbow, at a dangerous angle. He blinked like he wasn't really seeing me. "Knives."

I tried reassuring him. "I've double-checked and no one is here. Doors and windows are locked. You don't need a weapon."

He gave me a glare, fierce despite his loopiness. "My knives. In the car."

"The garage is locked too. They're fine."

"Go. Get them." He pushed higher, swaying like a branch in a high wind. A few more inches, and he'd end up face down on the unforgiving wood floor.

"If I do, will you stay put and go to sleep?" I couldn't believe I was bargaining with the guy I'd just rescued.

"Probably."

I snorted a laugh. "At least you're honest. Okay. I'm going, see? Now stay put."

I retraced my route to the garage and opened the car. "Knife, knife, where the heck would a civi keep one?" I muttered to myself. If it were one of us, the answer would be close at hand.

I didn't think civilians were that attached, but... I sat in the driver's seat, checking angles, then reached for the passenger seat. When that came up empty, I tried below the seat. My hand touched fabric. Another of the chef coats, open and covering a bundle shoved underneath.

Hauling it free, the bundle turned out to be leather, rolled into a tube, and heavier than it looked. I propped it against the steering wheel. When I unrolled it, knives gleamed back at me, nestled in slots inside the soft case. I eased one out. Not our kind of blade, but I knew well-crafted knives no matter the style. These felt perfectly weighted in my hand, the steel top quality, and edges as sharp as any of ours.

Respectfully, I slid them back in place. My fingers bumped over lettering. I tilted the leather more toward the light. *James Beard Winner, Chef, Northeast* was embossed on the top.

The case was the most personal thing I'd seen tonight. His knives were as precious to him as ours were to us. This was important, and said something about my vic.

I grabbed the case and jacket, then hesitated in the kitchen, where my load probably belonged. But if it were me, I'd want to be sure. I jogged up the steps, then checked my stride in case he was asleep.

He'd sunk to a braced forearm but was waiting. I knelt in

front of him, preventing any more inebriated acrobatics. "I found them. See?" I carefully unrolled the case as proof.

Nose almost touching the leather, he examined my offering. When he nodded, I re-rolled the case making sure I wrapped it the way I first found it, mostly.

I looked up from my task. Which put us nose to nose, in the tiny pool of light I'd turned on in the bath earlier, the rest of the room in shadow.

He tilted his head, that sharp, dark gaze slowly tracking over my highlighted face. "What happened tonight?"

For the first time, I wanted to be honest with a civilian. Instead, like a good C.O., I squashed that impossible urge. "Tonight was just a dream."

"Are you going to tell me you're a dream too?"

"Afraid so."

Lines creased his forehead. "You should be real, not imaginary. You shine."

Before I could process his statement, he settled back into his nest of pillows and blanket, finally well and truly passed out.

My phone vibrated from my pocket. I crept downstairs, made sure the garage was locked then let myself out the front, giving it the same treatment before jogging over to meet my team.

I climbed into the front passenger seat, dark night and disabled interior light meaning I didn't need to worry about flashing bystanders between the combo of my skirt and Liv's jacked-up tires.

Liv didn't put the truck in gear, craning to scan the property. "Has the Cleaner team already processed the vic? Did they take him to the hospital or HQ? Did they need to process any random witnesses?"

"Neither, and no other witnesses." I buckled in. "He wasn't injured, his cell didn't have any video or photos of the cryptid, and he's either so high or so drunk he'll put tonight down to a bad dream, if he remembers anything at all."

A soft snort came from the back. Kimi draped across our brother, taking her copper-tinged curls out of the haphazard topknot she'd jerked her hair into for the emergency patrol. She tossed the hairband, and hands free, leaned between the front seats and signed, her specialty since losing her voice. "Yeah, because scary, sentient animals they've never heard of can't be real. Oh, wait. They can. What was this hostile? "

I ignored her unusual level of snark. We had the best jobs in the world, but the entire team was flat-out tired.

Chewing at a hangnail, I sorted through my mental notes. "Did any of you notice the brunette in the shimmery snake-skin dress, hanging out at the bar?"

"There were a lot of brunettes in dresses out tonight." Josh rocked his leg hard, trying to shake Kimi off.

"At the east end of the bar, by the guy who entered as we started singing. I thought the dress was more of a sequin print," Liv said, checking for traffic then turning onto the main road.

Of course Liv had noticed where my attention had gone earlier in the evening, tuned into my body language the same as I was with hers, the product of training together all our lives.

"Didn't she seem off to you?"

Liv took a beat, analyzing opinions, before shaking her head. "I only noticed her because you were so intent on that spot. I didn't get any vampire tells from her."

"Me either," I admitted. "But she went by me as I was paying. Whatever it was, she felt weird. Not quite right."

"She the one who jumped the vic?"

"This is where things go off the rails. The thing that attacked him was humanoid but it was like her dress turned to scales."

"Details," Kimi signed.

"The creature's scales? Exactly the same color and pattern as the snakeskin-sequined dress."

"Are you sure it wasn't a desperate ghoul? Or a well-fed vampire in an ugly skirt?" Josh asked, his lip lifting in disgust, a sentiment we all shared.

Not an unreasonable question since we had a thriving ghoul population, even if they'd been oddly MIA recently. Cryptids' species-defining feature was a trait the Lab crew called the Chameleon Effect, the entirely too creepy ability to go unseen if you didn't already know they existed. However, none possessed psychic powers. A powered-up vampire could move fast enough to almost blur. They weren't true cryptids, their condition the result of a horrific virus, and definitely *could* play mind games. But that took more than a few seconds of contact, and faded in minutes.

"I don't know what it was, but I do know it wasn't a vampire. The claws were wrong—opalescent and hooked. Single row of serrated teeth. When it hit the building wall, it suctioned on like that gecko Jace snuck in during our last year as cadets." I made a serpentine, s-shaped move with my hand, mimicking the cryptid's gait. "We need to know more."

Josh slumped. "First no pizza, now no sleep."

Which summed up most of our recent Friday nights.

\* \* \*

I SHOVED ASIDE the empty doughnut wrapper, the last-minute convenience store stand-in for our lamented pizza, and sat my laptop in the middle of my desk. "This."

Josh leaned in from his spot on the other side of the desk, making a hasty grab for the oversized reference binder slipping out of his lap. "What the—"

"Take a look," Liv yelled, coming through the door with her tablet a second before Kimi and her laptop.

They lined their devices up beside mine. The files had different headings—I'd gone with chem resistant species, the very few who weren't susceptible to the Lab created chemical compound targeted to disrupt cryptid DNA. Liv dove into reptilian species. Information specialist that she was, Kimi had taken the largest group, rare and poorly documented species, i.e. those with few field notes or corroboration. And in true Kimi fashion, she had multiple tabs open, including hallucinogenic species and suspected psychics.

The creature in my and Liv's drawing, singular, since it was the same one, and Kimi's grainy black and white photo matched. "That's it. An anangoa."

Josh righted the encyclopedia, hitting the index and flipping pages to the creature's entry. "Man. One paragraph?"

Kimi tapped the scarred desktop for our attention, then launched into a succinct review. "From seven compiled sources, a humanoid reptilian cryptid of Southeast Asian origin, specifically Borneo and its outliers. Suspected extinct circa nineteen-ninety-eight, until four years ago when a Southeast Asian Asset brought in hatched shells with the distinctive sheen, and one un-hatched with a non-viable embryo. Strictly carnivorous with historic accounts of a mated pair bringing down a Sumatran rhino. Highly territorial, and especially aggressive when in rut or with hatchlings. Preferred habitat is deep rainforest and mountain ranges. Purported to partially shape-shift, which researchers now attribute to a biochemical agent causing moderate to severe hallucinations."

"Adding a note that the cryptid may exude an associated biochemical that increases susceptibility to suggestion, especially in confined spaces," Liv muttered, already keying information into the database to await HQ approval. A hundred-percent professional despite the filmy white hydrating mask plastered over her face.

Kimi resumed her debrief. "Rated Level One to Two for speed and agility. It will attack smaller, weaker, or previously injured prey directly, but prefers to envenomate prey, tracking it at a distance until it weakens—"

"Like a Komodo dragon?"

Kimi gave Josh a glare for interrupting, then resumed. "The mechanism for envenomating is undetermined, as well as the alleged toxin, and one footnote questions the translation of both terms as the report dates from the early nineteenth century."

"See? It could be a bite that causes an infection, thus infection slows the prey, thus? Ko. Mo. Do," Josh finished on an *I told you so* flourish.

Unease slithered down my spine. "How do they track their prey—line of sight or by scent? And what kind of radius are we talking?"

"It's theorized there's another pheromone marker, possibly related to the hallucinogenic agent it secretes, and range is unknown. Multiple accounts corroborate that they won't stop searching for prey they've marked until the prey is dispatched." Kimi checked with Liv, then Josh for anything on their end but both shook their heads.

"The vic?" Josh asked what we were all thinking.

"I'm ninety-five percent sure he wasn't bitten or stung. He did swear he wasn't drunk and didn't take anything, although, coordination and confusion suggested otherwise." I hadn't found so much as an aspirin in his house though.

"Or, he'd been envenomated already. The most realistic scenario being this marking thing mentioned in reality also causes confusion and disassociation. Track your prey until the compound fully kicks in, then finish them off easily," Liv finished for me.

"The anangoa stood right beside him at the bar. Way too close for a stranger, especially by Western standards." Close enough to touch him or brush up against him, possibly even deposit a drop of the venom in his drink.

Now, he was in a house with floor to ceiling windows and a convenient balcony facing the desert. Alone and unconscious, where I'd left him.

"Weapon up."

# CHAPTER 3

## BRUCE

What felt like a Carnival parade stomped through Bruce's head. He groaned, which intensified the stomping and banging. His stomach pitched in response.

He held still, hoping to hell the nauseating pitching and pounding would stop. After a minor eternity his stomach settled back where it belonged, despite the swamp-and-sulfur taste coating his tongue.

Since he hadn't booked a trip to Rio, this sure as hell wasn't the result of a week-long celebration. He cracked one eyelid, in slow motion, and recognized the outline of a bedroom.

*How the hell much had he had to drink?*

His abused brain gradually came back online. He hadn't been buzzed, much less drunk, since his twenty-first birthday and learning his lesson about binge drinking, closing in on a decade ago. Which begged the question of how he'd ended up in this state.

He poked at his scattered memories. Walking out on the dumbass restaurateur was clear, but after… There had been a phone call from someone. Then...a woman? Wild brunette waves and an attitude mixed with an ass-ugly dress. Two women?

Something about his knife case mixed in with the black-out stew. He jerked up, and immediately regretted it, stomach and head double-teaming him.

He got both under control, the softness of his favorite sheets and the funk of old cigarette smoke registering. Shit. There had been a bar, to go along with the two hazy women. Had he brought one of them home? That wasn't his habit, but neither was black-out drunk.

He pried both gritty eyes open and rolled to check. The bed was empty except for his solitary ass, and he still had pants and shirt on. The latter smelling of kitchen service. No shoes though. He felt sideways then remembered the night-stand was on the left in this rental. His fingers closed over his glasses and he slipped them on. Nothing else was on the stand.

By the bathroom light he rarely left on, he spotted his key ring glinting from on top of the dresser. His wallet and phone rested beside it.

He stood and made it to the dresser. When he flipped through the wallet, all but one of the twenties he'd stuck inside at the first of the week were still there, along with his credit cards. He swiped his phone screen and logged onto his accounts. No activity on any, including his debit, at least.

The place felt empty but he paused at the top of the stairs to double check before descending. Empty living area and empty kitchen, the sun rising over the view he'd paid extra for his only companion.

He filled the teakettle, then pulled out a mug and the green tea blend he was never without, packing pungent leaves in a diffuser. To the soft burble of the heating water, he took a second to remember which cabinet held what and fished out the vitamins, adding an extra B-complex. His morning smoothie would have to wait until the tea and detox did their work.

While water boiled, he checked his social media feed. A tracker alert for his name popped up, and when he clicked, multiple videos opened. One of him tossing the plating station at the sanctimonious sell-out owner, obviously taken by kitchen staff on the down-low. Several more were from the night's diners, taken as he'd flipped the owner off and left through the dining room. Both had a healthy ten-k plus hits. His mood lifted and he sent the best video to his stories then tapped out a message.

*Fuck The Cellar. Don't bother with a reservation unless you want assaulted by flavorless garbage masquerading as authentic, heritage plates.*

He tagged it with the #BruceTheBastardsNation hashtag from his most rabid fans. Comments flooded in as he added a shot of the sunrise and *'Last look at Scottsdale. Watch out Tàos.'* He'd had an old friend bugging the shit out of him to do a month-long pop-up there and now was as good a time as any.

He poured water over the infuser, inhaling the burst of lightly floral steam, and added agave syrup. Then quit stalling and did the one thing he'd been afraid to since waking up. The knife case lay centered on the island. The wrapping was secured with some complicated-assed knot instead of his double loop though.

If some jerkoff had been in it…he rolled the leather flat. The full complement of handles filled the slots. He took each out, all in the same pristine condition he'd left them. He finished his survey with the smallest and oldest. The first real blade he'd bought himself, the one his grandfather had planned to gift him on graduation but hadn't lived long enough to fulfill his promise.

Like a sentimental dumbass, he still kissed his fingertips then touched them to the blade. He angled to sheath the knife.

A sharp *ping* echoed off the window. Then the house's mountain view shattered into a thousand kaleidoscopic pieces. He ducked but glass peppered his arms and head in a stinging rain.

Something hit the floor, the impact shaking the entire house. Tea kettle and cup skittered, the cup crashing to join the other debris.

He grabbed onto the edge of the island, swearing, and yelled. "If this is some vandalism as payback bullshit for quitting, I will sue your hack ass, Lewis."

Instead of a brick chucked through the glass, someone rose and whirled. A weirdo in a freaking Godzilla costume faced him.

Then the guy hissed. A forked tongue flicked out, slit-pupil eyes fixing on Bruce.

"What the fu—"

The freak lunged.

Another, lighter thump hit, followed by the crunch of glass as a second vandal joined the party.

Bruce spun for his phone and nine-one-one. Two people out for his ass was one too many.

A knife slashed down, inches from his outstretched fingers. The blade imbedded in the granite, counter chipping. He jerked back.

A tongue flicked over his cheek, realistic as fuck. Hot. Alive. Some instinctual part of his brain roared awake, smarter than his modern brain, and he froze. Holding his breath even as a snort reeking of rotting meat blasted over his face.

A shrill whistle split the air. The person—because it had to be a person outfitted in some horror movie-grade makeup and prosthesis—twisted in a whiplash-fast move. Jerking their knife free, counter cracking like broken ice. The knife that was somehow attached to the weirdo's damn *hand*.

Over the costumed stuntman's back, Bruce caught a glimpse of the second guy. This one dressed head to toe in mottled black and gray clothing. And holding a gun that seemed too damn real.

True fear splashed through Bruce. "Hey, no. Whatever you want, take it."

"Shut. Up," the gun nut barked at him. But he holstered the gun in some ridiculously complex weapon's rig on his thigh. An improvement, until he whipped out a knife longer than Bruce's forearm. The guy whistled again.

In reply, the costumed weirdo hissed. The sound raised every hair on Bruce's body.

It—him, the costumed one—repeated the ungodly sound. The noise climbing up and down the vocal register. Like it was trading insults.

In a flash, it coiled and sprang. Flying at the second guy, like it was prepared to tackle and bulldoze him through the wall.

The gunman crouched, knife blade reflecting back the morning sun in a blinding pattern. At what looked like the last damn second, he rolled and slashed out.

The costumed combatant flew over him, unable to stop. They hooked a knife-claw downward. The rip of fabric was almost lost under a furious roar. Reddish-green goo splashed from the freak's stomach. Hella realistic goo.

Bruce's gut heaved in response.

Wood and more glass imploded behind Bruce. He jerked, slamming his back into the cold metal of the fridge as another black and gray clad fanatic stormed through what remained of Bruce's front door.

The man barked, "Six-o-clock," whatever the fuck that meant.

The first shooter was back on his feet. Knife flashing at dizzying speed, sun refracting back from the gleaming blade. Pressing into the freak's space. Dodging vicious swipes from its prosthetic claw-blade. The funky blood-goo splattered, again and again. Hisses and growls created a backdrop as the costumed one twisted and swiped, attacking back.

The second gunman surged past Bruce, gun in both hands and level, like he knew what he was doing. "Don't move," he ordered over the noise of the fight.

With an "I'm clear" that must've been aimed at his uniformed twin, the guy stepped right.

The first gunman kept moving. Slicing and feinting, moving as smoothly as the freak despite its costume. The pair flowed together and apart in some horribly beautiful performance.

Costume-guy feinted, then darted for the opposite side. The soldier was there before it finished the move. The other's legs bent, muscles bunching and clearly defined in the tight costume. Their head swung left.

In a flash, Bruce understood. The violent, costumed one was trying to reach a wall and some-damn-how climb it. Get over the soldier and his knife. The soldier was hell-bent on preventing its plan, even as another sharp *rip* of fabric marked the costumed, and obviously high as fuck on some drug, guy getting in a hit.

The soldier still closed in. Shoving right at the huge mass of costumed muscle and hooked knives in a burst of speed that set Bruce's nerves on edge in response. Inside costume-guy's reach, the soldier feinted, then dove straight for the center mass, both hands on the knife.

Bruce swore, waiting for claws to dig in and tear the suicidal soldier in half.

Instead, the soldier slammed the enormous blade into a costumed thigh, and ducked. The tip continuing through as the wounded guy gave an earsplitting wail. He swiped at the soldier, air whistling.

The soldier grabbed, latching on to a costumed arm, using the bigger person's backswing to flip over its shoulder. Rolling across the kitchen island, landing on his feet. Right in front of Bruce.

The soldier snapped "Clear!" More of their code, then slid the gun out without evening looking at the holster.

Sharp barks assaulted Bruce's ears and sent him shoving against the fridge, wishing he could shove through it. Have some kind of barrier between him and the madness. The guns spat again, the shooters angled on either end of his island, out of each other's way, both aimed at the same target.

Bullets hit the costumed guy.

Who jerked and swatted. Then swung in an arc, bone crunching as he pulled the knife free of his leg, blood trickling from his mouth.

Bruce's gut squeezed. The soldiers were killing someone, right in front of him.

Bruce scrambled, abandoning the fridge, bolting for the door. Tripping and coming up hard, granite island edge grinding into his ribs.

The tail prosthetic part of the bionic get-up swept at him, tip curling like it was another limb. Bruce fumbled for something to throw at it. His hand hit the familiar composite of a knife hilt and he grabbed it. Rammed it through the tail coming at his face. The blade pierced nauseatingly realistic muscle-like filling and broke free, hitting granite underneath.

Bruce let go, falling on his ass in a teeth-rattling impact as another shot barked from beside him.

"Motherfucking son of a bitch." His swearing was

suddenly loud, in the absence of animalistic growls, military commands, and gunfire.

A shadow fell over him and he scrabbled backward until his shoulders hit cabinets. "What the ever-loving hell is this?"

His position put him staring up into brown eyes. They tickled a memory loose, of those eyes with their lighter flecks glowing in the low light from his bedside lamp. Bruce's brain finally got in gear, popping up an image. "You!"

The soldier—her, the uninhibited woman, the one from the bar, the lead karaoke singer, who had charged down a street last night then brought his knife case in—pulled the balaclava mask up, baring her face. Then held out a short-nailed hand to him. "Me," she agreed. Instead of apology and explanation for shooting another person, or fear of police arriving, or any normal damn emotion, her reply held amusement.

"What. The. Fuck." The yell came from the very bottom of Bruce's lungs.

"We have a problem." The second shooter pulled a matching balaclava off, and fuck him if it wasn't the first's karaoke backup singer, the wavy haired brunette. She stopped on his other side, brown skin ridiculously flawless as a model's in the sun coming through the gaping hole that used to be his window.

"A problem? You fucking think?" He ignored the hand the first one offered and hauled himself up, glaring at the pair.

The second didn't bother replying to him, addressing his tormentor. "Are you certain the cryptid you reported was female?"

"The one that lured him into the street was most definitely female."

"I wasn't lured, damn it." They acted like they hadn't heard his testy answer.

The second used a booted foot to finish rolling the

collapsed, costumed victim on its back, genitals clear. "Yeah, definitely male."

Bruce couldn't wrap his head around…they'd killed some drugged-up sexual fetishist?

The pair continued their conversation. "Was there any footnote on gender morphing? Like with fish? Reptiles—alligators do it under certain circumstances, right?"

The first frowned like their gibberish meant something, absently swiping at a strand that had come loose from her tight bun. "None listed. I think alligators only do it in the shell and it's a response to some environmental catalyst. So."

"So," the second agreed.

Bruce hit his limit.

His bellow rang off chrome and glass, nearly as loud as the sex freak's had. The sex freak who had tried to kill Bruce. "One of you two fucking explain this shit." He jabbed his finger at *her*. Karaoke Girl. "You. Start talking right the fuck now."

"What would you like to talk about first?" Her eyes held a familiar glee. The same look he got when he was seeing how hard and how far he could push someone.

And damn, but something in him, underneath the fear, confusion, and anger, responded. Excitement mixed with the other emotions, even as he tried shoving the distraction down.

Glaring at her, he barked, "Do not fuck with me. Either I'm still tripping from whatever that woman—"

"Cryptid," she cut in. Her innocently helpful expression at odds with the devil in her eyes, the tiniest crinkle at the edges giving away her amusement.

"Tripping from whatever that *person* slipped into my beer." There had to be a semi-logical explanation. There couldn't, could not, be a murdered person in thousands of dollars worth of special effects gear on his rental floor. "Or alternately, you two are pulling some elaborate prank, which some hidden camera you've planted is recording. If it's that dick Cunningham, I'll finally kick his ass the way he's been begging for since he stole my best line cook during that food week rush."

"Or, option three," she said. Fucking poking harder.

He kept his mouth clamped shut.

"Or?" She prodded. "Here, I'll say it for you." She patted the freaky, meaty fake tail draped over his ruined rental's kitchen island. "Or this is a cryptid. A biological organism whose existence isn't known to mainstream zoology. I.E., creatures too niche and too dangerous for civilian society, a few of which society has had such profoundly unpleasant run-ins with, that they're dubbed folktales or the super-natural."

"No."

"Umm, yes."

"There are no such things as Godzilla lizard monsters. No."

"Anangoa, sub-species unknown." She leaned in, coming within inches of him. Close enough the stray lock of hair wisped over his cheek, a whisper of something like cocoa butter temporarily beating out the stomach-curdling tang of blood. Then grabbed and popped his knife out of the freak. "And yes."

She tilted the knife, and where there had been oiled, honed Japanese steel, now the edges were chipped and the tip broken off. For the first time, what looked like concern drew her brows together.

Flipping the knife hilt first, she offered it to him. "I'm sorry," she said, like she understood the blade was emotion-ally important to him.

Boot rubber squeaked, and they both twitched, putting space between them. He grabbed his broken knife.

With a minute of no one attempting to kill anyone, his adrenalin-soaked brain focused on something more than saving his skin and caught up with the situation. This wasn't a prank, that wasn't special effects blood decorating the island, and these were well-armed, well-trained soldiers.

She turned to catch the other women's eye. "Cleaners?"

Perfect Skin tucked a chunky, matte black phone into one of the multitude of pockets on her pants. "On their way. Are we processing him?"

*Hell* no. He snatched the biggest knife in his case, one meant for butchering. "Fuck that. You're not turning me into human pulled-pork." Phone, phone, where had he dropped the damn thing? Nine-one-one time.

The second, taller soldier was in front of him in a smooth move, her hand whipping out and connecting with his. Pain shot through his wrist, and his knife clattered to the floor.

"Seriously?" Karaoke Girl flicked her finger, and the other stepped back. His current tormentor propped her rear against the counter, arms crossed. "Why would anyone jump to the conclusion that being processed equaled turning a civilian into horror movie barbeque? That is twisted."

He rotated his aching wrist, and gave his wrist-bashing attacker a pointed look. Then looked from the science experiment bleeding out on his floor to Karaoke. He crossed his arms in mirror imitation of her pose, point made.

At his defiance, that spark of daring shone from her eyes again.

"Why?" His temper crested. "Let's start with because people conducting illegal research prefer to cover their tracks, and you are the para-military security thugs paid to do the covering."

"Thugs?" That came from the second one, an insulted undercurrent to the word.

"We are the good guys." Indignation laced Karaoke's response.

"Bullshit. You're muscle for some multibillion-dollar corporation, probably big pharma, doing illegal research which violates every FDA and other applicable government law, and is undoubtedly banned in all developed nations. That," he jabbed his finger at the creature, "is a godawful lab experiment that got loose. Now, you're disappearing any evidence. Namely, that corpse and me, who you are about to turn into a corpse."

She whistled. "Dang. That's a really good conspiracy theory."

"Maybe we should add it to our explanation rotation," the other said.

"Is big business experiment better than supernatural monster or UFO?"

The other lifted one shoulder in a shrug. "We could run it by HQ Legal."

At their casual fucking discussion, his eyelid twitched. These two...

Karaoke pushed off the counter.

He stepped back, adrenalin flooding him again. Although what chance he thought he had against a pair of corporate mercenaries, he wasn't sure.

All she did was squat by the mutant's head, flicking out a small knife from somewhere, and Jesus Christ, she must have more on her than were in his case. "Look at this, and I mean really look." Using the blade, she lifted its lip, showing teeth that belonged on nothing human, and no animal he'd ever seen. "Stop thinking practical jokes and drug companies, and concentrate."

He ground his teeth, but stared at the corpse. Seconds ticked by and he opened his mouth to call her on her bullshit, and the body...blurred. When he blinked, instead of a tight-fitting latex suit and special effects knives or a genetically manipulated Komodo dragon, iridescent scales shimmered. The claws did the same, thicker and opalescent. The joints and structure weren't a clumsy experiment. The creature was as lithe and powerful and natural as the lions he'd seen on a safari trip.

She met his eyes. "This is a cryptid. It's a murderous predator that sees humans as prey."

"Fuck." He slid down, back bumping along the cabinet, and laced his fingers over his head. "Holy fucking shit. Give me a minute here."

Apparently, they were literal about time. A couple of heartbeats later, Karaoke knelt in front of him, keeping her hands to herself. "Do you need medical help?"

"What I need are facts. Okay. That's a real monster. Meaning you are what?"

"Part of a force that contains and eliminates cryptids, occasionally to prevent their existence from becoming known to those unscrupulous corporate, homegrown, or foreign government entities that might weaponize cryptid biology and use it as a destabilizing social lever. Fundamentally though, our mandate is to always protect civilians from harm."

"And last night was what? Were you already after that thing?"

"No. Last night we, and you, just got lucky."

"That isn't a sane person's definition of lucky, but all right. Monster. Monster eliminating SWAT team."

She nodded.

"This thing is dead, end of that story. So what, exactly, is processing?"

She sighed and lifted her hand toward her face, like it was a habit, then wrinkled her nose at the goo-stained cuticles and dropped her fingers. "This isn't the creature from last night."

So he'd heard. He made a *get on with it* gesture.

"Concrete information on anangoa is scarce. What we have gleaned is that they are aggressive, and form strong mating bonds, likely for life. I'm guessing here, but we got a visit from the male today instead of the female because I wounded her last night." She tipped her head at the dead creature. "They have some biochemical means to influence how prey perceives them in order to get close and then further disorient prey, as well as track their target over long distances, and for extended periods of time when necessary. Once they tag prey, they don't stop until it's dead—probably an evolutionary adaptation to deal with food scarcity."

She let him sit with the implications, her expression serious. This shit just got better and better.

"The other one of this pair is still loose, and you're saying it can find me. Putting anyone around me in danger?" He made the last a question, hoping it wasn't true, knowing it was.

She nodded, her expression softer. Undoubtedly the hint of admiration was all in his head. "Processing involves getting you to a secure location where you, and the public, can be protected until we eliminate the threat."

"Where is considered a secure location?"

She exchanged a long, coded look with the other—he assumed soldier was the correct term after all—then spoke like she was continuing a conversation. "HQ has the resources, but there's still the Office division to consider, and Medical is full with an incident from the Cali region."

"Plus, the whole Southwestern Region's cadet class is in attendance for their fourth-year eval and graduation." Miss Perfect Skin rubbed at her temples, skin there already taut from what looked like hair pulled into headache-inducingly tight bun. "That might not technically count as a lockdown emergency, but for once, I disagree."

"I second that. I'm unilaterally calling this a potential HQ security threat. Better it target us."

"I'll start the report." The other soldier sighed.

If they kept on with their cryptic fucking tangents—he narrowed his eyes at Karaoke. "Meaning?"

"We can keep you safe at our base."

"Like an army base? You have an army."

"We have two more team members."

He waited for the punch line. They only stared back at him.

Instead of hiding him at an institution that had an army of Karaoke Girls, his rescuers were instead choosing a place defended by only four people. Like diverting the greater danger their way was standard operating procedure. "Fucking hell. What's your name?"

"Commander Victoria Ramirez, Region Two. Vee for short." She motioned over her shoulder at the other. "Lieutenant Olivia Muñez. Liv, if you don't annoy her."

He had a feeling he was already annoying the fuck out of her.

Karaoke Girl—Ramirez—rose, moving as smoothly as she'd fought. She backed away, giving him time and room to think. But hell, there wasn't anything to think about.

The house directly across from him had three kids, nearly as cute as his nieces, running around every afternoon after pre-school. The house to his left had an older lady who reminded him of his nana, if his nana had stood on a balcony painting desert still-lifes.

He was a dick, but not enough of one to risk a blood-thirsty lizard-monster rampaging through their lives when he had the power to prevent it.

He held out his hand and Ramirez took it like she'd been

certain of this exact outcome, hauling him to his feet and putting them close to eye to eye. For all her command and power, she wasn't even as tall as he was. Life, energy, some electric force seemed to flow from her, right through their clasped hands, into him. It felt like a circuit closing.

When she let go, he bent and retrieved his knife, wiping monster gunk off then slotting it and his fucked beyond repair first blade in his case. "Give me ten minutes to pack, then show me my new digs."

# CHAPTER 4

## VEE

$O$ur newest...guest? Refugee? Whatever he was, he pushed past us, hopefully done swearing about the compound's biosensors, which yes, had claxoned when we rolled into the garage with a warm body whose DNA wasn't on file in our database. Then he'd sworn more about the infrared and decontamination breezeway-chamber between the garage and house proper. Thankfully we hadn't been required to haul the anangoa in. The cryptid alarm was about ten times louder.

"How can anyone's vocabulary consist of that many swear words?" Liv asked under her breath.

Danged if I knew. Aside from his current display, he'd cussed when he had to ride in the back of the SUV. Then again, and at length, when we'd left the city limits behind.

Liv had given Kimi and Josh a heads-up as far as our arriving with a houseguest. Words didn't exactly do him justice. I sprinted and followed on his heels, ready to mitigate any issues. Issues. Disasters. Close enough.

Josh stood in the odd connector space where the breezeway fed into infirmary, kitchen, or the y-shaped halls containing our rooms and my office. Aside from his grumpiness at missing out on pizza, Josh was the most outgoing and personable of us, and often handled dealing with stressed civilians and vics. Dimpled smile in place, he'd parked himself here as welcoming committee.

Kimi leaned against the opposite wall, equally curious but always under the radar.

Josh held out his hand. "Hey, man. I'm Josh, this is Kimi."

When our guest gave Josh a slitty-eyed stare a lot like the anangoa's and didn't bother answering, I stepped in. "Guys, this is Robert."

"Bruce," he snapped. "Not Robert."

Josh tried to smooth things over, his go-to since we were kids. "Let me show you where your room is, then I'll give you a hand bringing in your gear. If you guys didn't have time to grab your personal stuff, the Cleaners will box it and have it here by evening. They'll bring your car at the same time."

"Show me the kitchen." He addressed that around Josh to Kimi.

She tipped her head left-ish.

Bruce stomped past and Josh wheeled to follow him. I hurried after Josh.

"Jesus Fucking Christ," echoed back at me as I stepped into our huge kitchen and dining area combo. The room was a relic from the bad old days, when teams were three times our size, before science and modern weaponry leveled the playing field between cryptids and humans.

Bruce switched his glare to me. "This? You call this a kitchen?"

Brow wrinkled, Josh asked, "What's wrong with it?"

If we were going by the probably state of the art kitchen Bruce had left behind, a lot.

"Not a fucking thing. If you're into turn of the last century survivalist para-military chic." He placed his knife case on the counter and unrolled it, like it was his tic, or the knives truly were that important to him.

He ran his fingers over each in turn and gave me a hard look when his hand landed on the anangoa-toasted knife. "You are paying for a replacement."

I couldn't argue with his logic. "What about the smaller one?"

"It can't be replaced." He rolled the case up, looping the tie around it. Done, he prowled from the two-stool eat-in bar closest to the hall, and past the giant oak table. From there to the stove, which got a derisive snort, then to the brown enamel fridge. Without asking, he opened it. "Son of a bitch."

I had zero idea what was wrong with our fridge. It was as spotless as our armory, and the rest of the house and compound, and stocked as full as it ever got. The bulk was milk, juice, and sports drinks. A few beers and condiments, plus a box of leftover chile rellenos from one of our rotation of favorite food trucks, and something that was probably General Tso's Chicken.

Hopefully, the freezer would make him happier.

He jerked it open, then slammed it even faster, nostrils flaring.

So, no on the freezer.

"You're a cook?" Josh tried forging a bond again.

"I'm a chef, you steroid-abusing asshole." Spotting the pantry, an entire room to itself, he veered inside.

The team crowded around me as another volley of creative swearing bounced back to us.

"This guy—" Kimi signed.

"Is going to be a challenge," I admitted, signing back.

Following my lead, Liv also used our ASL and Company hybrid. "Getting him wound up earlier didn't help."

Which was Liv's way of calling me out. And, fine, I had challenged him. "Kind and nurturing wasn't the approach he

44

needed last night or today. You saw him. He can handle blunt and truthful. He didn't react like any civilian we've encountered."

I edged closer. "He was freaked but not in the usual terrified and crying way. Even last night he demanded and argued." Then checked to see if I was okay. "He was close to fearless."

Which had been, and still was, exciting.

Like she heard the unspoken, unsigned last bit, Liv's brows went up. Civilians were an unavoidable complication but always held at arm's length. Honestly, three or four arms' length.

Bruce storming back in, air of absolute authority trailing behind him, saved me. "I'm positive I'll quickly regret the request, but show me my damn room."

One of Liv's brows went higher. Kimi caught her attention, signing agreement.

I ducked around them. "Come on, Mister Chef." I didn't check to see if he followed me. I wouldn't have let the taunt go.

Neither did he, right beside me as I pointed at the hall on the left of the y-shaped intersection. "Josh, Kimi, and Liv's rooms." I tipped my head at the hallway on the right. "This is home."

He stepped in like he was royalty claiming his conquest. "I see the survivalist theme continued here. I've seen nicer by-the-hour motels." Arms crossed, colorful biceps bulging, he dared me to reply.

Our kitchen might not be chef quality, but the place had been constructed well over two-hundred years ago, and added onto over the decades. It was roomy, comfortable, and full of what were undoubtedly antiques by now.

I invited myself into his personal space and put us temper to temper. "I get that this situation isn't ideal from your point of view, nor is it the style you prefer. As soon as we neutralize the last anangoa—"

"You're going to zap me and erase my memory seconds later."

My laugh popped out before I considered ramifications. "What, *Men in Black* you? The newest one is the best, and Kimi and I will fight anyone who claims otherwise."

He blinked, temporarily shocked silent by my laughing at him or my knowledge of pop culture.

I took the opportunity and kept going. "There will be no memory tampering. There will be a mandatory session with one of our psychologists, an in-depth evaluation and complete physical exam, and then a meeting with Legal and signing a non-disclosure agreement. HQ will provide you with a solid cover story and the necessary documents to support it. I'll warn you now that HQ enforces the NDA, rigorously. Your daily life will also be observed for a period of time after. I'd advise against ever meeting with any of those big pharma corporations you mentioned earlier. Highly."

His shock wore off fast. "That's it? Therapist and documents are supposed to cover up my disappearance, a rampaging Godzilla knock-off, and its corpse? Bullshit. The scene in my rental alone will have police and forensics crawling over the entire state. You can't cover something of this magnitude up."

"You've seen a cryptid." I made a circular motion with my finger. "You've seen our tech and this base. There won't be a cryptid or inexplicable DNA at your rental. Sometimes, we stage an especially awkward scene as a robbery, assault, drug bust, whatever fits the narrative. Yours had minimal damage and will be like new by nightfall. Probably sooner."

He opened his mouth.

I talked over him. "This is what we do. There's a flawless

system in place. So yes. A psych eval, corroborating documents, and a stringent NDA are the plan."

"*A* cryptid." He let go of the *MIB* tangent, aiming for a new topic, expression shrewd.

I'd already figured out he was one of those people who paid attention and went after knowledge. "Ask, and I'll tell you everything that isn't above your clearance level. Like I said, we're the good guys."

"You're government."

"Government adjacent, and on a need to know basis." As C.O., I was cleared for levels several steps higher than even the most in the know government functionary. However, there were levels within the Company I couldn't access either. "Company Alpha Cryptid Containment, Company for short. A central Oversight, then satellite HQ's for each geographical area, which train, assign, and support division teams for their regions."

He grunted, already formulating his next question. A trickle of anticipation, the same kind as before a mission, pulsed through me.

He didn't disappoint me. "Let's start with the other monsters out there."

"Cryptids."

"Same difference."

"I think monsters are technically paranormal or supernatural. Maybe alien, which, not real."

I took a very non-C.O. bit of joy from the way his bearded jaw clenched. He forced it to relax. "Tell me about *cryptids*, Ramirez."

"I can't cover every species and sub-species. There are only a few that are extant, local, and classified as lethal. Ghouls, which aren't dead. They're nasty tempered bipedal scavengers and opportunists. They prefer feeding on any corpse, but will take live prey if it's weak or wounded. In

47

leaner times, they go after anything living. In the dark and with a hoodie or jacket, they can pass long enough to get close to humans."

"Keep going."

"Also indigenous to this region are windigos, no relation to the First Nation's wendigo. 'Digos are a step down from ghouls. They're...think canid mated with a really big, really aggressive skunk. They're where the stories of hellhounds come from." I shrugged. "There are a few more smaller species classified primarily as pests, like chupacabra."

"Werewolves? Vampires?"

"No such thing as a werewolf, although there are a few more advanced humanoid cryptids with traits that kinda vaguely align with a mainstream animal."

He tilted his head, a fire lighting in his ultra-brown eyes. "You're avoiding the vampire question."

My turn to grit my teeth. I considered shutting him down. He straightened like he sensed my intent. I had agreed to explain, so I had no one to blame but myself. "Vampires are a conditional yes. That's not their scientific name and the Lab crew get snarky if you slip up in front of them. They're enough like European legends that they get the nickname."

"Transylvania? Are you fucking with me?" He straightened, disbelief radiating off him.

"They aren't true cryptids. They're the product of a virus."

"Which does what and to who? Don't hold out on me now."

"A virus that attacks human DNA and twists and mutates and fucks with it. Then, those—" agents "—people aren't people anymore. They are as close to your definition of monster as anything a writer ever dreamed up, and it's our goal to make that virus as extinct as the plague. That's where today's lesson ends."

"Fuck. I'm going to need a minute again." He scrubbed a

hand over his beard, face underneath paling at what he'd heard in my voice. He paced the room. "All of those things are real and out there?"

"More, but not here. Some are extinct, some are under the purview of Indigenous councils, some are so specialized they can't survive outside of their tiny ecological niche. Does it make it better if I say think of them like...like a tiger? A tiger isn't going to pack a bag and move to London. It doesn't have some ulterior plan. Same with the cryptids. They're animals. Freaky animals but not some unified monster coalition." Except a pair of anangoa had seemingly packed their murderous bags and somehow made it from a Southeast Asian island to Arizona.

We needed a new topic.

"Can you still have your processing minute while taking off your shirt?" Medical was primarily Kimi's job, but he hadn't exactly endeared himself to my sister.

Suspicion chased the last of the interest off his face and he halted in front of me. "No matter what you mistakenly believe, I didn't follow some woman into an alley for a quickie, and I'm sure as hell not interested in getting off in a cut-rate army base with a G.I. Jane."

"Are all civilians such jerks?" Our experience was limited, but dang.

A remembered lecture snippet from my Academy days and a civi media course surfaced. This was a case of mixed signals. The Company didn't have that kind of #MeToo thing and weird gender power imbalance culture but we'd watched enough Netflix to follow along.

"Oh! Oh, sorry. I should've been clearer. This isn't sexual or an advance," I hurried to reassure him. "I only need to do a quick exam to verify you weren't envenomated last night."

For the first time in our twenty-ish hour acquaintance, a wash of color tinted his lightly tanned neck and face. Then darkened further as his volume rose. "What the fuck? Envenomated? You can't use 'envenomated' and 'only' in the same sentence."

"I don't believe you were. Like, a ninety-nine percent certainty. Honestly though, we don't have enough reliable data or field notes to understand how anangoa physiology and marking work. Whatever it secreted worked as a mild hallucinogenic and sedative on you, which we suspect is what the original notation considered a venom."

"It touched me. While I was at the bar it brushed against me. I assumed that *was* meant as a sexual advance, FYI, and ignored it." He pulled his polo off, a thin silver chain and a stylized charm I was pretty sure was a Star of David glinting against lighter skin and a nicely smooth chest.

"Where did it make contact?"

"My right side."

I circled around him, leaning close since the colorful ink, which did extend across his chest, might hide a small wound.

Back where I started, I pulled out the blood tube, tourniquet, and syringe I'd pocketed and held them up for his approval. "May I touch you?"

"Go for it," he said, tone gruff.

I ran my hand down his right arm, hairs crisp under my fingers as I double-checked for wounds, rashes, or stings. All I found were nicks and raised pink marks on his hand and lower arm.

When I glanced up, he caught my unspoken question. "Cuts and burns, the hazards of working in a kitchen."

"Ahh. We have typical in the line of duty marks, too." I fit the tourniquet and slid the needle in on the first try, blood filling the tube. "I don't think bloodwork will turn up anything concerning, but there may be traces of the substance still in your bloodstream, and along with the male's cadaver, might help calculate half-life. Anything we can add to the species profile will be helpful for future teams."

"I thought these lizards were rare." His breath tickled over my forehead.

"So did we." I was beginning to wonder what else we didn't know. And how it fit into the cryptid uptick no one but me was willing to call a concerning pattern. I loosed the tourniquet and slid the needle out, pressing a band-aid over the puncture. While I'd worked, he had bent closer to watch. When I straightened, we were very much in each other's space.

Despite his volume and attitude, this had to be a stressful experience. "We've all had in-depth triage and EMT training, and I truly believe you're fine. Otherwise, I would have had you in HQ's med center with our specialists, I promise. We'll keep an eye open for symptoms, and please, please tell me if you feel at all off in the next forty-eight hours. Deal?"

He huffed out a breath. "Yeah, deal. Listen—"

Whatever he'd been about to add, Kimi's rap on the door-frame announcing her arrival stopped cold.

She held out his phone. Which she'd lifted as soon as he'd brushed by her on arrival.

He stared at the phone like he'd never seen it before. "The hell?" He patted at his pockets.

At Kimi's shrug, red flooded his face.

He slammed the door in ours.

"Maybe you should have asked instead of going straight to pick-pocketing."

She gave me the same answer she always did. "It's not like I didn't return it." Then added, "We need to catch that lizard ASAP."

As in, before it targeted another victim.

Or my team ran out of patience with the current vic.

# CHAPTER 5

## BRUCE

*A*s four pairs of boots pounded up the outdoor walkway, metal clanging, Bruce stood his ground, blocking their progress any further into...the house, the barracks, whatever the correct fucking term was. He'd watched the four soldiers clatter out onto the narrow deck that ran the length of the building and down to the yard, obnoxiously lively for the crack of dawn. Normally, he'd have only been in bed an hour or two at that point after closing out a successful service. As if he needed more proof that normal had gone out the window.

Now, *she* led the group, back from whatever deeply disturbing activity monster-hunting private soldiers performed. All of them were in some sweaty version of gray on gray, tee or tanks and shorts. Basketball style for the too tall, too pretty, too damn talkative male member and barely-there running shorts on the women.

No way in hell was he noticing the way *her* shorts cupped her ass and set off her legs.

"Here." He tossed a handwritten list at her.

When she plucked it out of the air almost before it left his hand, he added a glare. "Go get everything on that list. Don't substitute anything. Don't forget anything."

The damn klepto, loose curls forming a halo at complete odds with her un-angelic talent for theft, looked to the bane of his existence and signed, "Is he for real?"

He stomped the floor hard, relying on the vibration to get the klepto's attention, along with the rest of the pack's. When she jerked her bambi-eyed gaze his way, he pulled out his dusty ASL skills, hoping her obvious lip reading covered any slip-ups, and signed back, "Yes, I am serious, Klepto. While you bunch may revel in living the cult survivalist lifestyle, I don't, and won't." The lack of any viable breakfast option and tea fed his annoyance.

His bane separated from the herd, again taking the lead. A quirk which sent equal parts annoyance and adrenalin swimming through his antioxidant-deprived blood stream, further irritating the fuck out of him.

She gave him a level look. "My office, now. You know, one of the doors you tried earlier. In case you aren't up on the minimal acceptable behavior when visiting other's homes, attempting to jimmy locked doors doesn't fall in the previously referenced category."

He didn't back down from challenges in the kitchen or anywhere else, and he'd learned early to establish that he wasn't a target, hard, fast, and first. He got in her face, close enough to pick out the darker band around her brown eyes. "Fuck. You."

She moved before the echo of his insult died and pain streaked up his arm, now in her grip and cranked behind his back in a shoulder lock.

He jerked hard, then quit as her grip tightened, pain amping up into a burn in his shoulder. She turned him and marched him past the common rooms and kitchen, then to the shortest hall.

Showing off some damn military multi-tasking skill, she kept him jacked up and palmed one of the decorative yellow tin panels on the thick door. The panel popped and slid sideways, exposing a science fiction-worthy electronic screen that she swiped her thumb across, then keyed in a code.

The door clicked open and she aimed him into the room, kicking the door closed behind them. At the solid thump locking them in, she let go of him.

He lunged back out of her reach. Searching for anything resembling a weapon before she beat his ass, he hefted a book heavy enough to give him a hernia and swung around.

She'd perched on the edge of a monstrosity of weathered wood and embossed iron posing as a desk, arms crossed. Fucking sitting there, looking him up and down without uttering one word, implying she was patiently waiting for *him* to act reasonable.

He clenched his jaw hard enough to horrify his parents and their years of orthodontist payments. Crossing his arms, he mirrored her but stayed standing. Hopefully far enough away to escape if she lost her cool.

"First, you'll apologize to the team, immediately."

He got as far as opening his mouth, and she dipped her chin, one damn fraction, and he might as well have been thirteen and standing in his Hebrew teacher's office, busted for another infraction.

He shut his mouth.

She continued. "Second, the team—Josh, Kimi, and Liv, not *Klepto*, *steroid-abusing asshole* and *hey, you*—aren't the enemy so stop treating them like hostiles. We didn't get you into this trouble. That was sucky, random bad luck. We are trying to get you out of this situation as quickly and safely as possible."

He ground his teeth hard enough his temples throbbed, but, damn it. Every word she said was pure truth.

"Third. Good job with the signing. It's primarily ASL, but we've added some of our own terms and shorthand. Kimi isn't hearing impaired or deaf. She lost her ability to speak when we were younger. Thank you for making the effort to communicate though."

If he didn't know himself better, he'd call the feeling that ambushed him guilt. He didn't do guilt. He also didn't do many apologies. He did believe in being honest with himself though and owning his actions, brilliant, good, or fucked up. "Look, I'm a dick pretty reliably. I'll make the effort to dial it back but it's a reflex. Yeah, I explored, and maybe I do push the rules. Am I under some version of arrest?"

"Of course not." She tilted her head, loosely braided ponytail swinging, like he hadn't been the definition of an asshole and she couldn't fathom why he'd have to ask. "However, locked areas are secured for a reason." She rapped her knuckles on the desk. "You don't belong in my office, the armory, and the annex and second garage attached to the gym."

He tensed, ready to come out swinging at the jab about not belonging in the gym. It wasn't the first time he'd come up against bullshit ideas that cooking and kitchens equaled weak, and he wasn't in the mood for some outdated, macho military definition of what being a man meant.

She kept talking though. "Aside from those areas, anything else is fair game. If I wasn't clear yesterday, you could have asked."

"Yeah, well. I subscribe to the better to ask forgiveness than permission school of thought." He temporarily tabled his knee-jerk reaction as potentially his mistake

When that almost-smile tilted the corners of her eyes, he went all in. Pulling his phone out of his pocket, he flashed the screen at her. "Let's talk about the fact that I can't send or receive messages or access any social media."

"Do I really need to tell you it's a security issue?" Her cheek dented in like she was biting the inside and thinking. "If—if—you can follow the rules, no GPS pins, no hints about where you really are, what you're doing, anything at all remotely traceable by association, or with us or the compound in the background, I'll see what I can do. Your device will be monitored though."

He'd never been shy about asks. "Calls and texts too?"

"HQ is working up your cover story. Give them another twenty-four hours to get details in place and you to memorize the key points, and then you can contact employers, friends, family, anyone who'll be concerned or suspicious of your absence, as long as you stick to the official script." She gave an apologetic shrug. "Everything will be monitored, both here and at HQ. If you can—"

"—not be a dick—"

"—I'll see what I can do about speeding up the process," she finished, the hinted-at smile blossoming into impish reality.

That naughty smile. Damned if it didn't mellow out the worst of his fuck you-ness. "I can't promise complete dickish containment, but I'll also do my best."

"So, you're food famous? Like reality cooking shows?"

Thrown by the lightning change of topic, he stumbled. "I…how the hell did you know that?"

"I checked the data we cloned from your phone after the code was cracked." She said it like both the ability to hack a password, and the balls to casually admit she had, were nothing.

"When? You didn't have it yesterday, Klepto did."

"Kimi," she said firmly. "So called klepto-like tendencies are part of the psychological profile for intelligence specialists. Standard procedure. You wouldn't answer your door, and I was checking for your possible houseguests, appointments scheduled for that residence, or social engagements that would put others at risk. You'd be surprised how often those things slip people's minds following a violent incident. Who remembers the A/C repair person appointment on the heels of almost being eaten by an unknown predator?"

Just like that, his burgeoning anger and self-righteousness tanked. He hoped like hell whoever created his fictional cover story was better at subterfuge than her. He doubted she could lie. No, he doubted she ever *thought* to lie.

"No television gigs for me. I was in Scottsdale because a hospitality group annoyed the hell out of me until I agreed to, theoretically as it turns out, revamp The Cellar. They fucked their chances at a James Beard nomination when I walked out though."

Her brow furrowed, exactly like someone trying to parse a foreign language spoken by a native speaker, when all the listener had ever heard was the high school class version. Confused, but too embarrassed to ask.

The sheer absurdity of the conversation hit him. Because what were the odds of people who carried restricted weapons and what had to be dark web tech, knowing or caring whether restaurant award nominations were political. He laughed, the first real one in days rocking him. "Shit. Ignore everything that came after 'no television gigs.' From the state of your kitchen, I'd already guessed none of you were gourmands."

The lines between her brows scrunched tighter. "What's wrong with our kitchen?"

His automatic snark died in the face of her earnestness and confusion.

He pulled his glasses off, pinching the bridge of his nose, searching for a semi-polite response. All he came up with was, "Where the fuck do I start? *Chemical* and *processed* are not food groups."

She reached into the inner waistband of her shorts, presumably into one of the minuscule pockets women's wear had, and out of politeness, he focused on the ugly-assed wall clock over her shoulder. At the crinkle of paper, he checked back.

She held up his list. "Then...this?"

"Absolute basic necessities," he said firmly enough to impress upon her his seriousness.

She scanned his handwriting. "What's wrong with our coffee and dish soap?"

"The coffee isn't free trade for starters and the soap is a potential carcinogen. Even if you don't want responsibly grown coffee, that doesn't taste like diluted cat piss as an added benefit, you do need to replace the soap. All of your cleaning supplies, as a matter of fact."

"Where do I even find these things?"

"If you don't want to go into Phoenix, Scottsdale has a decent farmer's market. It's Monday, Wednesday, and Saturday, on the east end of town."

That earned him another blank look.

"How do I, who have been in town less than a month, know this and you, who live here, don't?"

She did one of those *no biggie* shoulder lifts. "We've never had a call-out or mission there, pursued a cryptid into that area, or documented any problematic activity there via our street contacts along the eastern corridor. It doesn't fit any real or projected hunting ground profiles."

Her expression perked up. "We do know the twenty-four hour diners, all the pizza places, and the best food trucks, especially the street corn vendors. Oh, and the delivery schedule for the convenience stores."

He felt the imminent twitching of an eyelid coming on. He didn't know what was more horrific—talk of neighborhoods as hunting grounds or consuming any food that originated from a convenience store. "Holy hell. All right, regrouping here. What are the chances you or anyone on this base can identify what's on that list?"

"What are the chances you can identify what's in my armory?" That devilish gleam was back. Daring him.

He couldn't help his lips curving up for a millisecond any more than he could the laugh earlier. Nor could he help the urge to see how far their sparring might go.

From the satisfied lift of her brow, she'd noted his amusement, too damn observant. If they were keeping score, she was two for two.

She let it go though. "Real talk? Unless it's shelved and labeled, the chances are low. Like, not even breaking double-digits low."

"New idea. What are the odds we—" he motioned between them "—go together to the market?" He wasn't going to insult either of them by acting as if he didn't appreciate the risks she took in her job, her leadership position, or dance around the fact that he wouldn't be going anywhere without an armed companion for the duration.

Her cheek dented in again. "The whole alley incident turned out to be helpful. The time from encountering the female, until the male located and attacked you gave the Lab a baseline."

He snorted. "Glad my trauma was useful. How is that answering my market question?"

"According to the Lab's newest projection, using your attack, data from natural species, and what they've analyzed from the specimen, it looks like once prey is out of easy sight and scent range, it requires prey staying in a location for four to eight hours before there's enough of a scent pool for detection. Terrain, weather, and population movement always factor in, too. I'm saying three, three and a half hours to err on the side of safety."

"Our trip won't take that long." He sensed an opening, and evaluated her body language, looking for clues on which way to go. "What else? Talk to me."

"Technically, a civilian isn't to go off site until their DNA has been processed and logged at HQ, as well as here."

He would've seen the rule as flexible and worked on how far he could bend without technically breaking it. From the way she shifted her weight, the energy and intensity that he'd already learned were part of her, so did she. "I hear a *but* in there, Ramirez."

"Your DNA has been on file in our security system since I took blood yesterday. Our lab also doesn't waste time. You've been processed and the official notice will hit my and Liv's inbox by lunch."

"Let's go."

She closed the few feet between them, that unconscious air of authority manifesting. "If you're thinking this excursion is your chance to bolt, I'm sorry but I'll have to stop you. You aren't a prisoner but you are a potential danger to others, and we do not endanger civilians. Plus, you'll lose your free pass here."

*That's no big loss* automatically popped into his head, on its way to his big mouth. He pushed back against the reflex. She'd been accommodating, and he didn't have a valid reason to bitch. "I have a damn good imagination. I've also had a night of staring at the ceiling and envisioning the damage that Godzilla-wannabe could do. I'm acknowledging that I'm shit at playing well with others when I'm not the one in charge. I'm guessing I'm not the only one." He dipped his chin at her, and earned another of those micro-smiles.

"However, I'm going with your expertise in this situation. Not to mention, I'm lousy at—"

"Staying still," she finished for him. "I recognized the signs." She leaned around him and opened the door. "Meet

60

me in fifteen minutes. Leave the phone. You don't want me patting you down."

That perverse thrill shot through him again. He was tempted to keep the phone to see if she followed through with the threat.

# CHAPTER 6

## VEE

"*W*hat happens if he makes a run for it?" Liv reclined on the plush, two-person beanbag pillow by Kimi's closet as I flipped through hangers.

"Or you *accidentally* let him go," Kimi signed. "Misplace him. It happens."

"Too much paperwork," Liv said, fluffing damp hair that was drying into killer waves.

I found the shirt I wanted, pulled off the plain tee I'd grabbed post-shower, and slipped the flowy tank on. Turning side to side in front of the full-length mirror, I made sure the bellyband holster didn't leave an imprint.

"Don't steal my favorite shirt," Kimi signed.

"That's my shirt, which you stole first," Liv said, sinking deeper in the pillow.

I ignored their complaints and tightened my ankle sheath and pulled the cuffed jean leg down, double checking that it and the knife weren't visible either. It was too hot for jeans, but security over comfort. "He isn't that bad."

Kimi snorted. "He is that bad."

I felt Liv's gaze on me as I stood. Like she saw under

disputed clothes and skin, to the bit of me that liked our temporary resident's bark. The part that was curious if his bite was as much fun as his bark.

All she said was, "Bring back a couple of pizzas. Josh is inventorying so a food reward is in order."

Officially, Liv should be the one ponying up the reward since as lieutenant, inventory was on her list. That wasn't how things worked here though. We were all in it together. Josh did inventory. She reviewed the satellite photos on my desk. Kimi switched out the SUV tire that had been patched once too often. I brought back pizza. Teamwork.

I gave them a thumbs-up and went searching for our guest.

It was a short search. He'd taken over one of the barstools at the eat-in, guarding the way out like he thought I'd stealth past him. Correction, past him and the plug-in cooler keeping him company, which I'd last seen in our pantry. "Really?

He hopped off his sentinel seat, tucking his prize under his arm. "You snooped through my phone, I snooped through your compound. Besides, we'll need this."

Fair enough. I tapped in my code and the series for a non-call out trip, and the door to the garage clicked open. He hustled, getting to the SUV first. I kept going, out and around to the personal bay. Once he saw our objective, he repeated the maneuver. He stood by the driver's door, one hand out, one on the truck door. "Unlike some people, I know the layout of Scottsdale."

I removed his hand from the door handle. "Not a chance, Mister Kantor. This is Liv's baby, and my sister doesn't play."

"Then let's take yours."

"I'm not a car person. I use our Company SUV or Liv's ride." I climbed in and only then unlocked the other doors.

He took a minute to stash the cooler in the back seat, then

settled in. He stayed silent as I pulled out, cleared the gate, and took what basically amounted to our driveway since we were the only building on the road.

I could practically hear the gears in his head whirling though. Biting down on my natural inclination, I kept quiet, curious what he'd come up with next.

It was worth the wait when he said, "Is today casual Friday?" He glanced at the truck, then at my clothes.

"Mmm-hmm."

He scowled at me and my lack of details. Then went at satisfying his curiosity from a different angle. "Ramirez. Muñez. Your sister."

"Yep. Kimi is Kimora Albisu. Our brother is Joshua Silva."

He frowned hard enough I should've heard his brows clack against each other. "You're fucking going to make me ask outright."

"Hmm?" This was way more fun than talking.

He ground his teeth, then caved, less than graceful. "You fucking win. If you are siblings—and, sure, I can definitely buy that with you three, and maybe with Steroid Boy— what's with the last names?"

"Josh. Not Steroid Boy, remember?"

"Josh. Now keep talking."

"Most of us aren't biologically sibling-siblings or half sibs. We're raised that way though. That's all that matters."

"Somehow you ended up working together? When did you make that decision?" Skepticism dripped off the question. He flicked a finger at the truck, apparently the stand in for the team and Company.

"We didn't decide. We were raised and trained to be this." I mimicked his finger wave.

"There is no damn way your orphanage or foster parents or adoptive parents could anticipate this military monster squad."

I took my eyes off the road, met his, and raised a brow. Not as accomplished as Liv, but going by the flush creeping up his neck, good enough.

"The fu—"

"Left or right?" I asked

His mouth snapped shut on his question and he pointed.

Right it was.

The next few miles were limited to terse commands, and an order to park closer to the market entrance—a huge space with tables, tenting, and a crowd.

I ignored the last demand, parking well back and away from the other vehicles. The need to avoid close quarters and blind spots that could act as ambush points ran too deep. So did keeping civilians as far away from conflicts as possible. At Bruce's scowl, I left it at "Protocol."

He made a retaliatory stab at one-upsmanship, bailing and heading for the entrance while I locked the truck. I stuck the fob in my pocket and caught up by cutting in front of him and stopping. "Don't do that again."

"Try to keep up next time."

I grabbed his wrist as he side-stepped. "I'm responsible for you."

"I've been taking care of myself since—"

"Anangoa."

His nostrils pinched then flared.

"Also, I'm responsible for the safety of everyone in this crowd today. Don't complicate my job."

He tilted his head back, gazing at the cloudless sky. "Fuck."

"Is that a yes?"

"I'll dial it back."

"Where do we go first?" One of us had to be graceful about agreeing, and I was the C.O. Plus, this place was potentially awesome.

"Dry goods first, then produce."

The venue was even more packed close up, but people were polite, no pushing or trying to cut between us or crowding so that we had to walk single file.

I kept half my attention locked on basics—weird shifts in the crowd, odd smells, someone searching for a lost child. The indefinable something that said cryptid problem.

All I got was good vibes, allowing the other half of my attention to follow my charge, who had not lied about his familiarity with the layout. Now I was the one lagging behind, forcing him to wait for me. At least he quit glaring after the first few tables. I glanced up from a display of goat's milk soaps and lotions, including one for chapped hands and cuticles, to see him watching.

I set the parchment and ribbon wrapped container down. "Sorry."

He shook his head, but not like he was annoyed. "Never apologize for your curiosity and desire to learn, or to experience life instead of sleepwalking through it."

I wasn't positive what that meant.

Like he understood, he dropped back beside me. "Most people are dull as fuck. They walk through life only seeing a fraction of what's there, the way researcher's claim most people only use a fraction of their brain's potential."

"It's easy to find interesting things here," I said. "Farmer's markets are cool. The place is a tactical nightmare if there was a cryptid attack. Too little structure, no clearly delineated exits and security, and way too much potential for collateral damage."

"I'm married to my fucking work, but even I take a damn day off." He scowled as we bypassed a couple of vendors who didn't interest him, then stopped mid-crowd. "Do you like ice cream?"

"Is there really any other answer than yes?"

"Here." He used his elbow, nudging me to the left. This stall was more of an intricate complex, almost a complete building. One lined with glass-fronted freezers, and tall displays of bottles and jars. A huge blackboard hung behind the counter area, *Flavor of the Day* done in pink and green chalk, and under that, *Cactus Flower and Agave*.

"They're a local dairy and creamery. No antibiotics and all grass fed cattle. No stalls or pens."

"Happy cows?"

"Fucking ecstatic cows. Pick a flavor." He stuck me in line, and headed for one of the cooler cases, coming back with cheeses not sliced and wrapped in plastic, while I puzzled through flavors I'd never heard of.

The family in front of us paid, both dads busy with a stroller and a toddler. They missed it when the older kid caught her toe. She didn't fall but her cone paid the price.

"Have you decided?" Bruce checked with me.

Instead of answering him, I addressed the woman in a cow-print apron behind the counter. "Could you do a cone of whatever she had?"

The cashier followed my discrete motion, leaning far enough over the counter to see. "Double mint chip? Sure."

Instead of ordering next, Bruce stayed silent. Watching me.

"Three ninety-nine, please."

I paid then pointed at the parents who had just figured out their ice cream crisis. "Could you?"

The cashier smiled and cut in front, walking out to hand one of the dads a cone, and nod in my direction.

The guy pressed both hands together like he was praying and mouthed "thank you."

"Your turn."

At Bruce's gruff command, I spoke to the returned cashier. "Today's special, please."

"Two of them." He handed her cash but watched me. "You like cactus flower?"

"Let's find out. It sounded interesting."

Bruce handed me my cone, then joined me, stepping out of the flow of traffic, still more focused on me than his cone as I taste tested.

"Whoa." I took a second taste and confirmed my results. "Ecstatic cows make great ice cream."

The family behind us laughed, the mom adding, "This is our favorite spot every Saturday."

It took me a second to realize she was talking to me.

As she moved away, I whispered, "That will never not be weird."

"The ice cream?"

"No, the ice cream is great. I mean the people thing." We rejoined the busy crowd. "No one is screaming, or crying, or afraid of me. Those are the top three responses with most of our encounters when people see us-see us. We don't really have regular contact with civilians. Karaoke night, or grabbing food aside, it is in and out fast. For most items we do regularly need, we order online and have them sent to a postal delivery box. For all others, we rotate among stores and gas stations, instead of always buying from one favorite or close store. Like that. We can't draw too much attention and have people remember us."

Bruce swore under his breath, at least respectful of the mixed company.

I tried explaining. "If people remember us, then they might start asking questions we can't answer. When we're around civilians, ninety-percent of the time it's due to a cryptid incursion. Even if we've saved everyone involved, they're still freaked, so they kind of lump us in with the danger."

"Hanging out with a short guy in hipster-ish glasses is the

epitome of non-threatening, Ramirez." His voice did that odd gruff thing again. "When you're not in military gear and armed to the teeth, all people see is a beautiful woman out on a date." For a second, he looked like he wished he could take it back, then shrugged.

"Thank you, Mister Kantor."

"Bruce. We've stabbed Godzilla and bought non-GMO ice cream together. We're in first fucking name territory."

"You just don't want to call me commander."

He shifted bags and motioned me to speed up. "Yeah, that too."

# CHAPTER 7

## BRUCE

*F*ucking hell. Scottsdale wasn't a city, but a time machine that catapulted him back to the most awkward part of his teen years.

He should have bitten his tongue off. Shoved ice cream in his face until his brain froze and forgot how to send messages to his vocal cords. Anything to prevent his runaway mouth from speaking.

But, hell. He hadn't done anything other than state a fact. Ramirez—Vee—was curious, she was gorgeous, and she had a spark. It hit him...she was present in the moment, savoring every experience.

He didn't actually regret his comment. She deserved better than expecting people to run from her or lump her in with the monsters, even if he was the only person available to fill that slot. The realization that he'd treated her more or less the same as multitudes of ungrateful people before him slapped him. To compound his guilt, he had also bitched and moaned and insulted her, her home, and what passed for her family.

At least he didn't have to add sexual harassment to his list of crimes. She hadn't taken his blurted comment as anything but what it was intended as—a statement of fact. She already seemed to have forgotten about it.

He needed to be glad, as opposed to the curl of disappointment currently lodged somewhere in his chest. The last thing he needed was sexual tension to complicate an already surreal situation. He hadn't processed the last forty-eight hours yet, jumping from one tense moment to the next. Realistically, he was still in survival mode. The monsters, government sanctioned cover-ups, and continuing danger were going to hit him soon, and he hadn't been kidding about accepting a therapist appointment. He reached in his pocket for his phone to check on the closest synagogue and rabbi. Then swore, because his phone was non-functional and at a military base, the exact things he'd want to discuss.

If secret government factions had medical headquarters and therapists, why not provisions for religious needs as well? He turned to ask Vee.

He almost blurted out the question about black ops religious structures to the cranky-looking elderly codger by his elbow, in the spot where Vee should be. He spun, searching stalls for a petite brunette in an ocean-blue shirt.

His quarry was two yards away, staring down at her phone. She shoved it in her back pocket and locked eyes with him, perfectly aware of his location. She skirted the other shoppers, not glancing at colorful table displays or checking out interesting people, back beside him too fast.

"What's wrong?"

She shook her head, and motioned him to follow her. Pace too brisk, expression too neutral.

Unease replaced his curiosity. Feet from the truck, she tapped the key fob, lights blinking and unlocking doors. She slid in without a word.

He shoved food in the cooler and climbed in. "Godzilla Junior?"

The truck's motor rumbled to life. "No, you're safe. However, we do have a call-out. There's a problem." She pulled out of the lot and turned north.

The base was to the west. "Ramirez?" When she didn't answer, he tried again. "Vee?"

"I don't have time to take you back to the compound." She finally looked his way.

His gut clenched. "Holy fucking shit. I did not sign up for this. Turn this truck around."

"I really wish I could. Our intel is a windigo pack, and the rest of the team is already enroute."

"You said windigos were basically dogs with a hygiene issue. Let the other three round them up."

"This is too close to a residential area." From the way she chewed at a cuticle, there was more to it than leashing devil dogs. She was holding out on him.

Before he could demand more, she made a sharp right, and he grabbed for the oh-shit handle as his ass slid sideways. She accelerated through stop signs, and he finally focused on the scenery. The desert lay out this way but they were currently surrounded by green, in a land of rock and sand landscapes. This was a pocket neighborhood, one with a fucking park and elementary school.

Vee cut left and a sprawling brick campus vista filled the windshield. Gut-clenching horror gave way to relief. This was a Saturday. No classes, no kids.

The relief evaporated as Vee navigated the parking area, and the school marquee with a Dust Devils logo and below it in removable letters *Booster game, three p.m.*

The place was an hour away from being flooded with players, coaches, and families.

Vee executed an illegal maneuver, driving over the manicured grass, and stopped. Stands, empty for now, threw shadows over them. The sharpness of crushed grass blew in, Vee's door already standing open. Her shadow lay long over the grass and concrete, twice her size and ominous. The back driver door opened and a minute later, a flutter of blue landed on the seat, the shirt she'd worn today.

"The hell, Vee?"

The rasp of velcro answered, and fuck it, he twisted and hung between the seats, ready for answers. One of the long-sleeved, black and gray urban camo shirts he'd first seen in his cryptid-infested kitchen replaced her swingy blouse. He watched as she strapped what looked like jointed, matt-black Kevlar over the shirt. She kept the jeans but shed her sandals and stomped into boots.

"The truck has reinforced panels and bullet proof glass, light but enough to keep windigos out. Stay inside this truck. No matter what you see, no matter what you hear, no matter if you'd bet every knife you own that the fight is over and there's nothing more dangerous than sand spurs out here. Stay. Inside. Understand?" She finally looked up at him, not seeming to need her full concentration to secure the webbing and straps to both thighs. "Kantor?"

"Bruce," came out automatically. "Fuck. Yeah, okay. Staying put I can do. I'm fucking secure in my masculinity."

She tossed him the keys. "I'm trusting you. I think you're too smart to bail and risk unleashing that anangoa on civilians."

She shoved the back seat sideways, in a direction the manufacturer had never envisioned, then tapped another of those high-tech pads, the truck floor revolving and a metal unit rising. Giving him a clear view of a row of matte-black guns, which Vee pulled out, expertly checked, then added to the holsters on both legs, before selecting two knives that resembled the illegitimate offspring from a machete and butcher's cleaver's one night stand. The blades shone a strange color, too silver in the middle.

Vee hesitated, hand hovering over the smallest handgun in the rack. "Have you ever used a gun?"

He held both palms up. "No, and I'm honest enough to tell you I'd probably end up accidentally shooting myself."

A trace of a smile pushed the calculating professionalism aside for a brief second. "See? Smart."

As the whine of tires on asphalt announced the arrival of the big-assed SUV he'd ridden in only days before, her humor vanished. "Lock the doors. Stay inside. One of us will let you know when it's over."

"*You'll* let me know."

She pulled her hair into a tail, then wrapped it into a tight bun. "Probably. Locks."

He swore but hit the controls. Satisfied, she jogged over, the other three soldiers bailing out of their truck and joining her. If he'd had doubts as to who was in charge, the scene in front of him provided the answer. Smallest one there, she was the center of the storm and the rest faced her, fixed on whatever orders she gave. Their body language altered. Still standing in a high school field, but in one breath they'd gone from relaxed to coiled potential.

They wheeled, splitting into two groups.

Vee and the pickpocket scaled the bleachers like gravity didn't apply to them. The other two stayed on the ground, moving parallel, headed for the flat building in front housing the gym and locker rooms.

A tree lizard, plentiful enough that they might as well be the state's official mascot, shimmied up the bleacher base, intent on lizard business. The air already heating under the

74

afternoon sun and perfect Arizona sky, he toyed with the idea of cracking windows. A fraction to allow air in couldn't be that big a deal. They'd find the dog-thing. Wrap up this situation the way they had the cryptid in his rental, and boom, get back to what passed for their normal. He'd get the artisan mozzarella he'd dumped in the shitty cooler into a real fridge before it lost consistency.

As his finger touched the window button, the earth boiled and came alive.

He blinked hard and the scene changed, and it was no longer the heat-shimmering blacktop parking lot going seismic. Dirty gray things poured across the drowsy complex, like storm clouds on four legs.

An eerie wail rose, the noise climbing higher and higher, and his skin made an effort to crawl off his body, primitive survival instincts rising.

As easily as Vee had climbed the seat scaffolding, a trio of the things scrambled after her. One fucking standing, legs jointed wrong, but upright. Walking, then tensing and leaping on those nightmare legs, grabbing bars feet above Vee.

Its teeth—freaking fangs—caught the sun. Vee grabbed a seat base and used her momentum, swinging at the huge monster. Her foot took it under the jaw, snapping its head back.

Two more scrambled over its twitching body.

To his untrained eyes, the fight devolved into teeth and knives. Arcs of the same foul red-green tinted blood as from the anangoa splashed seats and ground. The team's arms rose, and cut in merciless sweeps. Creatures fell, some headless, others with parts severed. More kept coming, climbing on and over the bodies.

He tried keeping track, but monsters and soldiers moved

too fast. The monsters clustering and the humans disappearing behind the moving wall of evil.

Whatever Vee claimed about cryptids being natural species couldn't be true. Even through the truck's protective glass and metal, the windings unnaturalness, their sheer wrongness, coated his skin in an oily wash.

An eternity later, he picked humans out among the chaos. Mounds of dead creatures outnumbered the living. A body hurtled from the sky, hitting the ground in a wet crunch, and he jumped, heart slamming. He bashed the shit out of his head, because he'd ended up practically fused with the windshield, nose pressed against the glass.

The body had been a creature falling. He revised that—a creature getting tossed. Vee came into view at the top of the bleachers. She flicked one of the huge blades, gunk flying. She had tossed or kicked the monster off the stands.

The other soldier, her sister, gave her a thumbs-up from a row lower. The risers were clear, nothing except the two women moving. He dragged his attention to ground level. The rest of the team stood in a ragged circle of unmoving creatures and creature bits. They gave Vee the same thumbs-up gesture.

One of the black mounds twitched, a foreleg reaching out, claws scoring the ground. Attempting to pull itself free. The soldiers whirled like they were connected, blades slicing into the not-quite-dead monster.

A flash of movement where there should only be grass caught Bruce's attention. A dirty-gray streak resolving into a last creature, easily twice as large as the others. It rocketed from the risers at an angle. The pair on the ground were busy dispatching the dying cryptid, their backs to the approaching danger. Right in the monster's path.

He swore and pounded on the window. "Look up, damn it! Fucking look."

Neither heard, the monster now only feet away. Silent, not baying like the others, red eyes slitted, jaws open.

Another body plummeted from the sky. One in camo body armor. Vee. She'd jumped from the top of the bleachers, a good twenty feet up.

She landed on the monster. Grabbing and pulling herself firmly astride it. Its bellow-bay rattled the truck mirrors. The monster bucked like an infuriated rodeo bull. Vee slid, then caught herself. Her legs locked around its thick neck.

The pair whirled in a mad tornado of monster and human. Green-tinged blood flew. Brighter red droplets hit the ground. Human blood. Bruce broke out in a clammy sweat.

The monster reared straight up, kept going, falling backward like a horse in a bad western. The beast and Vee rolled. First one on top, then the other. The soldiers on the ground circled, but even Bruce could tell they couldn't get a window to strike.

At a sharp bark of gunfire, he jumped again. The thing jerked, blood erupting from its hindquarters.

Vee wrapped her arm around the creature's neck, her face inches from its teeth. Bruce's racing pulse threatened to pump free of his body. Metal flashed and Vee drove her knife through the thing's eye.

It bucked, rearing onto its back legs. Then fell, collapsing. Vee rolled free and came up on one knee, gun in her hand, sighted on the creature. Twin pops echoed. Bullets slammed into the monster's head. Half of its face pulped.

The creature quivered, then didn't move again.

"FuckFuckFuck." His chant was loud in the sudden silence. Metal clattered and the thief, Kimi, hopped down from bleacher level to bleacher level, gun in hand. She'd been the source of the second shot.

She jumped the last few feet, landing beside her sister.

She offered Vee a hand and hauled her up. The other two loped over, joining the pair.

And tapped knuckles. Like this was some fucking game they'd won, not a bloody, gory life and death fight.

Like she felt Bruce's glare, or heard him still swearing, she looked toward the truck. Then made the universal sign for stay the hell put. He flipped her his favorite universal sign.

As she lowered her arm, red and rust brown showed, her sleeve shredded and skin visible. Giving the world a peek at pink shit that shouldn't be exposed.

Indifferent, she checked a pocket then made a face. Vee motioned and the guy tossed her his phone. The call barely lasted long enough to qualify before she tossed the phone back. The group split, her brother and the klepto jogging his way, Vee and her other sister switching out used gun for new, then they went opposite directions, weapons out.

He half fell out of the seat at a rap on the window. He glared at the klepto, now by the driver's window.

She signed, "Pop the locks."

For a second he considered not complying then got the fuck over himself, hitting the button and bouncing back to his seat, despite the guy standing outside of it. Fuck if he was getting in the second row of seats, and since he had a fuckton of questions, the front made a more strategic site for grilling.

The guy retreated and opened the back door at the same time his sister opened the front.

The smell that invaded the truck—the ice cream from earlier threatened to come up, and he flung his door open to gag. Which only allowed more of the decaying garbage on a hot day stench in. He slammed the door and fought his gag reflex.

Seatbelts clicked and the motor turned over, cold air blasting from the vents. He wiped watering eyes and took a breath.

"Sorry, man." Vee's brother hung over the back of Bruce's seat. "Breathe around it."

"What the hell is that?" Vee said the creatures smelled. That was an understatement on par with saying nuclear waste in your backyard lowered your property value.

"'Digos,'" the guy supplied, entirely too damn cheerful. "They are rank."

"They stink worse dead," Klepto signed. "How is that even fair?" She flipped the visor down and used the mirror to check out her brother. "Also, you are wearing 'digo gunk on your cuff."

The guy collapsed back in his seat. "Liv's gonna have a meltdown."

"Liv is going to make you detail this entire truck until it's de-grossed to her specs." She gave a rough snort-laugh, and put the truck in gear.

"Hold the fuck up. You aren't going anywhere. " Bruce whirled on the klepto and grabbed her arm.

Blazing pain flared in his wrist, hard enough he gasped, his hand empty and twisted close to the breaking point.

Once she had his attention, she increased the pressure a fraction.

"Apologize." Her brother's voice was cold and flat, all goofing gone.

"You can't leave Vee here," Bruce gritted out. Which wasn't exactly an apology, but her grip loosened, and she tilted her head.

Fuck if it didn't feel like his sister was here in person, interrogating his ass.

"Liv and Vee are securing the area and beginning cleanup," her brother said.

"Vee is bleeding." Bruce glared at her sister, then at the guy. "Hell, you've both already got bruises showing. Get that cleaning service you used on my rental in here instead."

The grip on his wrist let go. The truck backed up and turned for the exit.

The guy talked over Bruce's swearing. "We can't wait for Cleaners. Your house was a contained scene. This is too open and public, so the risk of civilian exposure is over acceptable limits." The guy glanced from his legs, knees almost in his face from lack of leg room, to Bruce. "Hey, you mind?"

Only the fact that the guy had a bruise the size of a dinner plate, or one of those hell hound's paws, blooming along his jaw convinced Bruce to scoot his seat forward. "Keep talking, and tell me why you aren't the one staying. I saw Vee's shoulder from fifty yards away."

"Protocol," he said, like that explained everything. "Vee is the C.O., Liv is Lieutenant."

He turned to her sister, because at least she seemed to have a brain. Mostly one handed, she signed, "The C.O. watches out for the public first, then the team second. It's their responsibility to take the more difficult aspects."

"We all have our part." Josh took over so his sister could concentrate on the road. "Kimi will send out drones as soon as we hit base, to confirm no 'digos followed us and that there aren't any viable targets left in the area. Then she'll mess with traffic signal times or whatever else is needed to keep civilians or LEO's, law enforcement organizations, out of the way. I'll restock the truck and our personal weapons. Sometimes calls come back to back, and weapons are priority one."

Priority one.

Not getting medical help, not taking care of themselves, but restocking guns and bullets.

If he'd needed another reason to get the hell out of here, he'd just heard it.

Public first. Team second. As if they weren't equally valuable, and their comfort and safety didn't matter.

Vee's sister had turned the radio on, playing with lists until she found one that suited her. Her fingers tapped out the rhythm while her brother mangled lyrics, singing off key about being wanted dead or alive, as Bruce tried and failed to wrap his head around thinking your sole value was being sent out to repeatedly get the hell beat out of you, or worse.

# CHAPTER 8

## VEE

*I* backspaced, erasing the last line, which more closely resembled a chupacabra having walked across the keyboard than a coherent sentence, then retyped what I actually meant, highlighting the sheer numbers of windigos we'd taken down.

Seeing it on the page made the total even less believable. Liv and I had counted though, then recounted independently twice more. The whole encounter had that implausible feel, starting with the pack size and ending with the alpha's unnatural behavior.

This wasn't the first windigo weirdness, just the most startling. It wouldn't be enough for HQ to call the mission anything other than *an isolated anomaly*, the heading they had filed the other reports under, where I'd noted oddities.

The team wasn't convinced, either. This went under my heading of a potentially brewing crisis, though. I switched tabs, entering the aberrations into the ever-expanding spreadsheet in my personal set of research files, notes, and sorta-theories. The first two I had tons of. The third, not so much.

I tabbed back to the official report and hit send as a ghost of a knock filtered in. "Enter," I yelled because the office's thick oak and adobe were topnotch soundproofing, another throwback to a time when large teams meant a strict hierarchy and need to know mindset.

Our guest opened the door, as fast and aggressive as he did everything else, walking in like he was sure of his place and his welcome.

And yeah, that confidence, bordering on arrogance, had started off attractive, and only got more appealing each time I saw it. Especially since we'd signed our peace treaty by way of the market trip.

His gaze tracked over me, stopping at my shoulder and the neat line of stitches. I wouldn't have bothered but they were in a spot I couldn't easily not use, which could reopen them.

Lines creased his brow.

"Was everything okay?" There was only one reason I could think of that he would be here and upset—if the farmer's market purchases hadn't made it through the mission. Maybe a promise to go the next day they were open would hold him over.

"Was what okay?"

"The stuff from the market today. Did it make it in the cooler while the truck was off?"

The lines cut deeper, at odds with his eyes. "Yes."

Ooookay. Time for attempt number two at communicating with civilians. "Do you need something?"

The muscle in his jaw flexed. He came the rest of the way into the room. "Here." He shoved the lamp over and sat a bowl and spoon in front of me.

I leaned and sniffed, enticing vanilla rising in a warm stream. "What is this?"

"Pudding."

It didn't resemble any pudding we'd ever had, not in a plastic cup, and warm instead of refrigerated. I double-checked with him.

"I made enough for everyone but you've been sequestered in here ever since getting that." He gestured at my patched shoulder.

"Thus the hand delivery?"

"Yeah." The frown was back. "I can put it in the fridge if you have to get back to whatever it is you're working on. The pudding is better when it's warm though." He reached for the bowl.

I didn't exactly snatch it out of his reach—more picked it up quickly. I'd missed lunch, and dinner had been a granola bar from my desk, and whatever he'd made, my stomach grumbled, ready to try the contents of the bowl. Hopefully, warm pudding was flan's close cousin.

Satisfaction smoothed his forehead. He didn't make any move to leave. "Private military has bullshit paperwork too, I see."

"The C.O. gets stuck doing the detailed debrief report for every mission, no less than six hours post-mission."

He settled against the edge of my desk, facing me with his arms crossed. The move pulled his polo tight, highlighting muscles underneath. "Eat and talk."

Since crossed arms seemed more default than an indication of anger with him, I did. "Archives are invaluable for research and training. This one took longer than usual. Weird always does."

"Since my definition of weird is a black ops assault on skunk-scented, partially bipedal hell hounds, you're going to have to elaborate."

I picked through for what I could tell him. "Sadly, the decayed skunk thing is disgustingly normal. The rest..." I tapped the spoon against the desk, thinking. "Cryptids have crazy-effective means of evading detection. The Chameleon Effect is what the zoology crew calls it, and it is one of the defining features that move a species into the cryptid classification. Aside from that, they are like any other animal. Predictable. They act, and react, predictably."

That. That was what had been nagging at me the hardest.

"Today wasn't normal, I take it?" He grasped the issue as quickly as an agent versed in biology and tactics, no need to point out my thought process.

"Windigos skirt the line between lower animals and more self-aware ones. The zoology crew say that's what the occasional bi-pedal thing is, some kind of pre-cursor to an evolutionary change. They're rarely that far into populated areas. People kinda notice the odor, so the element of surprise is lost. You don't want to know how many times we've cleaned a horde out of dumps and sewer treatment plants."

Bruce made an encouraging noise.

"The size of that horde was four times normal. Then when bodies start falling, the rest of the horde always, *always* turns and runs, no fighting unless cornered." I nibbled at my nail. Having an audience who didn't automatically discount my finds as no big was refreshing. It was also bringing new connections and ideas into being. That was how I came up with my best stuff, random facts and events cooking away in my subconscious 'til the perfect theory or idea popped out, fully grown. "The horde leader was oversized, too. It also should have led the attack, not been hiding or holding back, then lead the retreat when the fight turned against them."

"The thing that attacked you at the end? It sure as fuck wasn't running."

"I noticed. Anyway, there isn't enough to speak to a macro-level change in behavior. Only micro." When I glanced up, his weird scowl was back in place. Hearing the people responsible for your safety had questions couldn't be reassuring. Time for a new subject.

I angled the spoon and cradled the bowl in both hands, inhaling again. "Pudding, huh? Is it medicinal or something?"

He stared at me like I was as unfamiliar as a 'digo. "Jesus H Christ. No, it's not medicinal. It's—it tastes good. Period. It's comfort food."

I took a bite, sweetness and vanilla exploding across my taste buds, but layered, not like the one note of what I'd thought until now was my favorite pudding. I groaned. "This is even better than the ice cream."

"Of course it is. I made it." Satisfaction softened his expression.

"Your turn. Tell me about comfort food."

He settled in like he had no intention of leaving, or like he actually enjoyed being in here with me.

"It was a thing, when we had a cold, wiped out on a bike, had a wisdom tooth out, shit like that." He laughed. "Maybe it did have a medicinal use after all—for hiding pills or as a bribe to take some foul concoction and not drive the adults over the edge fighting to get medicine into a squirming toddler."

"Cool. Most of what I, all of us, know about civilian life comes from movies and television. Not exactly peer-reviewed sources, right? It's hard to know what's common in real life and what's a writer or actor taking liberties, or even pure imagination."

"You go out in the real world. If you didn't, I wouldn't be around for us to have this conversation, because I'd be a lizard amuse-bouche."

I made a note to look up amuse-bouche. "Sure, we can have a group night out. Shopping. Food. We only have to keep it superficial. "

"What constitutes superficial?"

"We aren't supposed to be memorable. Basically, not develop close ties with anyone who would notice those in the line of duty injuries you mentioned, or who might know more about our cover occupations than we do, or expect to visit our apartment or job." I dragged my spoon through the pudding and considered rules, and what constituted merely bending as opposed to technically breaking.

"Ramirez?" he snapped his fingers. "Vee? Are you okay? Do you need a real doctor?"

"See? This is an example of why we have minimal-fraternization rules. I get that pudding equals comfort to you. But I don't understand why you would think I need a doctor."

He stared at me for a minute across a gulf of alien experiences, before pulling his glasses off and rubbing them on his shirt.

This felt like a good time to redirect the conversation. He was interesting. Interesting and easy to talk to and I wasn't ready for our conversation to end. "Who made you feel-better pudding?" I scooped up another bite, savoring it.

Bruce relaxed a fraction, and I made a note. Whether he knew it or not people enjoying his food put him in a better mood. "My grandmothers. Well, my nona. My other, my bubbe, went more with magma-hot chicken soup to boil the germs out."

I made a go-on noise, licking pudding off the back of my spoon, drawing the novel experience out.

His gaze followed my motion, and he cleared his throat. "I learned a lot from both sets of grandparents."

"Were they cooks, too? Chefs." I quickly corrected, his attitude when Josh made that mistake still fresh.

"No, and neither side was especially taken with my choice although they respected that it was my choice to make."

"Why didn't they want you taking this career path?"

He laughed but not like he was amused. "My mom's a

lawyer like her father. So is my brother. My sister is a stock-broker, like my dad. Our grandparents were either immi-grants and poor, or regular working class poor. They worked hard, and wanted better for their kids."

I got that some jobs paid more. The finer points of why, not so much. "A chef wasn't better?"

"They don't see, or refuse to see, that cook and chef aren't synonymous. As far as they're concerned, what I do isn't prestigious or important. Nor do they consider it a stable occupation."

"But feeding people is a necessity. On the scale of needs it's a core requirement, like safety."

He looked at me, almost startled. Then did that gruff thing, shrugging. "Creative people and non-creative people, and never the twain shall meet. Some people value stability over any other experience. They're willing to sacrifice what makes life worth living in exchange for the guarantee of safety."

I wondered which side agents fell on. From birth, we were guaranteed a future by the Company.

"What about your parents, or foster parents, I guess?" Bruce watched me, back to relaxed.

"I don't have parents. No one on this team does."

"I need some kind of secret agent- to-normal translation guide. Everyone has parents or at least parental figures even if the biological parents aren't in the picture."

"We don't."

He made a *keep going* gesture.

At least I was picking those up fast. "Everyone in the Company is like us. We're a mix of scouring orphanages and taking in abandoned and unwanted infants in lots of countries. Like, those where it's poverty level subsistence or society is in upheaval because of civil and military conflict, especially if there's no safety net for people. Double down on that in places where female children aren't desirable. HQ does good works, and saves us. I mean, a few of us are agents' kids. All we do is based on merit and skill though not parentage. A few of us know who our parents are but it's not like knowing matters."

Bruce stared at me, and not with the interested air he'd had since he walked in. His face had lost color. "They do what?"

Clearly, I wasn't explaining for crap. I needed one of those translation guides, too. "We have instructors. That's all we need. Our strongest ties are meant to be with each other —our year group and then with our team. Remember when I said we were raised for this? Our teams come together as kids. We know who our family is early on."

"You aren't allowed contact with your damn *parents*?" For once he lacked the volume and edge I'd assumed were Basic Bruce. His voice was too soft, and felt...wrong.

"Why would we want that? We have what we need. They have what they need with their team. The teams have looser ties with each other so we can coordinate and work together as needed. Anything else might divide loyalties."

I didn't need to know what he was thinking to understand we weren't on the same page. The mix of disbelief and horror on his face was clear, and I didn't know where I was going wrong in order to course-correct.

I scrambled to change topics as the safer option. "Did you get hurt a lot as a kid?"

He ran a hand over his face like he was trying to wipe something away. When he spoke he sounded distracted. "What?"

I raised my bowl by way of explanation. "The pudding is amazing so you must have had it often for it to be meaningful and for you to master the skill."

His expression sharpened. "What the hell is that supposed to mean?"

Sometimes, attractive confidence tipped over into—not attractive. My irritation roused into life at his attitude. At least *I* tried to understand new things before making assumptions. "I mean—"

"Never fucking mind, Ramirez. I get the idea. Put the bowl in the dishwasher when you're done. I'm not your damn domestic help, and I refuse to live in a disgusting shit hole full of crusty dishes." He slammed the door behind him before I figured out a response.

I shoved the bowl aside, and went back to researching for other windigo anomalies that no one one else believed in.

Cryptids were hella easier to understand than civilians.

# CHAPTER 9

## BRUCE

*B*ruce slammed his notebook closed. For once, sketching out potential new dishes and restaurant concepts couldn't hold his attention. Fuck only knew when he would get out of here and to Taos anyway. The never completely dormant itch to discover a new horizon, absorb a different experience, then turn it into inspiration for his next project was already rising under his skin.

Tossing the notebook onto the lumpy excuse for a bed, he stomped out into the main living area. As usual, the place was empty. This bunch spent daylight hours outdoors, doing shit involving firing ranges, training courses, and learning to be even more brainwashed cogs in a morally questionable machine.

He glared at the lived-in surroundings, proof fucking decades of abuse had occurred, repeated again and again through the generations. There wasn't any other word to describe ripping kids away from families and *training* them instead of raising them. Denying them a childhood, comfort, and free will, all to create more malleable soldiers.

The entire place screamed utilitarian. Emotionless.

Without imagination, and minus a soul. He strode past the group showers, paused to list another dozen ways the excuse for a kitchen fell short, and then kept going.

He took his restlessness into the game room-library-what-the-fucking-ever, hoping for one book he hadn't read. He skirted the ugly ass bucket chairs and floor pillows, bending to grab one of the gaming controls threatening to trip the unwary, namely him. This—this was the only area that had a modicum of personality.

He paused mid-reach. Straightening, he left the controller and backed up to the arched doorway, and let himself absorb the room and its feel as he would on walking into a new restaurant.

This spot felt...he narrowed the vibe down to relaxed. Relaxation and fun.

It contained every gaming console on the market, set up around a flat screen rivaling a sports complex's Jumbotron. The chairs clustered around it in a semicircle. More huge pillows sat on the floor, on either side of the couch, all aimed at the screen instead of following an aesthetic placement plan. None of the décor even tried for a cohesive palette, instead a riot of clashing colors and fabrics.

He prowled, starting at the left and the pool table. The green velvet showed its age, worn thin in spots. The Foosball table across from it was equally beat up, although an indoor electronic basketball hoop hanging over the recycling box dated from at least the last three years. He trailed fingers over the built-in bookcases packed full of volumes covering every genre, from embossed leather-bound sets that were probably limited editions, all the way down to cheap paper-backs with cracked spines. The lower shelves held stacks of colorful boxes and he squatted, sorting through classic board games he recognized and new ones he hadn't even heard of.

He tapped one smaller box aimlessly, considering what

kind of unimaginative soldiers bought—and played regularly, from the scuffed edges—nineties TV trivia? He replaced the games and rose.

Afternoon sun blinded him as he exited outside and he took a second on the pipe rail walkway, eyes adjusting. He'd seen the base's layout when he arrived. Now, he really looked, past the obviousness of the training courses with scaling walls, the forbidden armory, and gym that would elicit an Olympic trainer's envy, and the gun range further out to the north. After spending time with Vee, and now factoring in his morning explorations, the oddities stood out.

He descended to the yard. Scratch that, to the courtyard, since it was visually divided, a fact he'd nearly missed. A fairly modern outdoor bench faced a filled birdbath, one that had desert flora planted around its base. Cacti and succulents created a mixed texture and an ombre effect. That had taken time and dedication, not haphazardly grabbing a few plants on a whim and dropping them in the ground. Further out, a stocked bird feeder was situated so whoever sat on the bench had an unobstructed view.

A rhythmic thumping pulled him away from evaluating the visual artistry of the courtyard. He followed the sound to a leftover space on the end of the living quarters, the building's L-shape hiding it unless you knew to turn the corner.

A nearly regulation-length basketball court greeted him, goals at either end. Josh stood in front of the closest. The guy dribbled, and lined up his shot, ball swishing through the net. "Score."

The guy sounded as pumped as one of Bruce's nieces at making the shot.

Catching sight of Bruce on the rebound, Josh tucked the ball under his arm. "Hey, man. Need something?"

Bruce had figured out that the question wasn't a challenge or shorthand for fuck off in the way most people used it.

Every damn time someone here asked, they really wanted to know if they could provide something he needed or wanted. "Got anything for crushing boredom?"

Josh perked up. If he'd had a tail, it would've wagged like an excited puppy's. "Do you ball?"

Bruce eyed Josh's purple and gold jersey. "I ought to say hell no to anybody rooting for the Lakers, on principle. I'm desperate though, and willing to teach you and your grand-standers how real players roll."

"Who's your team?"

Bruce darted in, smacking the ball out of Josh's arms. "There's only one team. The Knicks."

The game took off from there, fast and intense

While Bruce ran and hiked when he had a chance, he wasn't a professional soldier. However, he'd learned to play hard, keep under bigger guys' reach, and drive through the middle. He also fucking hated losing.

When Josh finally called it, they were tied. Part of Bruce bristled, taking the time-out as stopping for Bruce's sake and ready to push the other guy. The smarter part settled for pulling the hem of his shirt up, scrubbing his sweaty face, and hunting for a dry patch to do the same for his glasses.

At Josh's whistle, Bruce slid glasses back on and focused.

Josh held up two bottles. "Wild Berry Blast or Blue Hawaiian? The Hawaiian is limited edition amazeballs. I've been rationing it."

Bruce checked his first reply. The stuff was artificially flavored shit in a bottle, but the guy was selflessly offering Bruce a favorite. "Got any water?"

Josh dug in the same cooler Bruce had lugged to the market, and tossed him water.

Bruce wrinkled his nose at the tang, but chugged it. "You guys have to get a filter, and individual filtered bottles."

"Yeah?" Josh tilted one of the water bottles like it held answers. "What's wrong with this brand?"

"For starters, it's marinating in BPA and plastic film, which you then ingest. Second, there's no such thing as environmentally friendly plastic packaging."

"You should tell Liv. She's over our supplies and provision choices." Josh didn't argue or do the hyper-masculine indestructible act. "Rematch tomorrow?"

"Are you that bored, too?"

"Nah. You're more fun to play against than Vee and Kimi. Fair warning, they play dirty." He sounded completely aggrieved. "Liv can straight-up kick all of our asses when she's in the mood, no tricks, no cheating."

Again, Bruce caught no posturing on the soldier's part, and no hesitation in stating one of the women was better than him.

"What the hell. Rematch tomorrow, Laker man."

Josh took that as an invitation, falling in beside Bruce and talking at him non-stop until they hit the house, and then peeling off in search of food.

Bruce took advantage of empty showers, letting the water wash away a part of his assumptions. The exercise had gotten him out of his head, too.

Re-centered, he stepped into the hall on his way to toss his stuff back in his room. Wherever he'd ended up, Josh had left his room door open. Bruce stopped, taking in the feel the way he had the common room.

A framed Kobe jersey graced one wall. A display of kicks on another, more gaming equipment, memorabilia for every damn sport that involved teams, and headphones draped on a laptop were scattered around the room's edges. A primary-blue and green abstract painting shaded in black took up the area over his bed.

The door on the other side of Josh's was cracked open.

Bruce knocked on the frame and got no response. They hadn't worried about his privacy so they'd set the precedent, not him, and he was only following their lead. He toed the door open but stayed outside. Examining was one thing. Invading was off the table.

This room held enough photo frames to start a store, books stacked on every other horizontal surface, and an e-reader and tablet on the table by the bed. He recognized the tablet cover, having seen Liv carrying it around earlier. Another abstract took up most of the wall by a closet, this one in steely blue-grays like the sky before a summer storm, then swirled into an unexpectedly vibrant yellow and orange center.

He tried the last door, Klepto's. It was locked and he snorted, amused despite his best effort. He played with possibilities, turning facts different ways, life-size puzzle pieces representing the team.

At a muffled *creak-thump*, he stopped. The noise repeated, coming from the connector area between the private residence halls. A rustic as hell ladder of wooden beams banded with iron was set into the wall. When he concentrated, the back and forth of a conversation filtered down from what had to be the attic.

He climbed the few steps and found the equally anti-quated handle. When he shoved it and lifted, sunlight streamed in. The ladder didn't lead to a basic attic but to one of the flat roofs he'd noticed on older homes all over the area.

The roof was anything but basic.

Liv and Klepto faced him, propped against either side of a huge, flat platform swing loaded with canvas pillows. Color-coordinated beanbags piled on one side of a flat table that held a hurricane jar and mostly burned down candle stubs, and an actual film camera.

"Hi." Liv left it at that.

He took her low-key response as permission and climbed the rest of the way, trapdoor thumping down behind him. He circled the generous space ringed with a twisted wrought iron railing that bore no resemblance to the ugly pipe rail on the walkway. This was ornamental, period. Same with the potted lemon tree in the corner shaded by the swing's frame.

They watched him prowl, seeming at ease with his curiosity. He tilted his head at the camera. "Which one of you is the shutterbug?"

"That would be me," Kimi signed.

"All of the paintings downstairs are yours." He didn't make it a question.

She made a *hmm* noise.

"They are really damn good. Have you had a gallery exhibit?"

"Exhibits aren't my thing."

Bull-fucking-shit. Her robbing the public of her talent was probably more of the Company's *don't be memorable* brainwashing. Again setting unnatural limitations on their lives.

He propped against the railing, facing them instead of the view. "Swings are military issue now?"

Liv stretched and glanced over her shoulder. "I like watching sunrises and sunsets. This is the best spot in the compound for both." She lounged back on her elbows, her carefree pose at odds with the laser-like gaze she trained on him. "Vee and I spent an entire day figuring out the logistics, and another setting it up when we first arrived at this post."

She used a toe against an upright and pushed the swing into motion. "We aren't all work all the time. When we have down time we make the most of it. I call it a sliding scale of blowing off steam. The night you were attacked we were there celebrating a flawless capture and relocate mission which rated margaritas and karaoke, about a four on the scale."

"Carpe Diem," Kim signed. "There's no party like a group post-mission party."

She and Liv shared a look, signing and saying "Galveston" at the same time.

Without a word, he left them laughing, because the only words he was capable of in the face of their energy were four letter, and foul even for him. Now that he'd gotten his head out of his ass and looked past the military shells they were forced to assume, their pure lust for life and joy and art, each in their different ways, filled him with awe. At the same time it also made him want to punch someone in the face.

This shit went past abusive straight into the realm of brutally criminal. Criminal was the only term that applied when forcing these bright, dedicated spirits into limited lives. Fuck his assumption about the Company never giving them freedom to pursue life—they hadn't even had the freedom to understand there was more out there.

He ended up the only place he'd ever been able to channel his anger into anything useful. Their antiquated kitchen was better than nothing in this case. He opened and closed cabinets he'd already thoroughly inspected, finally pulling out his purchases from the market. He hadn't bought with cooking for more than himself in mind, but he'd make do.

He started the lower warming drawer of the oven, and put the flour and yeast to good use. Bread was time-consuming and without a decent mixer, kneading was a workout. A combination that suited his needs.

Two hours later, the space smelled like a real kitchen.

At the muted squeak of a shoe on tile, he divided the second batch of dough into separate balls, and went with a simple, "Hey."

When he didn't snarl or snap, Vee ambled the rest of the

way into the kitchen. "Something smells incredible." She made an aimless circle around the big assed table to the built-in bar, slowly getting closer. Like easing up on some sort of unpredictable animal. "I feel like it's my duty to inform you that your actions will draw predators. By predators, I mean all of us."

He dusted flour on the board and worked the first batch of dough over. "That's the whole point." He flipped the dough and met her eyes. "Look, I'm an asshole. It's a permanent condition. Meaning I've had a shit-ton of occasions to apologize. I don't always avail myself of the opportunity but this once I am. The bread is for everyone. One look at your fridge and I could tell none of you are finicky or gluten-free so I'm betting bread is something you'd all probably enjoy."

Vee hooked her heel in the lowest rung of a bar stool, hands in her back pockets, and watched him.

Her attention had intent. Mass. He felt it like a weight on his skin.

"You apologize in food."

He let himself smile at the fact she was right and that she didn't shy away from embracing his fuck-up and his need to apologize. "It's my preferred medium and my method of communication." He wrapped the kneaded dough in a towel and switched to work on the second ball. "Like Josh with his sports, Kimi with her painting, Liv with her books." It didn't escape him that without thinking, he'd used their names instead of his shorthand insults.

"Most people don't see that about them so quickly. Or see it at all. Thank you." Her voice was soft and real, because he'd bet every knife he owned that she'd noticed, processed on the fly, and came to the same conclusion about his slip-up.

He cut her a glance. "Thanks for?" He wasn't questioning the reason why he wanted to hear her say it.

Her head was bent, tucking hair behind her ear while she

examined the toe of her sneakers. "For balling with Josh earlier. You couldn't have chosen a better way to bond with him."

His turn to focus on anything else, because hell, of course she'd gone deep. He stared the innocent dough down, and cleared his throat. "Sometimes I get it right. Except I have no idea what your thing is. Aside from saving belligerent and ungrateful assholes like me, and protecting the oblivious residents of Scottsdale. That and karaoke."

"You aren't that bad."

He snorted. "I am and I know it. My policy is self honesty and I'm honest about the brilliant and the bad."

The slap and knead of dough was the only sound for several minutes. But each one felt significant. Vee's attention was significant. He either fed on attention or was oblivious to it when he was immersed in cooking. Whatever it was with Vee though—it went both ways between them. Some sort of almost tangible connection he couldn't ignore.

"My karaoke, huh?"

He didn't know if he was relieved or frustrated that she'd retreated to safer ground. "I might have noticed your performance that night, pre-Godzilla. You'd have had to be comatose not to."

She laughed with no hint of self-consciousness. "We have more enthusiasm than talent, but it's fun."

"Yeah, you are terrible." He wrapped the last batch and deposited both in the drawer to rise. "Your tone-deafness wasn't what caught my attention though." He had claimed honesty, so time to put up or shut up. This was a good time to push himself—and Vee. "Your lack of vocal talent also wasn't what held my attention."

"Then what did?"

She was as blunt as he was. It probably said something deeply narcissistic about him that her attitude snared him.

Drew him in like some moth to a light. He stood up and met her head on. "You were one of the most alive people in that bar. You were the most alive person in all of Scottsdale that night. You weren't afraid to be loud, make mistakes, and be happy, fuck whoever was watching."

"I noticed you too." That barely-there smile that killed him and had him anticipating the shit she'd come up with curved her lips. "I mean when you first walked in, not when you were alley make-out session bound."

The thrill of a good sparring session sparked through him. An ex had accused him of thinking arguments were foreplay. "You're never going to let that shit go, are you?"

"Not a chance."

"Stubborn."

"Determined," she countered.

Without intending to move, somehow they were in each other's space. She'd abandoned the stool and he'd left the oven. "I was trained to analyze the situation, formulate a plan of action, and commit to the follow-through."

The air buzzed between them, the intensity tangible.

"Fuck quitters."

"Is that what you were taught?" She was close enough for him to see the darker brown rim around her eyes. Smell a hint of berries. He inhaled, and narrowed the sweetness down to a lip balm, a betraying sheen glistening on her lower lip. Practically begging him to taste.

"I taught myself. I wouldn't be where I am otherwise."

They angled as if by some unspoken agreement. Close enough that he could finally run his thumb over her mouth, the skin soft and slick, confirming his lip balm guess.

Those enticing lips parted. White teeth met, trapping the pad of his thumb. The pressure just short of painful, and his dick sprang to attention.

The clomp of un-fucking-wanted company, and the shrill beep of the oven timer acted like an unexpected cold shower.

Vee jerked back fast enough that Bruce stumbled.

He turned and stabbed the alarm, grabbing a dishtowel and hauling the door open. He pulled a crusty loaf out, for once hating a kitchen.

"Whoa, what is that?" And Josh, definitely hating enthusiastic, cock-blocking Josh.

Bruce turned and barked, "You won't get a chance to discover the answer until you use damn soap and water." He narrowed his eyes at Josh's jersey from their game. "Find deodorant while you're at it. Then tell Liv and Kimi there's fresh ciabatta and real butter and cheese waiting."

Bruce grabbed a bread knife from his rolled-out case, and Josh bounced out in another annoying squeak of rubber.

"Is this butter and cheese from ecstatic cows?" Vee asked in the momentary silence.

"Damn ecstatic artisan cows." He left the bread and knife on the counter and retrieved the sorry excuse for a platter he'd employed as a cheese tray. He layered butter on a slice of fragrant bread, and held it out. He wasn't done yet. "Come here."

Neither was Vee. She met him and instead of taking the crust, looked from it to him. As clear a challenge as he'd ever encountered. "Well?"

He raised the sample.

Vee took a bite, eyes widening as his carefully chosen flavors blended. He sucked in her hit of appreciation, her openness stoking his desire higher.

Her pocket blared, a harsh ringtone. The sound repeated, echoing from three other spots in the house. Vee chewed and swallowed fast enough his throat ached in sympathy, and held up a finger.

"Are you fucking kidding me?"

Instead of answering, she pulled the phone from her pocket. Whatever it showed, she left him standing like the previous five minutes never occurred. Her office door closed, leaving him alone with cooling bread.

The roof-door opened, followed by Kimi and Liv jumping down like they didn't have time to employee the last three steps. Both headed for the office.

Seconds later, Josh appeared, shirtless and water still slicking his chest, his shorts sticking where he's pulled them on over wet skin.

"What the hell is going on?"

Talkative, outgoing Josh swept by him like Bruce was invisible.

Bruce spun to intercept him and find out what the group call meant. Before he made it out of the kitchen, all four poured in from the hall, splitting off in the directions of their rooms.

He stepped in front of Vee. "Stop and tell me—"

"Find a place out of our way for now."

Instead, he paced, staring daggers at the closed doors.

Vee was out of a room first. The soldier who had crashed through his window was back. Clad in black and gray, in a long-sleeved shirt too heavy for the Scottsdale heat, the same multi-pocketed utility pants, and boots.

When she pointed at the kitchen with a short "Sit", he didn't bitch, commandeering the stool she'd abandoned. She and the other three soldiers filed out through the door leading to the courtyard.

The only place they could be bound was the armory. His stomach still pitched when they reentered with holster rigs on, guns and knives slotted into the harness sheaths. Josh also carried a sleek matte case, and a black and gray cap.

Bruce almost wished Vee would ignore him again. Then, he wouldn't have to hear what he knew was coming.

She stopped in front of him, not wasting time stating what was obvious. She held up her phone. "Starting from now if we aren't back in forty-eight hours call the number programmed into this phone." She held out a slip of paper. "The first is our team ID code. The second is my C.O. code. When the dispatcher answers, give them each code, in order. Then tell them forty-eight hours. That's all, no name, nothing else, then hang up."

"Which produces what result?" His question came out too sharp and accusatory.

"They gave us this call-out, so know we're in the field. The Company will come collect you once they confirm identity, transport you to HQ, and keep you safe."

"And? What about you?" Which he hadn't intended to ask and couldn't stop himself from saying any more than he could stop time.

"When we don't return, there will be a separate disaster response team dispatched. They will take out whatever we failed to, or reevaluate the need for a multi-team response, triage if applicable, retrieve bodies, and direct any necessary Cleaners."

The ground tilted the same as the precursor to one of the quakes that were the reason why he never stayed in California very long. "Is your number in that thing?"

"We don't make or take calls during a mission. The risk of hacking is slight but present. If we are successful and require them, we make one call to the Cleaners. They're armed, combat certified, and prepared in case the message is hacked en route or at arrival." Like there was nothing more to be said, she laid the phone on the counter and strode for the pass-through and SUV.

He followed and halted in the garage when Vee held up a hand. "The compound will go on automatic lockdown when we clear the gate. You can't leave but you will be safe, I promise." With that, she climbed in the front passenger seat and slammed the door, smoked windows robbing him of a last look.

He stood alone in the bay as doors rose, then dropped and sealed closed with a sharp finality. Watching four complex, vibrant people leave through the mechanical gate.

The reality he'd ignored shoved into the spotlight and took center stage. They might not ever come back through those gates.

The already unsteady ground he'd been balancing on bucked. He sank to his heels and put his head between his knees before light-headed turned to face-first into the concrete floor.

Vee might never come back through those gates.

# CHAPTER 10

## VEE

The garage's adapted UV halogen light flared bright enough that my eyes watered even through the protection of the truck's tinted windows.

"When are you going to disable those things?" Josh muttered, skin ashy and stretched over too-prominent cheekbones.

"I'm close," Kimi signed, not lifting her head from the headrest, no more oomph to her gestures than there was in Josh's voice.

We were all oomph-less, crusted in dried sweat and dehydrated, all our hydration consumed sixteen hours into the mission. The garage bay sealed and the anti-vampire UVs switched to plain lighting.

I exhaled, some of the weight lifting for the first time in nearly twenty-four hours. Beside me, Liv did the same. Muted clicks marked everyone unbuckling, all of us ready to be *done*. "You guys hit the showers first. I'll toss some burritos in the microwave."

Then, write up my account of the mission. It could serve as

additional anangoa insight. Which did nothing to lighten the black ball of failure hanging over my head. Over my heart. I got out and stretched, feeling every old fracture and new bruise.

Liv joined me. "We completed the mission. Our success rate is still thirty-percent above average."

Which wasn't any greater consolation for her than it was for me. "It still wasn't a win."

"I know." She rubbed at her temples, fingers accidentally catching and jerking hair free from her severe bun. Strands hung limp, even her nearly indestructible waves defeated. "How much drama do you think is waiting for us inside?"

I hadn't thought of the repercussions of telling Bruce to sit and stay and then locking him in, too lost in running different scenarios in my head. Still not finding one that would've provided the outcome we wanted—which was no excuse. Kimi and Josh shouldn't be the first through the door. If Bruce was bitching that was on me to deal with.

I hustled to catch up with them. They'd paused where the pass-through, halls, and kitchen met. I slid between them and braced. I'd pitch our guest into the annex and lock the cage if need be. My team wasn't a target for his frustration, end of story.

Bruce sat at the far end of the table, a mug by his elbow. He'd found one of Liv's questionable decks, and playing cards fanned the scuffed tabletop, a hand of solitaire in progress.

His gaze tracked over each of us, intent and methodical. The sharp intelligence behind his eyes cataloging...I wasn't sure what. He didn't attempt to disguise checking us out though.

His attention finally settled on me. It seemed like he exhaled, the same setting down of responsibilities Liv and I did when the bay doors sealed, our team home and alive.

"Can you eat?" He directed the question to the room, but didn't take his eyes off me.

"Once we change, yes." The oddity that had nagged at the back of my mind since I'd walked in came into focus. The compound smelled food-ish. The fading scent of yesterday's bread lingered, along with the cut-grass tang of Bruce's tea. Another fresher smell hung over those, similar to the take-out bag from our favorite Indian food truck.

The scents somehow melded and it wasn't simply food— it was a welcome.

Bruce gathered up cards, sliding them into their box. "All right. Get cleaned up, and patched up." He lingered on a scratch on Kimi's cheek. One she had already disinfected and dotted with antibiotic gel. "Late lunch will be ready when you are."

The order wasn't an order. Calm, with no bite, more of a statement.

"Lifesaver," Kimi signed while Josh thumped Bruce on the back in thanks as they passed. Liv tipped her chin at him as she exited. Bruce nodded back, like he already knew her shorthand for "Good job" and "Thanks."

I stopped in front of him. "You haven't done anything to apologize for. Even if you'd wanted to there aren't many destructive options open when the site is on lockdown. What is this?"

A shadow darkened his face. Sad-ish, which I didn't get, since we were all here and fine, casting my interpretation into doubt.

"This is lunch. You were all out busting your asses, and it's not as if what you do is some civilized nine-to-five job, or hell, even a twelve hour kitchen shift. Now you get a decent meal because you are hungry and too tired to prepare anything. If you aren't hungry, I'll put the food in the fridge for later."

All I had in return was "Oh." I didn't know how to say "Thanks for not being a drama llama" and "Wow" and "No one has ever welcomed us back" and "Thank you" all at once.

"Let me see." He motioned at me and held out his hand.

It took a second to understand what he meant. My stitched claw marks had opened on one end thanks to squeezing through a tight tunnel, adding a few more superficial scratches. I'd hacked the torn sleeve off and cleaned and patched at the same time Kimi had.

It was nothing.

I still found myself extending my arm for his inspection. Bruce cupped my hand, careful as if it were breakable. I tilted my shoulder to show him. "No biggie, see? The edges had time to knit thanks to the stitches. We have a gel that goes solid on application, and that's all I needed."

He frowned. His thumb swept over my knuckles. Back and forth, gentle in a way I wouldn't have said he was capable of. Also, kind of amazing. Like the contrast between loud, abrasive Bruce and this Bruce, a version that lay under the others.

The version I'd glimpsed when he asked if I was okay the night I took him home, my safety his last thought before he passed out from anangoa venom.

"Is this the worst of it?" His thumb kept up the soothing pattern.

"Yes. A scratch from a tight space for me, a nick from a flying brick chip for Kimi. Josh and Liv are fine, although we are all thirsty. And hungry," I added fast, not wanting him to think his work wasn't appreciated.

He kept that same soft-calm tone. "Go do what you need to. I'll be—lunch will be here when you're ready."

We still separated by degrees. His thumb sliding over the back of my hand as we parted, both of us oddly reluctant to break contact.

When I hit the hall, Liv stood by the shower room door with her official post mission indulgence, coconut body scrub and matching moisturizer. Since there was no shortage of facilities or hot water, she was waiting for me.

"This is different." One brow arched, the signal that *different* meant a potential problem.

"Different can be good. Since when is flexibility a drawback?" Which came out too defensive. Liv and I were C.O. and lieutenant. We balanced each other out. She had as much right to voice concerns as I did, and it was my job to listen and consider.

I undid my bun, massaging my sore scalp. "His reaction is unexpected. What's your take?"

"It's hard to read civis, and he isn't a typical civilian by any metric. Maybe this is his version of a thank you."

"Makes sense." Obscurely relieved, I pushed myself into motion, ready for my shower, the private bath a perk of being C.O.

Liv added a parting shot. "Then again maybe he's implying something more personal."

We both understood the danger of plunging into new or unknown situations without all the information. With Liv's observation rattling around in my head, I washed away sweat and grime accrued from hours of maintenance tunnels, empty and condemned buildings, avoiding scorpions, and tent communities. I played with what-if scenarios while I moisturized ashy skin, and dried my hair enough to braid it into a loose tail.

I wished that the too-valid worries cycling through my brain were as easy to clean up and put in order.

Bruce was interesting. Sure, part was the novelty of his being a civilian. A smart, unexpected, and impossible to predict civilian, which ticked a lot of my boxes.

So did the thick, ink-covered biceps and chest I'd gotten

up close with while checking him for anangoa damage. The glimpse the day before when he practically peeled his shirt off to mop up the sweat he'd earned going head-to-head with Josh only added to my fascination. Bruce had played like the game was the only thing in the world at that moment, and losing wasn't an option.

He was so different in most ways—but that single-minded dedication was a Company hallmark. The thing that always drew me to sex partners.

Fact One, Bruce was appealing.

Fact Two, Bruce wasn't Company.

Fact Three, I had never had a sexual partner who wasn't Company. Ridge, who was in our year group but not part of a team, had some kind of long-running thing with a Company Asset he'd met. I'd always assumed his civilian relationship was an attempt to make up for not having what the rest of us did. Otherwise, no other agent I knew had ever slept with a civi. Mostly, the opportunity wasn't there. Now, it was.

We binged on movies and reality shows because they were our version of fantasy. Bruce was proof that media was even less reliable in representing real civilian life and behavior than I'd thought.

Liv, and to a lesser extent, Kimi and Josh, avoided interaction with outsiders like the plague. For Liv, there was nothing worth her time outside the Company, and none of them got why civilians interested me. And the too brief, too pointed conversation we'd shared was her way of telling me that an outsider was teetering on interfering with my duty, our team, and our family.

And, okay. All the romantic, my one true person and sexual partner, soul-mate stuff—that seemed the sort of fairy tale civilians had to make up, because they didn't have the Company. We had the security and surety of knowing who our family was, who mattered and always would, and who supported us as wholeheartedly as we supported them.

And adding an outsider to my—our—lives? That would be like adding a new team member. Basically, unthinkable.

Bruce was right here and interaction with him had an automatic cut-off date, though. As soon as the anangoa was history, gone, the species extinct, no other option acceptable to me, so was he. If I was reading him right, and he was interested in sex, what was the real harm in satisfying our curiosity?

Both ideas improved my mood. Dwelling was an energy-drain, one we were conditioned to avoid. As a bonus, food waited for me.

I pulled on a snug, hanging-out tee, and cuffed shorts I'd re-stolen from Liv's closet.

First food.

Then reports.

Then finding out if Bruce and I were on the same page.

I followed the beckoning smells, stronger and tantalizing enough that my stomach growled like an annoyed windigo.

Bruce was reassuringly Bruce again, legs spread and arms crossed, glaring at a seated Josh across the expanse of our table. "It's. Pizza." Bruce enunciated.

"I don't think it is." Josh eyed the circle with the same wariness he gave Kimi when no other teams were available to game, and she challenged him to a *friendly* Cogs of War match.

"What's the problem?" I interceded before Liv, right behind me, could.

"That." Josh pointed at the circular-ish food in the center of the table. "That doesn't look pizza—y. It smells even less pizza—y."

"It. Is. A curry pizza. Naan crust topped with chicken curry. Chicken, black garlic, green curry paste, ginger, chili."

Josh checked with us.

"You do eat Indian." Liv rolled her lips, battling the smile at the least adventurous of us. Looking to one of us to try anything new first, apparently on the theory if we dropped dead, inedible. If not, dinnertime.

"Jesus Fucking Christ. I saw you eat a box of unidentifiable Chinese takeout that had to be at least a week old because it was already molding away in the refrigerator when I got here. You didn't even heat it first."

I joined Bruce, picked up the first plate stacked beside him, and held it out.

He cut the pizza with the precision and speed Liv reassembled and loaded her favorite Glock. He centered the slice perfectly, and I passed it to Liv, repeating the process four more times.

I took the last two plates, using my knee to nudge Bruce to a seat, and taking the one next to him.

Josh poked at his plate.

"Fucking put it in your mouth, chew, and swallow," Bruce growled. "Just because you've never met a fresh protein doesn't mean you'll keel over from it. It's chicken and dough. These are fucking baby steps, so shut up and eat."

I picked up mine, prepared to take one for my team. Flavors exploded over my palate. I took a second bite, also taking my time. Spices layered and mixed, as complex as the pudding but on a vaster scale. Sweet, bright, savory with heat at the end, and smoke from something Bruce had done to the dough. I wiped a bit of sauce from the corner of my mouth. Then sucked it off my finger, too awesome to waste even a drop.

Bruce followed the motion with a single-minded focus. Catching me watching, he jerked his attention to the plate.

"Well?" Josh leaned in, elbows on the table.

"This is possibly the best thing I've ever put in my mouth," I said.

Color climbed Bruce's neck.

"Are you only saying that because you don't want to referee if he loses his shit?" Josh hooked a thumb at Bruce.

Whose face went from pink to a dangerous crimson.

In answer, I reached for Josh's plate to claim his portion.

Not new to the maneuver, he snatched it to safety. With my seal of approval, he took a minuscule bite. His eyes widened, and he folded the generous piece in half and shoveled it in his mouth.

Bruce gave him a half-appalled, half-vindicated look.

"Curry pizza is better than ham and pineapple," Kimi signed, then went back to eating.

"Her highest praise," Liv said.

We finished with no additional conversation, our last food only a vague memory. I chased a bit of naan around, and licked it off my finger. When I checked, Bruce was focused on me again. "This really was amazing," I said.

"So I inferred from your inhaling it. Did you even stop to breathe?" Words aside, pleasure mellowed out his customary frown.

"We're usually starved after a mission." Liv took a polite sip of water, wiping fingers on her napkin, although her plate was equally spotless.

"You burn too many calories without taking in enough protein. I'm temporarily remedying that deficit." Bruce rose. "Put those plates in the damn dishwasher."

He circled behind me. At a cold draft chilling my back, I used the seat back and twisted to see where he'd gone. He held one of the heavy square dishes I didn't think we'd ever used, and closed the fridge with his foot.

"This is tiramisu. Don't tell me you're afraid of cookies, cocoa, and espresso." He aimed that at Josh.

I took in the concoction, layers as perfectly equal as if he'd used a ruler and level, top evenly dusted with chocolate powder. "Whoa. That looks like it should be in a photo."

"It's too simple to post." Denial aside, he still seemed pleased.

I crowded close as he cut slices. "This isn't protein. Is it?"

He paused mid-slice, that weird sorta sad thing resurfacing but with a trace of anger this time, beating out the mellowness. "For fuck's sake. How the hell have you all survived, much less performed the way your career demands, subsisting on trash a starving alley cat wouldn't touch? Plates," he ordered me.

I grabbed the small ones stacked on the counter.

He repeated the ruler-straight cuts and placement on the plate. "This is dessert, a course designed purely for the sake of enjoyment. Eat." He shoved the last plate at me.

I checked my phone. We'd spent almost two hours here, about one and a half longer than I usually allotted before starting my debrief. I touched Bruce's thick wrist in apology. "Could Liv and I get a rain check? It's past time for our reports." The scene we'd left behind eighteen hours earlier flashed through my head. All desire for food, even this picture-perfect one, fled.

Bruce glanced around the table as if he'd felt the shift in mood. Josh and Kimi's expressions had gone carefully bland, the mask we used on-scene with civilians.

Again, Bruce didn't get angry. "I'll wrap these and they'll be waiting for you."

# CHAPTER 11

## BRUCE

*B*ruce tucked the last two pieces of dessert into the fridge, centered on the top shelf so Vee wouldn't miss hers.

The only sound in the kitchen was the slide of spoons on pottery plates as Josh and Kimi scraped to get the last of the mascarpone. The atmosphere had changed when Vee mentioned the debrief. Entirely too damn serious for a report destined for some digital version of a dusty shelf, be it a black op's shelf or not.

He poured out the espresso he'd brewed to go with the tiramisu, admitting failure. So much for sitting around the table in a civilized manner. Instead, he put on water for tea.

While he waited, he turned to watch the pair of soldiers, Josh now loading everyone's plates in the dishwasher.

Bruce wasn't one-hundred-percent certain, but there might be a new bruise on the guy's dark forearm. He studied Kimi's scratch, Vee's explanation about a brick chip registering. Shards didn't fly unless hit, say, by a bullet.

"How did it go?" He tipped his head at the garage.

The two shared a silent, coded conversation. Josh stayed quiet, indecision as to what to say written on his face. Kimi stepped in, taking point. "We were too late. We also failed to eliminate the cryptid responsible."

It felt like the temperature dropped twenty degrees, chills raising the hairs on his arms. Instead of keeping his mouth shut, choosing to stay ignorant and pretend Kimi only referred to catching some generic monster, he did it. He asked, blowing purposeful ignorance out of the water. "Too late for some schmuck like me, whose biggest gripe was the ridiculous parking fees in downtown?"

Both of the soldiers' expressions went suspiciously bland, a mask probably perfected on dozens—hell, hundreds of panicked civilians over the years—hiding their true emotions.

"Are you sure you want to know?" Kimi folded her hands together. Her way of telling him that they could stop right there. Forget the question and pretend he hadn't pushed for more.

He was sure he didn't want to know. They didn't hide from hard truth though, and neither did he. "Tell me."

"The vics were a young family with three casualties—a husband, wife, and a child."

At a firm pressure on his shoulder, Bruce twitched. Josh had come up behind him, dropping a reassuring grip on Bruce's arm. Steam rose from the kettle behind them. He'd blanked long enough for the water to finish heating.

"Man, you're safe here. Nothing we don't want to get in will. There's always a therapist on call for us for emergency sessions. Give me a minute and I'll get them on the line."

"I may take you up on that, but not right now."

"No worries. If I'm not around when you're ready, just knock on my door."

Kimi stretched and stood, catching Bruce's attention.

"We're setting up for a Cogs of War game against another Company team. Want to join us?"

"Maybe later."

"You know where to find us, okay?" Josh gave him another squeeze, seconding his sister's offer, as they both left.

Bruce pushed the pot away. Tea wasn't going to cut it. He needed—fuck if he knew, except that it wasn't going to be found in the kitchen.

When he focused on his surroundings again, he was at Vee's door. He knocked and the not-completely-closed door swung wider. Giving him a glimpse of framed pop culture posters lined so close none of the wall showed between. Under them, a dresser took up space, covered in necklaces, all draped on stands at different heights and angles like an art installation. No Vee, though.

Before he lost his nerve he turned and strode to her office, the horrible *thing* building in his chest pushing him on. He knocked and opened the door without waiting.

Vee sat behind the desk, but with her legs crisscrossed and the chair pushed away. Liv had abandoned her desk chair altogether, perched on the rolled arm of the barge-sized couch dominating the other wall.

Either he'd entered fast enough they hadn't had time to master their expressions, or they were simply too tired. He saw it in the circles under Liv's eyes, in the weary slope of Vee's shoulders.

"Is this a thing now—personal dessert delivery?"

It punched him somewhere in the middle of his chest that after all they'd done in the last day, tired and busy as they were, Vee still tried to put him at ease.

"I can bring the plates to you two but that's not the reason I'm here. The creature you were called out for was the one after me." He made it a flat statement.

Deep down, he had known from the moment all four had walked into the kitchen armed to their teeth.

"You are—"

He cut Liv off. "Don't say safe. That's not what I'm asking." He pulled in a breath, acknowledging the body camera hooked to Vee's laptop, which he had purposely not looked at from the second he barged in. "Let me see. All of it."

Vee and Liv did the same wordless communication their brother and sister had.

Liv pinched the bridge of her nose like she was fighting a headache. "He has the right to know."

Vee was already on her feet and turning the screen his way.

It took him a minute to understand what he was seeing in the crisp digital photos. His brain unable or unwilling to put the red-brown splashes, and the chunks of pink and white, into any semblance of order. To see it as what was left of people. The small hand in the third photo was what sent him over the edge.

Metal screeched and Vee got the old trashcan in front of him just in time to catch every bite of his dinner.

His stomach quit rebelling at last but only because there was nothing left. White fluttered at his eye level and he reached sideways for the tissues Vee offered, wiping his watering eyes and mouth. Wishing it was that damn easy to wipe away the image of three people, and the only way he'd known that was how many there were was through Kimi's earlier statement, because there wasn't enough left intact to amount to three bodies. Three lives destroyed. More than three lives since there had to be people who loved them and would now mourn them.

"All—" He coughed, throat scalded by stomach acid. A water bottle appeared, by the same magic the tissues had. He took the bottle, looking up into Vee's eyes. Confronted with her sadness, probably that he'd had to see that side of her life, and what occurred when there wasn't a Vee hurtling down a dark street to save someone.

He rinsed his mouth, and after a brief check with his stomach, drank. He pushed to his feet, facing all of them, Kimi and Josh in the doorway now.

He cleared his throat and tried again. "All right. Tell me all of it. Don't try to make what happened, and what's going to happen, more palatable. Say what you'd say if it was another one of you standing here in my place."

Vee sat on the edge of her desk, inches from him. He caught his reflection in the laptop screen, his face chalk white, superimposed over the cryptid crime scene photos.

Without taking her attention off of him, Vee reached and closed the laptop. "This is the anangoa. We're waiting on DNA confirmation from the scales and saliva the Cleaners recovered, but it was the female you encountered.

"The species' typical range is isolated rain forest, few to no human incursions, but extensive options for camouflage. It's also one of the apex predators in its ecosystem. Prey is primarily nonhuman, requires effort to track, and time and effort to kill."

She crossed her arms, gaze drilling into him. "Meaning they don't yet understand urban environments provide an easily accessed, plentiful food supply, require stealth, or the importance of not drawing the attention of other predators." She didn't flinch at referring to people as food.

A trace of disapproval laced Josh's voice, the censure directed at Vee. "You can tap out of this conversation anytime, man. No shame in it."

"That's not going to stop anything," Bruce said. "The anangoa got away." Another statement no one disagreed with.

"It was gone well before we arrived on scene." Liv's

contained, professional facade spider-webbed, her exhaustion and frustration leaking out of the cracks.

Vee dipped her head in confirmation. "We were out so long because we were attempting to track it. We are almost as in the dark about its habits, identifiers, spoor, and what techniques work best as it is with a city hunting ground." Her jaw clenched, the same frustration as Liv's, and an edge of anger clear.

Josh seconded Bruce's interpretation. "This damn thing—we have decades of field notes plus our research reports for the species we police. There are weapons and techniques refined for our work. But with this thing, we've got nothing. We can't extrapolate rainforest tricks to Scottsdale."

Bruce caught Vee's flinch. Microscopic, but there. She was shouldering responsibility for not magically having all the answers, when none of them even knew what questions to ask.

She rubbed at the spot where neck met shoulder like it hurt. "I suspect that it either has offspring to feed, or will shortly. The one thing our skimpy intel all agrees on is that they do have a reptilian feeding physiology. A large kill, then weeks to digest before even considering hunting again. The exception being when they're supplying offspring."

He regretted the water he'd chugged, liquid sloshing and threatening to come up. More people would die horribly, and soon. More of these nightmares on legs would infest the city, turning it into their private killing ground.

His pulse pounded in his temples, swoosh of blood loud in his ears. Body warning brain of danger. He wasn't sure his lungs or vocal cords would even work. He unstuck his dry tongue. "Use me."

The words dropped into a total silence.

"You said this lizard has hiked its leg on me and claimed me as its prey, the reason that I'm bunking here and can't stay anywhere without monster proofing for more than a couple of hours. You can't find it. But it can find *me*."

He took a deep breath although he felt like he was suffocating, lungs crushed together and refusing to expand. "Lay some fucking brilliant government cryptid hunter trap, and use me as the bait."

The whir of the laptop exhaust was the only sound.

Had he even said it out loud, volunteering as a walking snack?

"Oh, hell no—" Josh exploded, morphing from curious to enraged in a blink, muscles bunching as he towered over the rest of the room's occupants.

Liv's, "You cannot be serious," clashed with Josh's protest, while Kimi's hands flew, signing so fast he missed most of it even with all his recent practice.

Their voices and opinions crashed together and blurred into white noise.

Only Vee didn't speak. Didn't move. Watching him despite the drama. He couldn't look away from her, couldn't break the circuit, as she saw straight inside him in a way no one else had ever had the power to.

She understood his resolve.

She still had to go through the motions though. "You got up close with the male at your rental. The females? They are larger and faster than the males." The melee died down as Vee spoke again. "I think you and I are only standing here because the female was still getting her legs under her, and acclimating that night. With offspring, it will be the definition of savage."

Liv flipped the laptop open, waking the screen with a rough swipe. "This is what you are naively tossing out as a clever idea." She stabbed a finger on the image centered on the screen, the most graphically macabre of the human puzzle pieces. "A massacre."

"I fucking know that." He forced himself to face the photos and not slam the case closed even if his voice rose, volume beyond his control.

"You don't know enough to be scared." She shoved the screen in his face.

"The hell I don't! My balls are trying to crawl back up in my body. Trust me—I fully comprehend the concept of being shredded like human taco filling." He pushed into Liv's space hating the raw concern under her anger, because it underscored his stupidity. His potentially lethal stupidity.

Josh joined in. "You don't. That windigo hunt was nothing. Missions aren't always like that and—"

"Get. Out. Of my face."

Vee held up her hand.

They all stopped, including him.

"Why?" She asked.

One word from Vee and he understood what she wanted to know. "I'm a loud, abrasive, egotistical dick and people annoy the fuck out of me. Including my family, who irritate me on the regular, and who I'd do any damn thing to keep safe." He glared at Liv and the laptop. "If you think my nightmares tonight won't put my family in the actual victims' places, you don't know anything about me."

He switched from pointing at Liv to pointing at Vee's raised hand, then at the team, all three automatically standing at attention and waiting on their C.O.'s command. "And because of this and your reaction to a single damn twitch from your chosen leader. I am fucking brilliant at what I do, and I don't ever take it easy on any restaurant or service just because I already have a reputation, or call it good enough, because *good* is not an option. Good is a lazy, offensive squandering of talent, training, and opportunity. The four of you are exactly the same. Exactly. You're all beating yourselves up after today's failure. You are going to be considering and revising plans so that you succeed when you go at it with that killer again, and when you do, you'll be balls-to-the-wall relentless."

"No matter how good we are—and we are arguably one of the best teams in the Southwestern region—and how prepared and how committed, we can't guarantee no injuries or fatalities on a mission. We take that chance each time we leave this compound," Vee said, like they were having a mundane conversation.

"I know that, too. Unlike you, I value my life. Highly."

"And you're trusting us with your life?" Kimi butted in, demanding clarity.

He didn't lie or cushion the rest's feelings. He looked at Vee and only at Vee. "You've kept me alive twice. I'm trusting you to come through a third time." He was truly a dick. Only a full-on, professional-grade dick would dump that pressure and responsibility directly on another person. Directly on Vee, who already took unrealistic responsibility for the whole damn world and was beating herself up over a perceived failure.

Liv looked from him to Vee. Then put herself between them, forcing him to step back and out of the conversation as she addressed her sister. "You have been fixated for months on oddities in the local cryptid population. I've seen your spreadsheet."

"I've never encrypted or restricted my personal files, so I assumed you had. You can't deny that between planned missions and emergency call-outs, we've been slammed. Ghouls are suddenly keeping their heads' down. The few we do find are because they've gone from scavenging to unprecedented daytime attacks on the homeless, while we've seen a seventy-percent increase in windigo activity, not even factoring in that horde at the school. We've taken out two unrelated vampires in two months where—"

"Where we only took out two vampires in total last year," Liv finished for her. "I'm not arguing those facts. Nor that they've put you on hyper-alert, which is a justifiable response. Now there's this anangoa issue and it is an oddity times a thousand. So I am asking, as your lieutenant and on the record, if your pursuit of this personal project is the basis of your considering putting a civilian on the front lines. Are you risking our charge's life in order to gather data toward formulating a hypothesis to submit to HQ?"

With her back turned to him, he couldn't see Liv's face, and thanks to her damn height, she also blocked his view of Vee's. His body froze, waiting for Vee to blow. His brain kicked into overdrive though, calculating whether he had the right to jump into the middle of an altercation between the pair of trained fighters.

He risked a look over his shoulder at Kimi and Josh, gauging their reactions as his barometer since they had more experience as far as Vee and her sister's dynamic. Josh was closest to the impending fight. Whatever Josh did, Bruce would back his play.

Both were still in that at-attention pose though, not giving him a fucking clue. The silence dragged over his nerves like a cheese grater.

As he settled on screw the consequences and ducked around Liv, Vee spoke. "Yesterday was a slaughter. I've been going over and over the extant field notes, and I can't find anything suggesting the behavior won't be repeated soon. And I can't come up with a way to locate the anangoa before that occurs. Have any of you?"

The question didn't sound like a challenge. More of a real request for input. Finally getting a clear look at Vee, her expression matched her tone, open and thoughtful, none of the anger or defensiveness he'd expected.

"No scenario I run gets us closer to the thing, not without

more crime scenes and the labs processing them to create a better picture of the anangoa's evolving behavior patterns." Liv's body language was equally open.

Frustration that felt more like it came from helplessness as opposed to disagreeing weighed down Josh's short, "No."

Catching motion from the corner of his eye, Bruce turned.

Kimi signed, "My calculations agree with Liv's."

"You're still willing?" Vee asked him, lines cutting her forehead.

"Yes and don't make me say it again."

A sigh shook Liv's tall frame. "I'll put the request for authorization through."

Just like that, the plan was a done deal from the other three's perspective.

Kimi signed, "I'm sending out our compound drone to augment the pair doing sweeps, this one patrolling between the previous confirmed sightings." She pulled a phone from her pocket, fingers dancing and commanding electronics to do her bidding. Then she put herself in his personal bubble and added, "I've got you. There won't be a hidey-hole in this town where we won't have eyes on you at all times."

Her statement was meant as reassurance. It had the opposite effect, his hands going clammy.

"C'mon," Josh took Kimi's place. "I'll walk you through some exercises. I never thought I'd say this to a civi, but you are solid. Volunteering is a Company thing to do, brother." Josh held knuckles out, expecting Bruce to tap.

Bruce glared at him, bad attitude a dangerously thin protective layer over the budding terror and doubt. "That's the fucking problem with herd mentality. It lowers your IQ. You forget to think for yourself, and do stupid shit. Hell, you *celebrate* stupidity. It's your bullshit religion."

Josh's expression hardened, an echo of the pissed off

soldier that had appeared when Bruce grabbed Kimi surfacing.

Fuck. Bruce didn't mean the tirade. At least, he partially didn't. He didn't agree but couldn't not respect the hell out of their dedication. Their bravery and loyalty to each other was astounding.

Vee slipped between them. "Josh, armory."

When he spun, back stiff, and exited, she turned on Bruce. "You. Take a break. Anywhere but near a member of this team." She gave the door a pointed look.

It fucking blew that he'd insulted Josh—against all odds, he liked the guy. It blew even harder that he'd insulted *her*. Insulted and disappointed her. Fuck him, but somewhere along the line, Vee Ramirez's approval had become important.

But, hell. He wasn't a joiner. It wasn't in his DNA. Whereas disappointing those he cared about—those that cared about him—was the dominant component of his genetic makeup.

# CHAPTER 12

## VEE

*B*ruce was in the same place he'd been since I put him and Josh in a timeout, pacing a never-ending loop around the inner yard.

He was caught up enough in his head that he didn't notice me until I blocked his path, and he nearly walked over me. He *oofed* as his chest hit my outstretched hand. Then blinked at me, frowning. His look more habitual expression than his real feelings at the moment, since I was pretty sure he wasn't really seeing me.

I could guess what he was seeing. The photos were burned in my brain, joining the gallery of similar cryptid crime scenes going back all the way from the slides we cut our teeth on at Academy, or on when we snuck into files above our year grade as a dare, through today's grisly addition.

Every cadet had a visceral reaction to their first cryptid kill scene, and they'd been exposed, trained, and prepared for eighteen-plus years. Bruce hadn't. That he was still upright, much less had proposed and volunteered for the mission that he had—lashing out at Josh was simple displacement on his part. Josh had probably already forgiven Bruce.

He blinked again, brain catching up with reality. Then he frowned, a confused one because the guy had a whole closet full of them for different occasions, presumably his confusion directed at the burner phone I held up. "I transferred all your contacts, and dubbed your number into this one, which is basically untraceable without an incredible amount of knowledge and technology, neither of which an anangoa possesses." I offered him the phone.

Taking the phone, his fingers brushed mine and didn't move away.

"Hell. Even after my mouthing off and shitting on Josh?"

"Everyone is inside so you'll have plenty of privacy. Call your sister and brother." I squeezed his hand and left him to it.

From her spot lounging on the den's preferred gaming chair, one leg over the opposite arm rest, Kimi gave me a thumbs-up. All while never missing a shot as she and Josh took on Jace, Josh's twin brother, and his team.

That was one person here who approved my decision. I'd gone over and over Liv's question since HQ granted the request to utilize a civilian, but I felt in my bones I'd made the correct decision. Data wasn't worth a civilian's life.

And if Bruce had asked to play bait out of a sense of duty or obligation to us, I would have swatted the idea down.

When he said he'd see his family in the victims' places, he meant it. His offer came from a soul-deep place. The same as the one that Kimi and Josh and Liv occupied in me.

Love and dedication shone from him today, all of his growling and arrogance gone, leaving no barrier between us and his feelings. The drive to protect his family was the same as mine.

I grabbed my laptop and took over the spot at the bar. It

was usually Liv's preferred domain. At the moment, I needed to be in the middle of Josh and Kimi's animated battle against Jace, another teammate yelling back. I worked to the backdrop of one of Liv's funky old school metal playlists, guitar riffs coming through her opened bedroom door.

The scene we'd walked into had sucked. The hours tracking the anangoa, moving painfully slow around building corners, waiting for a hostile whose habits we had next to no intel to sweep out, one of us constantly covering roofs, for an attack from above, while navigating the maze of an urban landscape and still not pinpointing the monster's location, making sure there were no more bloody scenes—that had sucked too.

I scowled at my dozenth typo, and rapped on the delete key. Even without him clearing his throat, I felt when Bruce entered the kitchen. Not looking up, I said, "If you have kitchen plans, I can bail."

"Thank you for this." He set the phone on the counter by my computer and spun it in a slow circle. "It's ridiculous as fuck—my family is a thousand miles away, and logically, I know there's no lizard monster tracking them down because it can't get to me."

"But still."

He blew out of breath. "But still."

"How did the call go?"

"Routine. I didn't have to say much. As soon as I answered, mom started grilling me about whether I'd lined up a new job, her lead-in to the usual offer of paying for a graduate program if I choose business or law as a major. Finance. Anything but food service."

"Not your thing, huh?"

He snorted a non-laugh. "I got a four-year degree in business, mostly via online courses. Restaurateurs need to understand more than food prep. There are plenty of things outside of the culinary world I was—and am—interested in learning about, too. None as a new career though, and sure as fuck not as the precursor to taking out a mortgage half an hour from their suburb and in a good school district."

"More of the non-joiner ethos."

He scrubbed a hand down his face. "I'll apologize to Josh."

"Yes, you will." I hit send and gave him my attention. "I'm not asking in order to start a fight. Call this my being interested in a subject. Why no joining or staying in an area long?"

"Are you getting an undergrad credit in Bruce Kantor?"

I pulled my knee up and propped my chin on it. "I enjoy learning, too."

"I believe that." He shrugged, but not like he was blowing me off. "Part of it is that I enjoy changing shit up. Part is that drive to take on new challenges. If I'm being honest though, after a few months of seeing the same kitchen and hearing the same people yammering about the same pointless minutia, I'm ready to slit my own throat. People annoy the fuck out of me, and I annoy the fuck out of them."

"I believe that."

He laughed, a short, real burst of surprise. "You are a shit."

"We don't stay here."

"Can you translate that into civilian English?" Bruce drifted to the dishwasher, opening it, snapping it closed when he found it empty and no clean dishes to put away, despite swearing that wasn't on his chore list.

"I mean this is our primary base, but we have others, and rotate through them. Theoretically randomly, so cryptids can't anticipate our patrol patterns."

"Like?" He swept his palm along the table. While it was scratched all to heck, it was also spotless. There was nothing for him to clean.

"Taos, Flagstaff, co-patrols in Vegas with another team— its kind of a district of its own. All of the Western and Southwestern teams have a larger area we're responsible for than teams in more population dense areas. I mean moving around like that."

"Yeah, okay. I can see that."

Somehow I doubted he really could, since he wasn't giving me his full attention. He was less frantic than before I'd given him means to reconnect with his family, but still restless. In that place with too much energy and too few outlets.

He checked the fridge top to bottom. Made a pass through the walk-in pantry, and out again. "How do you do it? This." With nothing left to check, he finally paused and motioned at my laptop and the room in general. "How do you deal with the part between planning to go get up close and personal with creatures that want nothing more than to kill you, with only three other people as backup, and actually going out those gates? If you've got any tips, I sure as hell am all ears."

"There may only be four of us but that's enough."

"Fuck. I'm not disparaging your skills or ability." He took his glasses off, seemed to forget why, and put them back on. "There are about a hundred different thoughts racing through my head right now, and I can't stop and concentrate on any of them." He finally looked-looked at me. "I've got nothing here. Toss me a bone, Vee."

Somewhere between the market and the windigo hunt, he'd switched from Ramirez to Vee. I liked the way my name sounded coming from him, and that same sizzle of desire I'd gotten from watching him on the ball court danced over my skin again. "If you've gotten over your dislike of GI Janes and big boots—"

"I didn't mean that shit. I say and do a lot of dumb things on reflex. It's an unfortunate side-effect of learning to hit before I got hit."

"Ah." I stretched, unkinking muscles, and Bruce followed my every move. Like he was...not exactly hypnotized. Fascinated, maybe. As fascinated by me as I was with him. "Was what you accidentally said about me at the market reflex or truth?"

"Caught that, huh?"

"Mmhm."

"I stand by what I said."

"In that case, I do have an idea to help you settle." I slid off the stool, putting us face-to-face. "Sex usually works for me."

He stared at me. Then blinked. "You're serious."

"You aren't interested?"

"I never said that. Damn, you are nothing if not direct."

I was only approaching sex the way any of us would. "Is direct a bad thing?"

"Hell no. More people should practice directness, but few do."

I rested a hand on his chest, then skated it lightly over his soft polo, getting a hint of what lay underneath the fabric.

Bruce caught my wrist, immobilizing my hand. "We're getting this out of the way now." He let go and spread his arms. "This is me. I'm not a professional soldier. My job doesn't require twelve hours of workouts daily. I'm a normal human with normal flaws. While we were visiting the topic, what you said the evening when I went out of my way to bring you food was a cheap shot, on top of being a shitty thank you."

I fast-forwarded through our interaction that night, searching for what he might perceive as a problem. "You shut me down and stomped out but I still don't know why. My best guess is crossed wires between our and civilian social cues." I chewed on my thumb cuticle.

"You're telling me the snark about the gym not being for me that first day, and a clumsy childhood resulting in well-honed kitchens skill wasn't a jab about my not being a fighter, and up to your standards in general?" He narrowed his eyes, challenging me.

"The discussion about our childhood seemed to set you off, so I tried changing the topic back to yours. You were cool talking about your family and experiences, and I like hearing about your life. I was only trying to keep the conversation going. If it was offensive, I apologize."

He studied me, then tilted his head back and spoke to the ceiling. "Fuck. Okay, that was on me, jumping to conclusions."

"To be clear, I like the way you look. I enjoyed watching you throw down on the court with Josh. Is it acceptable to say there was a lot I admired when you flashed the yard while wiping sweat off?"

"You could teach a master class on forgiveness." He caught my hand again taking it away from my face. He ran his fingers over my abused thumb, soothing the evidence of my bad habit. "Are we good?"

He said he came down on the side of directness. "Let's find out." I rested my free hand on his chest again and leaned in for a delayed kiss. I admitted to myself I'd wanted to do this since our verbal sparring match in his rental, excitement popping along my skin.

Bruce's lips parted in surprise. Wary of more mistakes, I brushed his lips in a light question, getting a hint of tea and mint. He made an interested noise and linked our fingers together.

Taking that as *keep going*, I traced the seam between his lips, caught in the sensation of soft lips and rough beard. That was Bruce, rough and grumbly on the surface but unexpectedly sweet too, all mixed together.

He used our joined hand and reeled me in. I worked my palm from his chest down, then ran my hand under his shirt, eager to keep exploring. My nails accidentally scraped over warm skin. Muscles clenched under my hand and Bruce leaned into me, pressing nails deeper. The same reaction as when he fed me bread, daring me to take what I wanted.

If he liked to play—I nibbled along his top lip, a hint of question. His grip tightened, and a hit of excitement coiled under my navel.

I caught his lower lip between my teeth, far less gentle. Hand in the small of my back, he fitted us tight together. The bulge in his shorts pressed against me.

I increased the pressure while pulling away, teeth skimming and bringing his lip with me until I gave a harder nip that would leave a mark, then let go.

Eyes closed, Bruce groaned. "Fuck. Me."

"That's a yes?"

He opened his eyes, expression dark and hungry. He abandoned the small of my back, catching the nape of my neck and bringing my lips where he wanted them, hard against his.

"You." He nipped my lower lip, echo of what I'd done to him. Mixing growled words and teeth. "Are." Nip. "The fucking sexiest." Nip. "Woman I've ever been saved by."

Done playing, he took over. Parting my lips and tongue invading. Showing me exactly what he intended to do next, fuck any further discussions. He ended with a crushing kiss that sent spirals of blistering heat racing through me. My skin felt too tight, nipples hardening.

He put an inch between us.

I licked my lips, tasting green tea and a promise.

His breath washed over my swollen, sensitive lips, his next question low and intense. "Is this still what you want?"

I leaned against his chest, letting him take my weight. Putting my lips by his ear, my teeth grazed the outer edge. "What do you think?"

A shudder ran through him but he held immobile. "This is one of those occasions when we have to be one-hundred-percent clear. You have to say it, Vee. No guessing."

I could do that. One hand still underneath his shirt, I flexed my fingers and drew my nails down his stomach hard enough to leave scratches. "I'd very much like to fuck until neither of us remember our names."

"Then we—"

"Where did you hide our dessert?" From out of nowhere, Liv circled the table, brows up in an innocent question. Unless you'd lived with her and her dry sense of humor your whole life, and the to-hell-with-the-rules streak that ran through her law and order personality. It was a quirk she only let family see.

"Fridge?" I checked with Bruce.

His, "Yes" came out sort of strangled.

"Fridge," I confirmed, my thigh sliding between Bruce's legs and pressing harder against his balls.

The shush of the fridge door and clink of silverware marked Liv locating her prize. Then humming quietly about being shook all night long as she took her time leaving.

Bruce blew out a breath and tilted his head in the direction my sister had gone. "Is this going to be a problem?"

"Of course not. However, unless you want a live, move-by-move performance review, we should take this private."

"You're all a bunch of little shits."

Complaint aside, when I stepped back, he reclaimed my hand, keeping us connected. He only let go when he needed both hands for the ladder, following me to the roof.

The door barely cleared his heels, before he found my hand, expertly twirling me under his arm. He eyed the platform swing. "I can work with this."

I backed toward the swing. The soft creak of the trap door stopped Bruce cold. "What the ever-loving hell?"

It only opened a few inches. Enough for Josh to toss a ribbon of condoms in and yell "Kimi told me to," the door thumping closed on my "Thanks!" as I scooped them up.

Bruce stared at me and I shrugged. "They're mine."

"You—all of you are...this is pathological."

"This is teamwork." I flashed the pack as proof.

"Does that door lock?"

"No, but they're done. Well, done for now. We'll have privacy."

Bruce turned and scanned like he was searching for something, then marched toward the center of the space. He grabbed the edge of the low, blocky table we used to hold candles, drinks, and the occasional laptop, dragging it to the entrance.

"Seriously?"

"Seriously," he grunted, positioning it on top of the trap door.

I rested my butt against the swing's wooden frame, admiring muscles clearly outlined under his polo as he wrestled the makeshift lock to his exacting specs.

He straightened and evaluated his work, then faced me. His expression shifted to another I couldn't translate. We were so done with miscommunicating. "What's wrong?"

"You." He shook his head like he was the confused party. "Shit, not you. Rather me figuring you out. What are you thinking right now?"

"That you're fun to watch and have a really attractive butt." I hurried to add, "Not just your butt," in case he took specific admiration as another form of criticism. Criticism by omission?

"You don't play games, do you?"

"I told you I noticed you at the bar. I mean, that's kind of a clear I-think-you're-attractive statement. Oh! Unless you're talking about sexual role-playing? I'm up for that, too."

Bruce crossed the space separating us in two strides. He caught the back of my neck again, his eyes a fascinating desperate-hungry. "I don't want you to be anyone other than who you are this time, because you are incredible." He dragged my face close.

This kiss. Whoa.

This was all blistering heat and urgency. Bruising, teeth clashing in our haste. I wrapped one leg around his hip and the bulge under his fly hit right where I wanted him. Except, I wanted us both naked.

His other hand went under my shirt. He found my nipple straining against my sports bra, and circled the bud with his fingers. When I pressed in, hungry for me, he pinched.

I gasped and arched into his hand. He swore against my mouth and increased the pressure. An inch short of painful, and freaking perfect. I ground against him.

His lips and tongue demanding, his fingers switched between nipples, pinching and rolling, and the heat that began in the kitchen during our flirting a day and a half earlier got a shot of oxygen and ignited like a blowtorch. Fast, scorching, and dangerous. Silky dampness slicked between my legs.

I found his waistband, the button popping free and worked my hand inside. Tracing down a neatly man-scaped trail, I caught his cock and circled the wide base in a tight grip.

His hips bucked. One handed, I shoved his shorts and boxers down. I slid my hand up his freed shaft, delighting in the velvet skin over the hard length.

Pants gone, I shifted focus to his shirt, tugging on the hem.

Bruce let go of me, grabbed fabric, and tore it off, no gentler than I'd been with his shorts.

I leaned in and pressed my lips against his ear. "I noticed

your ink that night in your bedroom. You had a—" I caught his earlobe, sinking teeth in lightly "—nice bed. Should I have stayed over and stripped you then?"

He swore again and replied via hauling my tee and sports bra over my head. I ducked as it caught my ponytail, helping him out. As soon as fabric cleared my head, he bent, catching a nipple and working it over with his teeth and tongue. He caught the other nipple between callused fingers, tweaking expertly. At the double-shot of sensation, I gripped his hair. Then caught myself, because we hadn't discussed that. But when I tried loosening my hold, he growled "tighter" against my breast, the demand vibrating through me.

I worked fingers down to his scalp and tugged. Tightening my circled fingers around his cock at the same time, running my hand from base to tip. Thumb tracing around the head. Sliding it back and forth using the drop of pre-cum I discovered.

He abandoned tweaking my nipple, dragging his splayed palm down my stomach to the top of my shorts. Instead of slipping inside, he kept going, then rotated his wrist, cupping between my legs. He circled the heel of his hand around, purposely not pressing into my clit. Teasing me.

I changed my grip, cupping his tight balls, weighing them. Circling each, then drawing a finger from underneath to the base of his cock again.

"Fuck, Vee."

"Yes, please." I let go of silky-rough hair, jerked my stretchy shorts and boy-cuts off, then felt for the condoms I'd tossed on the platform.

Bruce ran knuckles from one newly exposed hipbone across to the other, then dipped, thumb sliding between my folds, barely grazing me. Testing and teasing at the same time. He licked his lips, tasting my transferred lip balm. "I'm going down on you one day."

"Not now."

"Not now," he agreed, fingers following his thumb. A finger easing inside me while his thumb circled, gliding in my dampness.

My turn to demand. "More."

He added another finger, then a third. "Okay?"

"Yes."

He returned my earlier favor, nibbling along my ear, then caught the softer skin under my ear. Pulling an honest to Pete whimper out of me. Before I had to warn him against hickeys, he kept going. Nip-kissing down my throat, the scratch of his beard almost too much against skin that already felt like it was all exposed nerves.

Remembering what I held, I tore one packet off the strip, and more carefully than I'd done anything else, neatly ripped the top off the foil and offered it to Bruce.

He gave my clit a last flick, causing me to bite my lip. He rolled the condom on, his bigger hand gripping himself and snugging up the rubber. I added another thing I liked watching him do to my list.

He caught me watching, and slowed, stroking himself again, watching me watch him.

I used my calf to hook him again and urge him closer. "Now please?"

He double-checked our location, frowning at the wooden beam at my back. "Here? Your back is going to be—"

I caught the overhead section of the frame, pulling myself up with one arm, and positioned myself over his cock.

"Fucking hell, woman." He guided me onto him, careful now. His length filled me and I bent my other leg around his waist too, savoring his groan.

He wrapped his arm under my hips. "I can support you."

"That's not what I want from you." I locked my free hand

over his shoulder, one finger at a time. Purposely digging short nails in, feeling Bruce's excitement.

He didn't back down from a challenge. He switched, grabbing my hips in a bruising hold. Slamming into me exactly as hard as I needed, jerking my hips close.

I met him, matching his hard rhythm. Pushing him harder. Daring him. Giving way to pure sensation, the sun splashing on my head and bare shoulders, the burn of muscles in my arms working, Bruce filling me up, sweat already slicking our skin.

He jerked me into him with every thrust, like he couldn't get close enough, and I rode him in return, ankles digging into his back.

Neither of us looked away, still challenging each other. Despite the thick chains and massive posts and beams, the swing creaked and jittered, set into motion by our mutual hunger, a delicate spiral of pleasure spreading through me from where we joined. Branching out over my skin.

He pulled almost all the way out, then drove in again until balls bumped. Hitting that perfect spot. The look in his eyes saying he knew exactly what he'd done. Stoking me higher and higher.

Muscles in my core tightened, on the verge, so close, nails pressing deeper. Bruce's jaw tightened at the pressure, a light sheen of sweat on his chest.

The orgasm hit me, my back arching and crown of my head against the post. Pleasure flooding me, clenching hard around Bruce's cock.

A beat later he shuddered, muscles in his neck and arms taut, keeping my orgasm going as he came as hard as we'd fucked.

The release finally crested and receded in slow, lazy waves. My sigh and Bruce's harsh breathing all I could hear over the ringing in my ears.

I unkinked my fingers, then winced. I'd left more than nail marks, blood rising in one crescent-shaped indent, after refusing to let him mark me. "Sorry?"

"Don't ever apologize for taking what you want from life and savoring every moment." He kept one arm under my hips, but worked the other between us, catching the base of the condom.

I used both arms, and did a careful pull-up, raising off him.

He worked the condom free, knotting it, still paying more attention to me. "I'm beginning to see government training programs in a new light."

I unwrapped from his waist, thighs still a little quivery, and dropped to my feet. Stretching my arms overhead then behind, I shook out the knots. Spying my briefs, I bent and grabbed them and my bra, shimmying into them. I left shorts and tee for later.

"That's it?" Bruce watched my shimmy with a distinctly satisfied air.

"If you can fight in it, it's dressed enough."

He scowled, and I made another note for my ever-increasing list—work and mission related topics weren't his idea of pillow talk. Our fun and games today were about de-stressing him.

Mostly about de-stressing, with a side of sexy times and satisfying my curiosity.

"Want to?" I patted the swing and crawled on, content and muscles loose. "You didn't quite make it there earlier."

"You didn't quite make it, not me."

Since his tone was distracted because he was busy watching my butt, I didn't argue, just thumped the empty spot beside me. I relaxed and watch naked Bruce as he found clothes.

He glanced up from sorting and stepping into his shorts.

Shrewd eyes didn't miss my blatantly watching him move around, the same as I'd watched them earlier.

I didn't miss his blatant satisfaction either. He climbed onto the platform beside me, shirtless, and tucked one of the canvas pillows behind his back. I took it as mission accomplished when he stretched out, ankles crossed.

I tilted my face to the sun filtering down from the swing's cross-beam top. "Better?"

He nudged my ribs with his elbow. "Quit fishing for compliments."

"I don't need to fish."

His laugh vibrated through the wood and into me. "I appreciate your self-confidence."

"Is it self-confidence if it's just a fact?" I rolled onto my hip, genuinely curious.

He bent his arm behind his head. "The shit you come up with."

"Seriously. Like saying you make freaking amazing pizza. That's a verifiable fact. Is that what self-confidence is in the civilian world?"

He got that inexplicable sad-angry expression again, something about the way the faint lines at the corners of his eyes shifted and how his lips thinned. I rolled back straight. "If that's too personal or inappropriate, I apologize. Liv swears I'm a civilianophile. Like people are Anglophiles or Francophiles, I guess."

"You can ask me any damn thing you want," he said. "Don't ever apologize for curiosity and a thirst to learn, either."

Since the lines around his eyes had eased, I indulged myself. "Can I ask about these?" I skated a finger over the tattoo circling his wrist, a bent spoon that acted like a bracelet and the beginning of the sleeve on his right arm.

He caught the end of my braid where I flipped it over my

breast, and tugged. "Can I ask you to take this down?"

"You don't like my hair?"

"Braids are the new sexy as far as I'm concerned. I'll never look at the Swiss Miss girl the same again." He grinned and the open, teasing smile made my stomach do a weird flutter.

It wasn't simply because weight of his hand that close to still sensitive nipples stoked the embers south of my belly button back up, either.

Oblivious, he continued. "The first time I saw you, your hair was down."

I reached to pull the hair elastic off. There was enough breeze that it would catch loose hair and tickle, the reason I usually kept it in a braid or tail. I justified it as part of Mission: Distract Bruce from Valid Nightmares.

His hand closed over mine. "May I?"

With a nod I let go, and he set to work. He undid the band one loop at a time, forehead crinkled and absolute concentration like tugging was a crime. Band gone, he gave the braid the same laser-like attention, working from the bottom and methodically deconstructing my braiding.

When he finished, he worked his fingers in and gently fluffed, my hair resettling in waves. He rubbed a strand between thumb and forefinger.

"My turn." I tapped his arm.

He balanced it against my thigh, giving me complete access. "You're into ink?"

"You're the first partner I've slept with who had them. I think I am now." I kept going, over crisp hairs and corded muscles, tracing smaller designs that were kitchen implements. A larger one was the same emblem I'd seen on his knife case, a sepia-toned man's head in an oval. Spaces between were worked with green vines that snaked over his chest, connecting one sleeve to the other. "Do they mean something?"

"They're a narrative."

"Of?"

"What else? Me." Amusement colored his answer.

"This one?" I ran my finger over the spoon.

"I got it when I was sixteen. That was the year I forged my parent's signature and switched from AP English to a vocational class in food prep." his smile softened. "When my parents saw my first grade card, I was grounded through the entire holiday break. Other than for Hebrew class, it was straight to school then straight home. Except for the detour either getting my ass kicked because I was playing Betty Crocker with the girls and getting accused of doing it just to cozy up to some other guy's girl, because what guy would take cooking classes for any other reason, or the detour to detention when I got in the first punch before some jock or dipshit opened their mouth."

His expression turned fiercer. "I didn't drop the class when the beginning of the second semester rolled around. I used the Christmas and Hanukkah cash from my grandparents to pay for this." He rolled his wrist so the design was bathed in sunlight. "For the record, the kind of tattoo an underage kid with an attitude can get isn't pretty. I had the original incorporated into this one with my first serious paycheck a few years later."

I didn't entirely get everything he'd referred to—the not being truthful with his parents, which seemed pretty much our version of each year's guardian, and the fights over his specialization. Whatever our interest or strength was, that's naturally where we were placed.

I didn't want our conversation to end though. Bruce was fun to spar with. Fascinating to listen to. I also took a huge measure of relief and satisfaction that at least for now he was at ease.

"What about these?" I spread both hands and ran my

JANET WALDEN-WEST

palms past the bend of his elbow and his biceps, which flexed under my touch.

"I added one for each milestone—my first job in the kitchen." He fit his hand over mine and guided me from image to image as he spoke. "My first spot on a line. My first move to a station. One for each station I mastered. One for my first sous chef position." He rested my finger on the oval portrait. "Then, the awards. These let me measure how far I'd come every time I looked in a mirror."

That, I understood. We didn't do physical markers but we celebrated every technique mastered, every level advanced, and every new way to stop a predatory creature. On a personal level, Liv and I competed for the best scores too, pushing each other to be better.

I played over the vines and curlicues that swirled around his pecs and the top of the second sleeve. "Your right arm is impressive. Is it okay to say that your left is more artistic? Not better, but it looks like a single, unified thought." I glanced up into his face, inches from mine since I'd ended up half in his lap.

Bruce caught a chunk of hair that the breeze blew across his chest, playing with the strands. "I drew that out one night. I couldn't get it done all at once, but I kept the drawing and had sections finished whenever I was in a city with an especially good tattoo artist."

"These are more personal. They're more important." I felt that truth in the way he spoke about them.

Despite the heat, Bruce raised his arm and tucked me in closer, then left his arm over my shoulders. "The inter-locked stars are for my dad's parents. The matched figs for my mom's. Like I said before, they would have preferred a different career but they still supported me. My dad's father especially. Once he saw how passionate I was, he threw his approval behind me a thousand-percent. He went

146

head-to-head with my parents a couple of times on my behalf."

He cleared his throat, a ghost of the sadness back. "He never got to see me with my chef's jacket, and never got to see that I moved past being the family troublemaker."

The urge to lift his sadness swept in, as strong as the previous urge to get naked. Stronger than any reaction toward a civilian, no matter how horrible the cryptid event they'd been part of. "I don't really have any frame of reference, but it sounds like your grandfather never saw you as anything but a success."

"My family would disagree." He turned his head, nuzzling into the bend of my neck, then depositing a light kiss on my temple.

A kiss that felt sweeter, even more so than our first experimental brush of lips and elicited another desire I couldn't name.

Bruce continued. "They don't believe what I do is vital, or contributes in any way. Hell, probably none of you do either."

I let go of unnamable personal revelations. "Art is important no matter what form it takes." I nibbled on a cuticle, framing the half-formed ideas into something coherent. "Kimi's photography and painting are the kind of art everyone can agree on, right? But so is the way she makes connections and filters everything—data from a hundred sources—and twists and tailors it and creates codes out of nowhere, or the way Josh can frame a long-distance shot during a storm." I leaned more on him, weirdly happy to be sharing personal feelings about my family. "And Liv—I'm an excellent hand-to-hand fighter. But once you witness Liv with a blade? It's a dance. What I mean is that *art* covers a lot more than obvious. What you do, I get that it's art. I respect that. You're brave."

Bruce pulled back an inch and hesitated like he was

searching for words the way I'd been, or like whatever he first wanted to say, he changed his mind. "Our yardsticks are different. What qualifies as brave to you? As pissed as my parents were, they wouldn't have disowned me, and I always knew they loved me."

I wiggled to close the gap and Bruce tugged, positioning me even closer. "Living a civilian life is brave. You don't know what you're meant for from the time you can talk. You don't have that certainty or unflagging support and praise from literally everyone around you because they believe in the same purpose and goal you do. You don't have the reassurance of never thinking about a physical home, and never worrying about stuff like healthcare and finances—I really do not understand that. Why isn't that a civilian world thing?"

Bruce's jaw flexed and his arm had gone from relaxed to stiff. "I don't call lack of choice reassuring."

"We have choices." Again, somehow we weren't speaking the same language.

Bruce looked around, giving the locked gates a pointed glare. "You have rules. You've never slept with anyone with tattoos because your hookups were probably all damn soldiers, because you aren't allowed anyone else. And it's forbidden for any of you to get tattoos, isn't it? Don't try denying it. You, Kimi, Liv, you all have the same hairstyle. Josh has a boring as fuck, generic fade bordering on a military cut. None of you wear earrings, because your ears aren't pierced. Sure, not all U.S. women do. But playing the odds, at least one of you should, to go with the shit ton of jewelry I *did* see in your room."

"We aren't—"

"Supposed to stand out or be memorable. Yeah, I remember."

"Earrings? That's...nothing."

He angled so we were facing but putting distance between us, the easy almost-hug we'd shared now history. "The jewelry is a symptom of something worse, then. I'll grant that your job does need performed but only in the sense that so do firefighters or police or even military's. They, this HQ, shouldn't have the ability or jurisdiction to unilaterally take away your rights and freedom. No one has the right to dictate who you can or can't be. What you're going to be. Conscription isn't legal, and what you bunch do is so far past simply getting drafted, it's another world."

My confusion edged into frustration. "HQ and what? That's—all wrong. You misunderstand it, and us. They don't stop us or limit us or—I don't even know what you're, mistakenly, thinking. None of what you're saying is accurate."

"I'm dead-center-of-the-bullseye accurate, and that you don't recognize that and how you're being controlled and limited, *that is* the problem. Jesus. Aren't there things you want to do but can't?"

On the verge of denying the barb, I hesitated.

Bruce pounced. "There. Right there."

"Not traveling outside of our region or hitting the beach on a whim or trying out purple highlights can't compete with the importance of what we do." I shrugged. "All careers have minor drawbacks, right?"

Bruce scrubbed his hand over his face. "Okay. That's…it's a start. There are so, so many other adventures and experiences waiting for you. You haven't even been allowed to know what you're missing. If you want to go to a black sand beach in the Maldives, the only limit should be cash to do it."

"Sure, black sand does sound amazing."

Bruce grabbed my shoulders. "There's a world of amazing you've been robbed of." He squeezed my arms then jumped off the swing, grabbing his phone from where he'd left it on top of his shirt. "Lawyers first. Mom knows every player in New York City and D.C. Then this Company needs blown wide open, the shit they are doing brought into the light. I have contacts in the media. We can find a way to make this happen."

He spun back to me, phone in hand, purpose blazing from him. "We can get you out. Kimi, Liv, Josh, all of you. No way is what this HQ is doing constitutional. It also has to be a human rights violation." He punched at his phone. "Possibly kidnapping or even human trafficking, depending on how this bullshit save the orphans story they're peddling pans out."

I launched off the platform and caught the hand with his phone in it. "Stop. All of your calls, texts, and interactions are monitored." The penalty was...I wasn't sure, aside from Bruce's immediate relocation to HQ and Oversight's intervention, possibly handing him over to our contacts in other civilian policing agencies. The same for whoever opened his message. The tech crews would vanish any trace of his texts or calls, and I'd never see him again.

He covered my hand, sandwiching it between both of his and the phone. "I know, and I also know we'll have at least a couple of minutes before whatever dark web tech they have will shut me down. A few minutes is all I'll need. One well-constructed message, sent to everyone at the same instant will get out to at least a few people. Enough to blow this place wide open, no more hiding, no more secrecy, no more taking advantage."

Horror nearly choked me. I'd been so off. Instead of sharing, Bruce had been plotting. Instead of respect, he was prepared to ruin all he could touch here. "How can you have witnessed what you have, the anangoa attacks, the windigo horde, the latest anangoa massacre that had you puking your guts out from second-hand photos, and intend to stop us? To stop me?"

Instead of an outburst, Bruce's tone altered. "Policing cryptids is important. This isn't the way though. This organization's policies are as dangerous and destructive as anything you kill."

Pity. The new emotion I saw was Bruce pitying me. I broke his hold. "That you can say that tells me how little you understand."

He tried sliding in next to me. I sidestepped, and whatever he saw on my face, he didn't try again.

He kept talking at me though. "You don't get it. Hell, you can't because how the real world works has been kept from you. You don't know any better. The military does important work. The police do. Every damn day. The difference is, that they operate with full knowledge by the public and under public scrutiny."

"I'm well aware of other government agencies. It's part of our course load. Which is why I know their protocol isn't viable. That's not an option for us, and you don't have the right or the background to decide otherwise."

"Fuck, Vee, I do. I'm a citizen. That guarantees me certain rights and places restrictions on what the government can and can't do, and for a damn good reason. They fuck up, but that's why public scrutiny is vital—to force them to do better. The CIA and Homeland are sketchy as fuck, but even they are beholden to checks and balances."

"You keep forgetting that we study civilian mistakes. 'Do better' seems to be an illusion. I'm also versed in all those offices' failings. For instance, your government's response to how citizens who look like Josh are treated by police, and how children like my sisters and I are put in cages. And how long it takes for the simplest change to be decided on and implemented.

"Plus, how one elected official can single-handedly derail decades of an organization's work. Ignore qualified people, and kill programs or create new ones that are useless. All with a pen stroke, every four years.

"You are talking about human organizations, created and dedicated to dealing with humans, even humans who could be classified as monstrous. Cryptids aren't human. The same rules don't apply."

"No one is exempt from the rules, not even you." He crossed his arms, arrogance shining.

The reappearance of his temper made it easier for me. "That's the only thing you've gotten correct in your entire residency here." In one smooth move, I was in, tapping the nerves that ran along his wrist at the perfect angle, and claiming the phone as it dropped from his numb hand.

He swore and shook his arm.

"I'd say you'd get this back when you were behaving in an appropriate manner, however, I learn from my mistakes. You have no respect for us—" for me "—and I can't trust you." I gathered my clothes, stashing his phone in my bra.

"You accuse me of not seeing the bigger picture? You're the one only looking at one narrow part of a picture. You're wrong. You are so damn wrong this time, Vee."

I was.

I was wrong for imagining a civilian might take a peek inside at our lives and our cause, and be open-minded enough to understand why we did what we did, what teams and my commission meant, and the loyalty necessary to carry out our mission. How much I loved this job and this life.

I was even more wrong about considering sharing any part of my life and time with anyone outside the Company.

I'd been right once though—when I said civilians were a lot better as fictional characters than in reality.

# CHAPTER 13

## BRUCE

*H*e paced the circumference of the rooftop patio for the hundredth time. The repetitive busy work in the small space wasn't doing a damn thing to jump-start his brain. The limited room only underscored the limitations of Vee's life, pissing him off all over again.

Half of his anger was aimed at himself. You couldn't rush things. Rush prep, rush a dish, and you'd already fucked up. That was one of the first lessons he had learned in the kitchen. Instead, he'd let temper get the better of his brain. Hearing Vee talk about being used like it was some sort of pinnacle of achievement, like there wasn't more to life than waiting for some mission that she wouldn't walk away from, hell, that all four of them wouldn't, added another heaping measure of disgust and horror to the load that began with a lizard person on a dark street corner.

He hadn't intended to like any of his rescuers. That shit had snuck up on him.

Worse, he respected them. Instead of stereotypes, they were unique as hell, with their gaming battles, and shitty music, and pushing the boundaries of their sterile lives and finding creativity and wonder and their loyalty to each other. They'd shown the same loyalty toward him as well, even though he had been a dick for the majority of his stay.

They deserved better even if they didn't realize it. Better than cult indoctrination so complete they thought there was no separation between job and personal life.

He scrubbed both hands over his face and beard like that would wipe away this dumpster fire of a situation. If he was honest with himself, like it would wipe away the feel of Vee's lips on his, and the taste of cocoa butter and sun-touched skin on his tongue.

She knew what she wanted, and wasn't self-conscious about asking for it. She wasn't shy about challenging him either or meeting his challenges and upping the ante.

Sex with Vee wasn't *relaxing*. It was fucking energizing. She pushed all of his buttons, in the best way. He already saw how she could become addictive, fast.

He didn't do addictive. He'd witnessed too much of it in his industry. Alcohol to take the edge off the stress of bullshit hours, trying to maintain a relationship, and putting everything into a restaurant only to watch it tank. Drugs to get back up the next day and do another sixteen hours, six or seven days a week. He'd watched brilliant people fuck up careers and their lives.

Not repeating today's experiment went to the top of his to-do list. The argument had done him a solid, since the odds of Vee also wanting a repeat were zero. Fuck the stupid twinge that fact elicited.

He flipped the trap door and climbed down. He wasn't apologizing or backing down from his beliefs. He did need to find some sort of detente with Vee though, if for no other reason than neither one of them needed to be off their game with a lizard person mission looming.

Hell. Maybe he'd even planted a seed, and giving Vee a

few days might let what he said take hold. The lure of new places, black sand beaches, and fresh experiences might work.

He snorted an unfunny laugh. Nothing had ever knocked his convictions loose, and the theoretical ability to add a shit ton of body piercings wasn't going to alter Vee's either.

He stepped into the kitchen in time for Josh to close the decrepit refrigerator. He had a fork in one hand and one of the desserts in the other.

"Put that back," he said. If it was Liv's share, she hadn't pissed him off. If it was Vee's—he ignored the question of why he wasn't letting her brother abscond with her share.

Reading Bruce's mind, Josh said, "Vee said I could. She relinquished all claims."

Bruce also ignored the sting of her refusing his food. "Kimi says this, Vee says that. Are you a perpetual ten-year-old asking for mom's fucking permission?"

Josh plopped at the table, peeling the wrap off the tiramisu. He forked up a ridiculously large chunk and didn't answer until he finished it and swallowed. "Vee's the C.O. Her word is final. Liv's is pretty close, since her position is the C.O.'s replacement if Vee falls."

Bruce ground his teeth hard enough his jaw popped.

Josh finished off another quarter of the food in one bite. "I knew what I'd be living with from the time Vee was old enough to give orders. It's who she is." He lifted a shoulder in an in-fucking-furiating 'what can you do?' motion.

"I never especially wanted to be a leader. Neither did Kimi—she prefers indirect approaches. It works because Vee always takes everyone's voice into consideration. Every member of a team is expected to make their opinion known and have it heard. Vee is smart enough to listen to concerns or alternate ideas, and she doesn't let ego get in the way if someone else's idea is better."

Unless that someone was pointing out what a crock of shit she'd been indoctrinated with.

Josh polished off the cake and put his spoon down in a clink of cutlery on stoneware. "Which one was it?"

"What the hell are you talking about?"

"Man, I know that look. Which one pushed all your buttons? Kimi hacking all your passwords and replacing your screensavers with videos of octopuses mating, Liv quoting rules twenty-four-seven, or Vee turning things upside down with no warning?"

"Octopus mat—never mind. I don't want to know. How can you live here and be so laid-back? Because your level of chill is fucking unnatural."

"I have my own intense tics too, so fair's fair." Josh rose and put dishes in the dishwasher, motioning Bruce to follow him outdoors.

"Rematch?" Another game worked for him. Good intentions or not, he'd nuked plenty of apologies when his still-smoldering temper won. Facing Vee right now wouldn't end in anything other than Bruce versus Vee, part two.

Josh went right at the bottom of the steps, toward the other buildings instead of the court. "Basketball is for fun. The bag is for serious shit."

Josh opened the gym door and automatic lights powered on, giving Bruce his first real look inside.

No mystery why Josh had zero body fat and Vee could perform pull ups mid-sex. The enormous space held every piece of physical fitness equipment known to serious gym rats. Along with other equipment that he'd only seen in self-defense courses, and his nieces' dojo when he'd ferried them to classes once.

The rack of practice weapons along the back wall caught the overhead light and winked back like they were taunting him.

He forced his attention from them back to Josh. The guy squatted in one corner, amid different bags hanging out of each other's range. "Fair's fair, my ass. You take your shit out on these."

"Everybody does. I do log more time on the Big Brown Counselor." He grinned and flashed a roll of tape. "We all have our go-to's. Liv runs cross-country. Kimi tackles the obstacle course. Those are Vee's thing." He jutted his chin at the martial arts dummies on the opposite end of the building.

"You ever done this before?" Josh asked, winding the protective tape around Bruce's right hand first then switching to the left.

"No."

The next five minutes consisted of Josh running down a list of do's and don'ts, and coaching Bruce through combinations, before stepping back.

Bruce concentrated on jabs and keeping hits centered.

Josh watched, the picture of a private trainer.

"Vee obsesses over all things new and different."

One of those insufferably chatty private trainers.

"She's also crazy into pop culture and all your civilian trends." Josh tapped Bruce's forearm, correcting his form. "Our streaming queue is seventy-five percent reality shows, twenty-five percent rom-coms."

"How the hell do you know what a rom-com is?" Bruce grunted, most of his breath reserved for the actual pulling in of oxygen.

"Why wouldn't I? Those makeup scenes at the end get me every time, and *The Kissing Booth* ones are awesome. Anyway. She goes all in on whatever new thing catches her interest. She's intense—there's no halfway for her, so, yeah, she's probably annoying you, shaking you down for every deet about civilian life. Probably as foreplay."

"Do not. Discuss sex. And your sister. In the same

sentence. The same paragraph," he got out between jabs. "Or ever."

"All I'm trying to say is that if she treats you like her personal documentary, as soon as she learns her fill, she'll dial down the intensity and go back to directing her focus at her latest obsession with cryptid patterns and patrol schedules."

*Back to her real life* went unspoken. As did that Bruce was a one-off, simply a passing diversion for Vee.

The farmer's market scene sprang to mind, and her fascination with everything from bars of soap to the reaction of the dad when she sent the replacement cone.

Fuck all if he understood the sudden hollowness in his chest. He took his confusion out on the bag.

"I'm calling it." Josh held his arm in front of the bag, between it and Bruce. "You've got good upper-body strength, but you're still gonna hurt tomorrow. This works a new set of muscles. Hit the showers."

Ten minutes later, as Bruce tossed his toiletry bag on the bathroom shelf and plugged in his razor, Josh's warning echoed. *You're going to hurt—this is a new set of muscles.* The facts Bruce had ignored, but his asshole subconscious hadn't, punched him in the balls.

He hadn't gone into sex with Vee as a one-time thing to take the edge off and he was free to get on with his life. He hadn't had sex with her to get the justifiable mutual fascination out of his system either, and if he'd meant to, spectacular miscalculation. He was more invested than ever. He didn't do invested but here he stood, obsessed. The dumbass staring back at him from the steam-fogged mirror was obsessed.

He was as obsessed as Josh claimed Vee was. Not only did he still feel the way she clenched around him as she came, that memory-sensation led to others; the rapt way she listened to him, and for once the attention wasn't appealing because it fed his ego, but that she was so damn smart, so quick to grasp ideas, and his meaning like they already had a short hand. She was so damn curious about everything. She was the most interesting person he'd ever met, from the way her mind worked, to her inexplicable imagination, and offbeat sense of humor. She had the sexiest brain he'd ever encountered.

That string of revelations created a trail, like the steps of a math equation, finally equaling the answer. That A) He didn't have any intention of staying here, and the conflicting fact that B) He didn't have a desire to forget about Vee or stop spending time with her.

A plus B equaled he was so screwed.

# CHAPTER 14

## VEE

*L*ight cut across me in an arc, then disappeared as Liv and Kimi entered the armory. *Entered* also being known as tracking me down to hear all about my Bruce interlude.

I put the extra sniper rifle back together and replaced it with an already immaculate compact HK, taking the gun apart.

"That bad?" Kimi signed. "You never know with ultra-confident guys—fifty-percent chance they're confident for a reason, fifty-percent chance they can't find your clit even with a map and tutorial."

A valid enough assumption. "No. Sex was fine. Really great, actually."

"But?" Liv pulled out one of the beat up metal chairs and flipped it backward, arms across the top and chin propped on them. "There's some Bruce related reason you're breaking out your second favorite *I'm annoyed* habit."

I ran the cleaning brush through the barrel. "Why are civilians so...rigid? And self-centered? *Definitely* self-centered." I traded brush for polishing rag. "Also, they do *not*

160

approach sex like any rational person. Who knew orgasms turned them judge-y, and gave them the right to explain your own life to you?"

"Harsh." Kimi levered onto the table and folded her legs up.

"He doesn't even try to see another point of view or understand."

"It's not like this was anything but a one-time quickie," Kimi signed, then ignored me in favor of her phone.

"Just avoid the topic, or him, until he's out of here," Liv said. Her eyes narrowed. "Unless, of course, you were thinking of filing the request for him to become an Asset, and seeing him every time you were in the area and had need of *really great, actually* sex."

I glared at Liv, then the top of Kimi's bent head. This wasn't a casual dish session. This was a well-planned, tag team intervention.

Rule number two was never lying to your team. "Fine. I was considering the possibility."

Liv gave me a look.

"Considering strongly," I admitted.

"He's entitled to his opinion, no matter how wrong or offensive we find it," Liv said, tone softening. "This mission he proposed aside, I don't get the vibe that he's one of those civilians who is entranced by discovering cryptids and who can't let it go."

I didn't want to hear what Liv had to say. Which was exactly why I needed to. She was my voice of reason.

I gave a short nod, and she continued. "He isn't one of us and he wasn't raised to understand. He is one of that larger percentage who view our big revelation as a waking nightmare. That's his right."

"He doesn't have to like my career in order to stay under the Oversight umbrella." I looked to Kimi. She was our intelligence specialist because she had the ability to analytically sift through observations and facts and weigh them dispassionately. She saw what was, not what you hoped or wanted it to be.

"He's interesting, and I think I might like him." She handed me her phone.

The screen was open to one of Bruce's social media accounts. It was filled with gorgeous shots of plated food, most of which I couldn't identify, along with selfies of him with actors and sports figures who I did recognize. More photos, shots of cities, of other countries, and expensive rentals like the one he had in Scottsdale, of him at clubs and events. All had tons of likes and comments, and, wow, he had an army of followers.

Kimi flicked the screen. The links to articles and press releases, festivals, his opinion pieces, and awards that came up when searching for Bruce Kantor went on and on. Several were about his feud with another mouthy chef in Britain and his attitude in kitchens. "I kind of knew that chefs were more of a notoriety thing but not that he was famous-famous. He's basically a public figure." A bit of me was fiercely proud of his drive and success, especially after him sharing what he had to defy to get to the point of accolades and happiness. Or at least get to the point of fulfillment. I still didn't get how he could really be happy without strong ties and people he needed, who needed him, around every day.

My sisters had done their homework. Lots of it. And I got the feeling it stemmed from more than Kimi's habitual curiosity. Liv had no interest in civilians, aside from in a professional capacity.

"He's accustomed to being in charge. You are accustomed to being in charge," Kimi signed. "Neither of you are quitters."

"The two of you are combustible." Liv's body language left no doubt that she considered combustible a bad thing.

Kimi frowned, head cocked, and seemed on the verge of adding more. Whatever it was she changed her mind and kept it to herself, reclaiming her phone. She hopped to her feet.

"Where are you going?" I fit the gun back together and replaced it in its assigned spot.

"Jace's team had a mission call out. Some annoying ghoul sitch. They should be back at their base soon and then I can continue to remind him and Josh of their place in the gaming hierarchy."

"Namely, far beneath you."

"As is right and proper." Kimi somehow made an eyebrow wiggle devilish.

When the door closed, I slid in my seat until the back of my skull rested on the seat back. My sigh sort of snuck up on me.

Liv confiscated the last weapon on the table, one of her extra side pieces, and mindlessly disassembled and reassembled it. She took her time and the energy in the room shifted by the time she finally spoke. "Why are you so—" she waved her hand at me "—this. So you two go separate ways. He's just a guy and it's not like he's your only option for fun. There's always someone new at HQ taking their turn as Visiting Instructor when you are. There's Terrance, because you know we'll be teaming up with his crew at least once during the windigo migrations. There's Miguel. You guys were eyeing each other when we took the weekend in Galveston, and he's always fun."

All true. Josh was my brother so Jace was as well. The others weren't though. We all, in the general teams sense, hooked up for a fun one-off, or a weekend, or even a standing thing whenever someone from two teams worked together on joint missions once or twice a year. That was normal. Fun. Easy.

So, no, I had no idea why it mattered that Bruce wouldn't occasionally be available. Much less why the thought of Terrance and Miguel left me unmoved.

"Bruce has made it clear he isn't a joiner and he'll never get why we are. It wasn't fair of me to expect him to embrace my lifestyle and career." Without anything to clean, I picked at a hangnail.

"It's not fair for him to expect you to agree with him, or spend time and energy trying. We do not waste energy. You two are destined to butt heads endlessly. Like, the human equivalent of those Bighorn rams we saw when we did the training externship. Pointless, painful, and an energy suck."

Underneath the assessment was the unspoken. Bruce was my energy suck. Rule number one was never split your focus. Never let outside crap mess with your head. There shouldn't even be a question of anything significant outside your team. That led to divided attention, and inevitably, mistakes. We couldn't make mistakes.

That rule went three times as much for me, as C.O. Once for Josh's life, once more for Kimi's, and the third for Liv's.

Liv rose. "I'm running over a short list of sites for the anangoa trap again. We can cross-reference our top picks, and run the specs by Kimi for surveillance angles, then Josh for sniper locations he can work with."

I added a fourth to my math—four times as much responsibility as C.O now with Bruce not a team member, but willingly taking the risks we did. That should be, was, my priority right now. "I'll be there in a few."

Liv paused in the doorway, staring in confusion. Then snapped the door closed, her comment on the situation.

Yeah. I didn't get why I was acting this way, either.

# CHAPTER 15

## BRUCE

*B*ruce glared down the hall at the general direction of the kitchen and the voices he couldn't ignore any longer.

*That he didn't want to ignore.*

The stupid, traitorous part of his brain taking over at identifying one of the voices as Vee's. He had also had his fill of staring at the walls in his temporary room. He should've been *wiped* after twenty-four-hours straight without sleep.

He'd tried once the team left for their mission, but being comfortable—fucking safe and sleeping at all in their home—hadn't felt right. Not when they were out possibly coming face-to-face with something that wanted to kill them.

The emotional undercurrent he'd finally identified as concern for Vee wouldn't let his brain shut down even if he hadn't felt like a dick for sleeping when they couldn't.

Then, roof sex. Roof sex with Vee, which had rocked his damn world. Followed by the mother of all disagreements, if disagreement encompassed fundamental, basic as breathing, violently opposite ethos.

The gym workout should have finished him off. Instead, he felt like he'd mainlined a six-pack of those foul energy drinks on an empty stomach.

He hit the kitchen, ready for anything the team threw at him. Aside from a quick, out of everyone else's sight thumbs-up from Kimi, all four stayed fixated on some kind of three-D computer module he doubted even the Pentagon possessed.

"So we're looking at excellent line-of-sight on option A," Vee said.

"Yeah. There are at least three positions I can utilize, depending on wind shear." Josh used a fancy pen-wand device and tapped, illustrating. "Easy kill shots, since the street grid and business layout boxes the target in." Chilled-out Josh was gone, replaced with an intense version, eyes flat as he calculated how to kill, with icy professionalism.

"Surveillance?" Vee moved on to Kimi.

"Excellent terrestrial surfaces and camouflage points for the scooter. Equally unencumbered aerial space for drones. We'd have real-time imagery on everything larger than a Gila," Kimi signed.

Liv took over, their switching as perfectly orchestrated as a dance. "Five stop lights to synchronize. Offset by unpredictable civilian presence and limited means of controlling foot traffic, even by claiming a biohazard terrorist alert and filtering Homeland via local SWAT to hold a clear border for us."

Jesus Fucking Christ. Liv talked about terrorists and tossing local and national groups in at the team's orders like it was as easy as calling a HOA patrol.

"Site B. Terrain is inhospitable to the scooter. Only forty-percent of the site open to a drone." Liv held up fingers, ticking off points and folding one down for each. "Only two potential points for sniper setup. There is significant potential for subterranean infiltration."

Which sounded like huge drawbacks to Bruce, whatever the hell subterranean infiltration meant.

Liv held up her last finger. "Those facts offset by minimal civilian presence. Only one potential ingress and egress point, easily closed off by computer data manipulation. Chemical spill signage and warning to LEO is the likely scenario, stating the company responsible is utilizing a private hazmat crew for cleanup."

"Only a nineteen-point-three percent chance of civilians coming into play," Kimi signed.

"Site B, then." Tension hardened the line of Vee's jaw.

The only sign that as far as Bruce could tell, she had just chosen the most hazardous option.

"Site B." Liv flipped open a tablet and tapped. When she flipped it closed, Kimi touched a device, and the Star Wars-level simulation disappeared.

All four stretched, like they'd been at it for hours. Bruce checked the ancient clock over the bar which, yeah. They probably had.

Hours spent pinning down the site where he'd stand around with his thumb up his ass, hoping a monster would find him appealing. Praying four people he'd gotten to know took the hit meant for him. Fucking justifiable fear, and guilt, set up residence in his chest, making it hard to draw a breath.

"Firing Range?" Liv asked the room.

"Always," Josh answered as Kimi scooped up electronics and retreated to her tech den with a snort.

"After I unofficially file our plans with Terrance." Vee grabbed a cup and sipped. Her nose crinkled but she drank it anyway.

"Two words. Sports. Drinks." Josh laughed at her reaction. "Unlike your coffee they don't get bitter after sitting."

Josh caught sight of Bruce. "Any chance of another weird pizza later?"

"Do I look like your nanny? Fucking fix one yourself." Bruce regretted it even as his mouth kept moving, but the turmoil in him took the path of least resistance, keeping to old habits.

Vee's cup clunked on the table.

Bruce held up both hands. "I'm going, I'm going." He shouldered past Josh, escaping outside, where the only person he could be a dick to was himself.

He ended up on the bench, staring at the birdbath and plantings. Trying to will a measure of calm from the peaceful scene over his burning nerves. Trying equally hard not to picture Kimi out here, camera or sketchpad in hand, translating the art in her soul to a tangible form. Reminded he might be part of the reason that soon, she risked never coming home, never sitting here again. The sun moved and shadows changed, gunfire popping in the background from Liv and Josh's training. The disconnect between the two, beauty and violence, wrapped everything in a surreal haze.

The thump of gunshots got louder, knocking Bruce's efforts to the curb. A flash of movement from the corner of his eye startled him. He whirled, banging his knee on the bench arm. The sound wasn't gunshots but Josh, who pounded past him, something clutched in his hand. Two strides later, Liv sprinted by with her phone visible in her grip, the metal steps rattling like bones clacking as both charged up them.

Bruce bolted after them, catching the door before it closed. He jerked to a stop before he slammed into Liv's back, not prepared for warm bodies bottlenecking the entry.

Vee had Josh by the shoulders, her volume belying her calm tone. "He's alive. Stop. Breathe. Jace is alive. He is in medical right now."

She kept repeating the mantra as the wildness left Josh's expression.

Bruce moved to Kimi's. He kept his question low. "What's wrong?"

Most of her attention on Josh, she signed, "Jace. Jace is Josh's twin brother. Jace's team was on a mission." She spelled ghoul. "It should have been a gimme but something went wrong and—" She shook her head and didn't finish. Instead hurrying to catch up as Vee used her hold to turn Josh further into the house, to the left and her office.

No one closed the door so Bruce hovered in the opening. He didn't have any business joining them. He didn't get sucked into other people's drama, one of the reasons he couldn't stand staying in one kitchen and the suffocating gossip and worries, petty grudges and manufactured bullshit. At the first hint, his bags were packed, his car pointed to a more appealing destination.

Yet he couldn't make himself turn and leave.

"Ramirez?" A feminine voice came from the open laptop on Vee's desk. Instead of taking her seat, she turned the screen so the entire team had access. "We're all here."

A woman in medical scrubs, braids pulled back in a knot, nodded at the crew. There was no missing the red-brown streaks across one sleeve of her scrubs. "We got him stabilized and he's in surgery."

"How long? How long until he's out? Why aren't you in there? It's *Jace*—how could you not be in with him?" Josh pushed to the front, a raw edge to his barrage of demands, fists bunched and tendons standing out. The demands felt especially personal like Josh, or maybe his brother, had some relationship beyond medicine with the doctor.

"There are three surgical teams in the OR."

Josh flinched at the news and Bruce had to assume just

like in the real world, a packed operating room didn't bode well.

The woman continued. "Believe me, if I could offer anything, I would be in there. The circumstances call for specialists, not my generalized ER abilities."

Liv caught Josh's fist, cradling it between both of her hands.

"What about the rest of the team?" Vee took command.

The doctor's soft sigh caused Liv to take one hand off Josh and grab Kimi's, linking the three of them.

Disbelief shaded Vee's tone. "Michaela? Paulo? Alice?"

"Alice and Paulo were deceased on the crew's arrival. Michaela didn't make it through the med flight."

Bruce blinked, his brain fighting processing the facts. Three gone. Maybe four, from the doctor's grim recital. The same vibe as the doctor during his grandfather's illness. Talking treatment options and chemo scheduling, while the reality that none of it would change the ultimate outcome made every word a lie.

"How the hell did this happen? Jace said a ghoul. The intel was solid and there's no way, none, that Michaela let them go in unprepared." Vee's anger seemed to take up all the space in the room. "It was a lousy ghoul, not a nest of vampires."

He wanted to tell her that the anger was good, to hold onto it as long as she could. Because once it was gone, that's when the real pain hit.

"From what I could gather, it was ghouls, multiple."

"No fucking way." Kimi signed so emphatically her hand grazed the screen and Vee grabbed, saving the laptop from crashing to the floor.

"All I know is the chatter from the extraction crew."

"There will be an official pre-report circulated within an hour." Vee nodded at the doctor. "Thanks for calling so fast, Nandi."

"I'll update you as soon as I know anything." The screen went dark.

Leaving a reflection of tear-streaked faces. None of the team hid their grief, Josh ugly crying, eyes already red, drops rolling down Kimi and Liv's chins to hit the tile under their feet.

Vee closed her eyes and tilted her face up.

His assumptions crashed and rearranged themselves, in the same way they had when he realized that the brain dead Barbie-soldiers he had gotten stuck with were instead bright, complicated people.

They were the realest people he'd ever encountered and they felt every emotion on a level that made him ache in sympathy. He needed to do something. Help. Hold Vee, if she'd allow it. Give her any support he was capable of, all too aware it wasn't much since he couldn't bring their friends back or affect the outcome of their brother's surgery.

Using her thumbs, Vee wiped tears away. "It'll be a couple of hours, at least."

Like that was a coded message the other three headed his way, Vee behind like she was shepherding. She was getting them where they needed to be safely.

He stepped out of their way then fell in again behind Vee. Shoving his hands in his pockets to keep himself from reaching for her and interfering.

They all ended up in the game-filled common room. Bruce understood the reason once Josh sat, Kimi and Liv curled on either side of him. This was the only spot that held all of them comfortably. This room was the heart of their house.

Instead of fitting onto the bulky couch, Vee circled behind, tossing one of the pillows she grabbed from between it and the ugly corner chair to Liv, the other to Kimi. She hugged Josh from behind, and he wrapped his arm over the top of hers.

She laid her cheek on top of his head. "I'll hit Terrance up for any other chatter."

"'K." Josh let go and Vee dropped a kiss on his head, before standing straight.

When she passed by, her sadness drifted over Bruce like it was a cloud attached to her.

Impulse ruled and he touched her elbow. "Is there anything, anyway, I can help?"

Vee paused, more forgiving than he'd ever be and laid her hand over his like he was the one in need of comfort. "If there was, I'd take you up on the offer in a hot second. Thank you though." She glanced back at her family a last time before continuing on.

Bruce did the only thing he could.

When Vee came back out of her office, laptop in hand, twenty minutes later, he had the start of mise en place done.

She pulled out the stool and set her computer on the short bar.

He tipped his chin at the coffee maker. "It's fresh."

She poured a cup then relocated to the end of the table, chair at an awkward angle. The spot gave a clear view into the den. He watched her, while she watched her brother and sisters, only occasionally keying an entry into the spreadsheet.

Vee cradled her mug in both hands. "You were right."

For a heartbeat, wild hope flared. That this god-awful tragedy had convinced Vee to take the rest of her team and run, and to let him send that exposé text.

She tilted her cup his way. "This coffee is much better than our old convenience store brand."

He couldn't keep her safe any more than she could Jace's

team. He turned back to the range top, stirring a pot that didn't require attention.

"Pudding?"

He checked over his shoulder. Vee had given up any pretense of adding shit to an inventory spreadsheet.

He cleared his throat, because today's events call for a hell of a lot more than pudding. "My spin on matzo ball soup and babka." He'd brought out the big guns. Bonus that both dishes were time-intensive.

Vee wandered to the stove but kept her hands off lids, more polite than any of his family. "What does soup and bread say?"

"Pastry," he corrected. There was enough chocolate and dried black cherries in the dough to give the entire compound a sugar high. "Sometimes, carbs really are the best medicine."

He lifted the pot lid in invitation and Vee leaned over, inhaling.

"This is comfort food to me. Well, my version, and from one half of my family."

When Vee stayed close, he kept talking. "Food is important. It's not just fuel or about taste. It's an expression of culture and caring. Both sides of my family have food shorthand and their own necessities for celebrations, apologies, illnesses or—" He quit. Hearing about funerals and shiva buffets with the last damn visual he wanted to give Vee.

"For sadness?"

"Yes. Sometimes to try to cheer people up, sometimes to acknowledge the sadness when there's no recourse and you simply have to sit with the emotion."

She showed no inclination to leave, only turning until she faced the den again, parked at Bruce's side, which felt right. "I can understand that."

It killed him, how many times they had undoubtedly

repeated this scene and sat with sadness for other friends. Grief was universal. Food was universal. Damn if cooking a meal for these people, here and now, didn't feel right too.

So did having Vee in his space.

Song lyrics blared out, shattering the calm bubble. Vee lunged for her phone and swiped it open. "Nandi?"

The floor shook as the other three charged in and ringed Vee. Liv had Josh and Kimi's hands again.

Bruce's heart felt like it was trying to slam out of his chest. He didn't realize he'd slipped into Hebrew and uttered aloud the prayer running through his head on a loop until Liv glanced his way, before turning back to Vee.

She didn't say a word but Bruce knew. The expression on her face—he'd bet every knife in his case that this once, the outcome was good. They had kicked the odd's ass.

"Okay, thanks." Vee cut the call, looking a hundred years younger. "Jace is out of surgery. He has broken ribs that will take time, punctured lung that's repaired, pins in his left leg, but a couple months of PT and he'll be up and recertified. He's going to be okay, Josh. You can talk to him in the morning. He's alert and coherent enough to speak to Nandi, so no lasting damage from the concussion."

Josh scooped with his long arms and brought all three of his sisters in for a hug. The four clung together, sharing relief and comfort. No one spoke but they didn't need to, their silent communication palpable. Each knew what the others meant and what they needed.

For a second, he missed his family. They had lost that easy sense of understanding once one after another of them left for college. Then again, perhaps distance wasn't the problem so much as different mindsets, because Bruce had had that bond with his grandfather right up until the end. That hurt had mellowed into something softer but the view was suddenly hazy. He jerked his glasses off, swiping them against his shirt.

Replacing them, he caught Josh's eye, the group already separating into clumps.

It was as natural as breathing to grasp the soldier's arm, ending in a rough one-armed hug. "I'm glad your brother will be all right."

"Thanks, man." Josh let go.

Kimi inserted herself into her brother's slot without hesitation. Fuck it. Bruce reeled her in, the same as he did for his sister, and hugged the shit out of her. He didn't half-ass hugs any more than he did fights.

When he let her go it was only to do the same to Liv. The tear tracks down her face hit him hard, and he wished for a physical target and the ability to eviscerate anything that cracked composed, professional Liv's shell.

She *oofed* a soft breath but before he could loosen his hold or apologize, she hugged back, taking his comfort and offering him the same, his ribs protesting.

When they both stepped apart by mutual agreement, Vee was watching them. Her expression… he couldn't read her. He'd glimpsed underneath Liv's shell. This with Vee went deeper though. Like she was seeing him in a different way, too.

He cleared his throat and retreated to safer emotional territory. "Get in here. You need food and this broth needs served before it cools."

He grabbed for the bowls stacked in the cupboard but Vee nudged him aside. She pulled out bowls and plates while Liv gathered utensils and Kimi and Josh cleared the table of computer and phone.

Vee followed his short instructions, plating and serving in easy silence. The cloud of grief around her had altered. The sadness was there but cushioned in approval. Every time she brushed against him, handing over a bowl or taking a plate, her approval whispered along his skin.

Once food was distributed she took the seat by him. When she lifted her spoon, he held his hand over her bowl. "Give me one minute."

He closed his eyes and gave a simple thanks, acknowledging he'd asked for a miracle, and however it came about, his request was answered.

When he opened his eyes, the teams' were all on him, waiting for their cue, hands off of utensils. Respectful, even if they didn't understand. "Eat."

No one eyed the soup or asked what it was, either too wrung out to care or finally trusting him. "A twin brother, huh?"

After Bruce's prompt, he let the conversation flow, all four sharing memories. Jace wasn't just a good friend to them. The whole group, the stories, the tone—the guy was as much their brother as Josh was.

Soup gone, Liv started to rise with her empty. Bruce shook his head, stood and took his and Vee's, and worked his way around the table, letting the team keep talking. Letting them work through the shit-ton of emotions they'd cycled between in the last few hours.

As he accepted Liv's, she gave him a smile that primarily showed around her eyes. She let him see a bit more real Liv. He got a hit of the same approval he'd felt from Vee.

He arranged dessert plates and sliced babka, passing out servings on autopilot while he rolled these feelings around, examining them from all angles. It wasn't the admiration and acclaim he evoked in diners and other chefs that fed his ego. Even when Josh asked about Bruce's family and his brother, half of Bruce's attention gnawed at the puzzle while he answered.

As the team lingered over seconds on Josh and Vee's

parts, then over plates long ago picked clean, obviously needing this time to bond, it hit him.

He was feeding off of the approval and happiness. Not because of great food, but something more personal since that seemed to be the day's theme. Liv, and even more, Vee, appreciated him and his contributing to the team, and to caring about their siblings. Vee was happy *with* him.

Son of a bitch. It felt right. Worse, it felt good. On a par with any recognition he'd ever garnered, filling up some hole in him usually reserved for industry awards, and care packages with wavery grade school handwriting, addressed to Best Uncle Ever.

Which freaked him right the fuck out. What freaked him out more was the too-domestic scene didn't kick off the need to grab his bag and keys and pull up directions to a new gig.

"I'll help."

He started, jerked out of his head. Vee stood by his chair, the rest of the kitchen finally empty.

"I told them we would clean up," she added when he blinked at her. "But I can do it myself."

He shoved his seat back. He opened his mouth to tell her to go, that this once he had clean up. To get her and the vibe screwing with his head far away from him. Instead, "I'll help," came out.

They worked together like they'd done it hundreds of times, perfectly in sync. He caught himself rearranging cutlery like he gave a damn how they organized their mismatched forks. A glance over his shoulder showed Vee wiping down the chairs nobody had sat in.

He admitted to himself that they were both finding reasons to stay. Giving in, he filled the kettle and grabbed lavender chamomile tea because he sure as hell needed to chill, and Vee did too.

Like she read his intent, she folded the towel and dropped

it on the counter. She parked herself beside him, ass against the counter edge, facing the empty room.

While water came to a boil, he rested his ass beside hers, and tipped his chin at the second hallway. "Is Josh leaving tonight or in the morning for the hospital? Whatever you call your black ops version of a hospital, I guess."

Vee got that damn look, brows scrunched. The one that said he might as well be speaking a foreign language. "Of course not. We have a mission on the books."

He stared at her over a chasm that went beyond an unfamiliar language. On one side, where of-fucking-course Josh would be on his way to see his fresh from surgery brother. On the other, Josh, and the entire team expected to act like nothing happened and jump back into performing as a corrupt organization's expendable toys. They weren't even allowed time to catch their breath, much less mourn lost friends.

He looked at the ceiling, because if he looked at Vee with her eyes bloodshot from crying, he'd burn the compound down, and enunciated "Josh's. Fucking. Brother. Almost. Died today."

A warm hand wrapped around his. He brought his gaze down as Vee edged so that their sides touched. "All of this?" She reached sideways and tapped her closed laptop. "We are doing a deep, deep dive into terrain, power grids, traffic and foot traffic flow. Talking to our street contacts about any changes on the ground that building plans and aerial views don't show. We're also still collating anangoa information since Kimi reached the Asset who made the first-person report on them a year ago. We are tailoring this mission, and we'll keep tailoring it until the last minute, to form the absolute best plan."

She thought he was worried about the mission. "Damn it, Vee—"

She caught his other hand, squeezing both like she was trying to physically force reassurance into his veins. "I get it, okay? You just heard that three-quarters of a team was lost, then heard about Jace's injuries. Of course that scares you. Obviously, I can't promise you that missions never go wrong." Her grip tightened. "I can promise you that you are our first priority. We will protect you. *I* will protect you."

"I'm good at what I do in the same way that you are in your career." She mimicked him, tilting her head at the stove. "I spent thousands of hours learning and perfecting my skills, and I spend every day keeping them sharp, and pushing to improve. What Liv brought up earlier when you volunteered? She had the right to ask, but I will never view you as expendable. No matter what, we will be between you and that anangoa."

It wasn't going to exclude him from competing in the shittiest person of the year games, but he wasn't letting Vee carry the added weight of some weird guilt. "Hell, I know that." He flipped their hands, holding onto hers now. "I never doubted you or any of the team. Never."

The furrows between her brows eased a degree. "Forget clearances and rules. Ask me anything and I'll answer if it will help to reduce your anxiety."

Presented with a chance to satisfy his bottomless curiosity...he blanked. Brain as empty as a shuttered restaurant. He gave a rough laugh. "I've got nothing. Hell, I'm made of ideas. I have them in my sleep and wake up long enough to scribble them down, and then go back to sleep. But right now? That part of my brain is frozen solid."

"If it helps, your part of the mission is simple. The most dangerous as far as exposure to the anangoa, but the simplest. Crap." She let go and worried a cuticle. "That was not at all helpful or reassuring."

He smacked her hand, stopping her before she drew

blood. "Knock that shit off." He grabbed the cutting board and peppers destined for the next day's breakfast, and lied. "These need mincing. Get busy. Besides—"

"We think better when we're working," she finished for him.

He snorted. "Mince more, talk less." He pulled out greens that also didn't need prepped, as much to keep himself busy as to sell his bullshit claim.

A minute in, he side-eyed Vee and her technique, which he could only label *enthusiastic*. "You are fucking disturbing with a knife."

"Hey, we're both specialist with blades, just for different reasons." She stopped, blade halfway through a sliver of mangled vegetable, and blurted, "I could show you basic knife fighting technique." She glanced from her board to him and words rushed out. "You said you were used to getting in fights, starting when you were a kid, and okay, let's be honest, you are not diplomatic or polite, so I can't imagine that part has changed as an adult. Plus, I saw you playing ball against Josh, and you're agile and fast and aggressive. Kind of willing to cheat too."

He laid his knife down, tension pushing his shoulders tight. Beside him, Vee tensed up as well. "Why? Why teach me?"

"You're already familiar with them and it's the one weapon you'll always have close at hand. The ones in your kitchens, and in your case at home. You probably sleep with that case under your pillow."

He ignored her try at humor and distracting him. "Try again. Why?"

She slammed her knife through the pepper, its blade lodging in the wooden board, and faced him. "Because then you'll be able to defend yourself. When you leave here you'll be able to defend yourself in—non-human fights. You can yell at me about being bossy, and always having to be right, although you do that too, and that I'm not your C.O. and I'm way out of line but—you know what? Bite me. I'm entitled to my feelings, and yes, I'm going to worry." Color climbed her cheeks, her temper showing as she shoved into his personal space.

He surprised them both. "I'm not pissed about what you just did to my knife or your offer."

"Why?" Suspicion replaced her temper.

"Fuck if I know."

Her eyes narrowed. "Uh-uh. Try again. Why?"

"It was something Josh said. This—" he motioned between them "—this always feels as if we're equal. When you interact with the team, you see each personality and you respect it and you treat every one of them as an equal. You don't discount their opinion even if you don't agree, you don't discount their abilities, and you'll admit when they're better at something than you are. You don't make decisions for them." He glared on principle because she did take on guilt, whether she'd earned it or not. "I guess I'm saying there might be something to this looking out for each other thing of yours."

"Oh." She pulled her lower lip between her teeth, his outburst clearly not what she expected from him.

He took a deep breath. Her transparency deserved the whole truth from him even if the truth freaked him out. "Brace for more 'oh' action. I'm not calling your skills into question. I don't need to be familiar with what constitutes a skilled soldier to understand that you are fucking amazing. As good as you are, I'm still worried spitless about you and this mission."

When she didn't protest, he kept going to the bitter end. "I know I'm the weak link in this plan and having my civilian ass out there on a mission makes everything dicier for the whole team."

"No, listen—"

"Don't. Do not try to bullshit me," he warned.

"We factored you in, okay? No bs." Her fingers rubbed back and forth over his clenched fist.

They were discussing how he might screw up their lives, and she was still trying to reassure him. "If anything happened to you—" he had to clear his throat. "If anything happened to you, it would gut me. I'm not just talking about carrying the weight of that guilt either." He took one hand back and brushed his knuckles over her cheek.

"You'd be sad?"

"We're only discussing my never seeing you again in the most theoretical sense and it feels like there's a sucking black hole opening in my chest."

She frowned, because, hell. He'd dumped more responsibility on her instead of less. His reassurance game was shit.

Instead of pulling away, Vee did that thing, teeth leaving indents against her plump lower lip. It was a visual that shot him straight back to the roof, them, and those lips on skin.

He was already knocked off center when Vee's attention snapped to his face. "That's it."

Undoubtedly meaning 'You're a dick. Stop talking,' and he couldn't even work up a half-hearted reply.

Vee moved close enough that a sheet of rice paper wouldn't fit between them. "That's totally it."

"Help me out here, Vee. What are we talking about?"

"What you said. The sucking black hole thing." Her expression shifted to satisfaction, the look he'd observed when she settled on a plan or figured out a problem. "That's what it feels like when I think of you leaving some bar—"

"Damn it. For the last time, I wasn't drunk or following

anyone in order to have back alley sex," he barked. "It wasn't even an alley."

Vee waved, like facts weren't relevant. "Okay, when you leave work or anywhere *but* an alley late some night, and I'm not there, and anything, like *literally* anything bad, because hey anangoa, so who can guess what else is out there, is just waiting and—"

He caught her chin. "Focus. And fucking breathe."

She rolls her eyes but finished, "That weird, out of nowhere fear is exactly my reaction if anything awful happened to you. I've never encountered this with anyone we helped. I mean, yes, we didn't want them hurt, sure, but it was more...academic? People good, cryptids suck, you know? Some people were obviously nicer than others, and I always felt sympathetic. Not this though. Not where I'd ever think of teaching them self-defense tactics, or honestly, think about them at all once they processed into a safe house or HQ. What *is* this?"

His throat clogged. He made himself do just what he'd insisted Vee do and breathed, then finally got words out. "I have no idea."

Which was the biggest pile of bullshit he'd uttered in years. Plain fact, the knot in his chest felt a hell of a lot like the kind of worried that accompanied caring about another person. Long-term, wake up beside them more than once, caring about.

He was supposed to be immune to that fatal emotional entrapment. Another thing he'd been wrong about on a rapidly expanding list.

Vee tipped her head, searching his face for God only knew what.

He cupped her cheek, and traced under the softness of her lower lip with his thumb. Her eyes, that bottomless brown, pulled him in. Promising he could spend the rest of eternity swimming in their depths and still never stop finding new sides of Vee to explore.

Somewhere during his revelation, Vee's hand ended up on his chest, right over his heart. Like she could reach in and touch it. As natural as breathing, his free hand skimmed up her back, urging her closer.

Vee didn't live by half-measures any more than he did. She fit snug against him, arms going around his neck.

Hell, she had to need comfort after all she'd seen, and lost, in the last twenty-four hours. More comfort than a simple meal provided, and Bruce could give her that, too.

He brushed a kiss over her lips, asking in their shorthand what she needed from him.

She opened up, lips parting. He caught the sweetness of cherries and chocolate from his babka. He shut down the flare of possessiveness he had no right to, that the ghosts of his food on Vee's lips brought blazing out of nowhere. That wasn't what she'd asked for right now. Her inaudible sigh, like she wasn't allowed to be anything other than a stoic leader, wrecked him. He cupped the back of her head, working his fingers through her hair to cradle her.

Her arms tightened and a shiver-tremble went through her. Like maybe she was finally registering the emotional shitstorm she'd had to shove to the side in order to be there for Josh and her sisters. "I've got you," he whispered against her lips.

She gave the smallest nod, his fingers stroking along her scalp at the motion. "Whatever this is, you're really good at it," she whispered.

Which also should have set off all his alarm claxons. Instead, he kissed her again, because, hell, why not ride this night to wherever it led, especially if it helped Vee.

A chime sounded. Then a second time. They separated,

her hand going to her pocket and then swiping across her phone.

He tensed and caught her hands and phone. "Is it the hospital? Josh's brother?"

The universe couldn't be cruel enough to jerk that win from under Josh and his sisters.

"Just my alarm." She held up her screen as proof. "HQ set a meeting for all regional C.O.'s in order to decide how to reallocate resources since we're down a team."

He blinked at her, processing. If there had been some meeting called, it had happened hours earlier when she was still in her office.

They had scheduled a fucking business call while Josh's brother was still in surgery, long before anyone even knew if he'd survive. "Jesus, Vee."

She gave him an apologetic grimace. "HQ can't wait." She headed down the hall.

He started after her. Bodies weren't even cold yet. They hadn't had a chance to grieve. All the Company cared about was the Company. They used people like toys or game pieces. *Resources.* Cards to be shuffled at a dealer's whim, and Vee thought that was normal.

He backed up, like he could back away from the whole situation. He spun and kept going until he was in his room. Carefully, he closed the door. His suitcase, dropped off at the same time as his car by nameless Cleaners, sat like an accusation. He hauled off and kicked it across the room.

He was as stupid as he accused normal people of being.

There was nothing between him and Vee other than an in-a-foxhole-together emergency situation. They were together twenty-four-seven with no outside contact or conversations, instead stuck here going from one emotional high or crisis to another.

What he was feeling wasn't real. It was adrenalin, stress,

and proximity. They had nothing in common. No interests and sure as hell no shared background and values. Company agents were forbidden outside ties, not that Vee had given an ounce of indication she wanted ties, and he sure as hell didn't do relationships.

As soon as he left here, the false intimacy would vanish and his life would realign and return to normal.

# CHAPTER 16

## VEE

*I* double-checked the site map I'd already memorized, like any of the topographic details had changed or some safer spot to position Bruce in had magically been built in the last thirty minutes.

When the blueprint stayed depressingly the same, I rolled my hair into a bun, the last step of my pre-mission ritual.

Kimi checked on the drones, the blips steady dots on her laptop screen as were the darker green lines outlining the cul-de-sac and small city amphitheater.

She flipped the laptop closed. When she caught me looking, she signed, "All set. Drones up, perimeter lasers all steady."

Kimi and I had set the tiny lasers around every opening to the downtown trap. A combination of historic battle sites that couldn't be built over and a micro-park, it sat in an awkward L-shaped area between the modern office buildings ringing it on all four sides. A knee-high wrought iron fence surrounded a patch of sandy soil and a historical plaque, a couple of concrete tables with umbrellas and concrete seats taking up the rest of the square footage.

Since it couldn't be seen from the road or street, only employees of the businesses and the occasional die-hard history buff frequented it.

We'd had an underground water main emergency called in, the area blocked off by city saw horses and tape. We wouldn't pass as workers but there shouldn't be anyone working, with the buildings also closed to any extra-dedicated worker-bee types with a promise water would be restored by morning. HQ had access to the site's security cameras, plus their usual monitoring for civilian drones and tech.

One way or the other, the plaza would be empty by daybreak.

Kimi wrapped her braid around and twisted it into a topknot bun, her go-to. Done, she caught me chewing a cuticle. "Everything is perfect. Reals."

I knew that. She and I had climbed and walked every inch earlier, making sure our intel and drone reports matched what was really there as we placed the laser system, and pieces of Bruce's used pillowcase and sheets in areas with the best airflow, to draw the anangoa. At least theoretically. The Asset who reported on the live specimen said locals had used worn clothing when attempting to hunt anangoa, at least in all the stories she had heard. Second—or third—hand information didn't give me the greatest sense of confidence.

Either Bruce would get bored standing around all night because the lore wasn't accurate, or we'd end the threat and he'd be free to leave the compound, post-HQ briefing.

For whatever reason, the latter idea didn't fill me with the usual mission anticipation.

I wanted the creature dead, definitely. The part about Bruce leaving—I still wasn't sure why that was an issue. At least, it was an issue for me.

I hadn't seen him long enough to do more than ask for his

bedding. The kitchen was empty by the time I finished the division call the night before, and my soft knock hadn't brought Bruce to his door.

Today had been spent largely off-compound, Josh and Liv drilling tonight's plan into Bruce's head. Of course, he'd only given me a nod at breakfast, then vanished.

I needed to quit obsessing—either he'd be interested in hooking up when we were in the same area for patrols, or Liv had been right about him wanting to forget we existed once he left and he'd say no. He hadn't argued about our rooftop time being anything other than a way to blow off steam. Plus, still a judgmental jerk as far as our careers. I had zero illusions that blowup was behind us. We'd only temporarily tabled the argument.

Whatever he decided was a worry for Future Vee. It was time to get my head in the game.

Aside from eliminating our target, I'd sworn to keep Bruce safe. Civilians were always priority but this was the first time I knew the person, and promised to their face I wouldn't allow them to come to harm.

My only job today boiled down to—eliminate the target, keep the civilian I had a personal tie to intact, keep my team as safe as possible, all on terrain that didn't offer us the advantage.

There were too many points for the anangoa to hit us from above our heads. Josh had only two options as far as a sniper post. Leaving three for the cryptid to exploit. The anangoa's penchant for heights also meant Josh was at extra risk as well, leaving his back exposed to the possibility of it coming at him from a roof or upper-story office windows.

The perimeter lasers went along rooflines as well, so we at least had a warning if the creature targeted us from on high. As fast as it moved meant only a second's notice, but seconds were better than nothing.

Water and sewer lines that provided us our cover story also provided the anangoa a route to ambush from underneath and be in without tripping a laser, again with only seconds' notice. At least there was only one subterranean entry there. We had found a few suspect traces when we tracked it from the murdered family's home, but underground tunnels had to be where it was nesting, and its means of traveling without one damn sighting via our informants. Especially given that our site was close to the center of its hunting grid, using the bar, Bruce's previous abode, the murder scene, and the iffy reports of a shredded coyote pack our people called in, the wounds matching anangoa claw patterns.

The coyote slaughter made sense if the female was feeding offspring. She might be teaching hatchlings about prey if they were old enough to watch her hunt, or even practice on easy prey she wounded for them. That was the m.o. for other large predators. There was too much we didn't know and the pure guesswork aspect had all of us on edge.

Kimi nudged me with her elbow, hair mission-ready. "This op is our best chance at preventing another mass slaughter, and we all know that, okay? Aside from the fact you'd voluntarily give up your commission before you'd violate our mandate on protecting civvis, anyone can see these minor local incidents you're tracking and the anangoa issue aren't related." She leaned to grab tablets, then paused, signing "Unless—what if the anangoas arrived somewhere else in the Southwest, working their way here, and the 'digos and ghouls encountered them before we did? The presence of a strange mega-predator is the likely scenario for why they're temporarily acting off. It tracks."

Maybe. The explanation was logical, and better than anything I'd come up with. It didn't sit right though. Not any more so than everyone dismissing the cryptid behavioral changes as minor.

Of course, I might be as off base with my ideas on cryptids as I was in understanding Bruce.

I'd put Liv on Bruce-briefing duty partially because she hid her emotions better than I did. He was handling his decision amazingly well for a non-agent, but as Kimi and I left my office for the kitchen, Josh's voice carried down the hall.

"Listen, you can elect not to go. You can go and change your mind on the way or when we're on site, and stay in the truck."

Josh and Liv stood by the bar, fully weaponed up and obviously in the middle of a conversation. Bruce paced a circuit around the kitchen table, turning at the end and repeating the process.

"Are the sheets you took enough to lure Godzilla Junior in?" He asked without stopping his circuit.

Josh punted, looking to Liv. Part of her role as lieutenant was to take the harder decisions. "It's difficult to say."

Bruce stopped, glaring at Liv as I entered. "Yes or no?"

It was my job to take the hardest decisions though. "There's an excellent chance your scent is all over the plaza. However we don't know enough to say whether the biomarker on you transferred along with your scent. We also don't know how much of their hunting is done by scent or what the range for them detecting it is if they do."

None of which would be enough of an answer for Bruce because it wouldn't have been enough for me if our positions were reversed. "So, no. There's a high probability second-hand scent isn't sufficient. Josh is right—you can choose to sit this out at any point. We appreciate your willingness, but it's our job, not yours."

"Let's go." Bruce jerked a thumb at the three by the exit to move, took a deep breath, and headed after them.

I caught his elbow and he spun to face me. I held out the confiscated burner phone. "You know the drill—if we go down, you call the number programmed in and give them the codes you memorized last time. HQ knows you're going on-mission with us, they have our plan on file, and there's a tracker in the phone." I produced a second set of truck keys. "You can say no at any point."

Bruce pocketed the keys and phone. "Everybody is waiting."

He fell in beside me, nervous energy radiating off him. We passed through the decontamination breezeway and Bruce blurted, "When we get to the site don't ask me if I want to back out."

I took in his chalky face and set jaw, and nodded, respecting his determination. If he needed not to be offered an out that would knock him from whatever mental zone he got himself into, I understood.

I tilted my chin and gave Kimi my usual front seat, sliding into the second row across from Bruce while Liv cranked the motor to life. Josh chose to stay behind me in the last row so he could still see Bruce. Josh was treating him like a cadet on their first real mission, with full respect and support.

The three buildings fronting our objective came into sight, the trip feeling far shorter than when Kimi and I made it that morning.

Josh bailed, moving the blinking orange sawhorses blocking access to the buildings and parking. We parked in one of the half-dozen slots marked *Reserved* off to the side of the wide main office. Liv hopped out and the soft click of magnet on metal was her affixing the City of Scottsdale seal to the side doors in case of curious loiterers.

Kimi swiveled in her seat and gave Bruce a quick, "You've got this," before flipping open her tablet and exiting to check drones and lasers.

Josh stuck his front half in, grabbing his kit. He gave Bruce's shoulder a rough squeeze. "You remember the play?"

"I keep my ass at the first table and look like a history buff. Get under the table when the shooting starts." Bruce's voice was steady but he had the phone in a chokehold, all of his tension channeled into his grip.

"Don't—"

"Don't move beyond the table. I got that the first fifteen times you said it." A trace of his customary grouch came through.

"Nailed it." Josh said. He flipped his cap backwards and left.

I cupped Bruce's hand, my fingers over his on the phone.

"Vee," he warned, strain replacing his false-confident front.

"I'm not asking anything," I reassured him. "I'll have my eyes on you the entire time. We tailored this with you as priority. Ready?"

"Be careful."

I paused, hand on the door release. "What?"

"Be. Fucking. Careful," he gritted out. Then added, "please."

"It isn't our job to be careful, it's our job to be successful. You don't worry about us."

Bruce's answer was to slam the car door on his way out. He did wait for me but didn't say anything.

I scanned the small courtyard while Bruce took his spot. The fabric we'd planted was still tied around the base of the second table, another strip woven through a section of fence enclosing the historical marker. "Positions?"

Bruce jumped at my question.

"All clear," Liv said into my earpiece. "Lure untouched. Business egress-ingress doors locked." A series of Morse code-style clicks was Kimi's all-clear, the second set confirming drones were up, perimeter intact.

"I'm a go," came Josh's terse reply.

Nothing had crossed Kimi's laser boundaries, rooftops clear, and the caution tape I'd put across doorways as we left unbroken, the door still locked.

For Bruce's benefit, I said, "I'm taking my spot."

I flipped the rifle on its sling around. "You've already heard this speech but I'm going over it anyway. Stay right there. Don't move. Don't run. As long as you hold your position, I can protect you. If you bolt, you risk crossing sight lines and fouling our shots. I know it feels exposed out here, but it is the safest spot, I promise."

Bruce gave a shallow nod, his barkless agreement the surest sign he wasn't as together as he acted.

I broke my own protocol and caught his hand again. "I promise."

"I believe you." He flipped his clammy fingers around, grasping mine. I squeezed his hand, and then jogged to my spot in the longest end of the L-shaped courtyard, out of easy sight when I crouched behind a trio of freaking heavy vending machines Kimi and I had appropriated from the building's lobby.

Through the narrow space between the two center machines I'd left as my window, I stayed half focused on Bruce, the other part equally busy watching for shadows where there shouldn't be one, or air wafting over me when there wasn't a breeze. I was especially intent on the only outlet from underground, a manhole cover camouflaged by rocks right in the middle of the historical monument. That was the likeliest entry point, almost seventy-percent by Kimi's calculations.

Diagonally from Bruce, and across from me in the dead end space where three of the buildings joined, Liv blended with shadows and cream sandstone. Her attention was doing similar double-duty watching sides of buildings in case our target did the gecko-on-a-wall entrance, and watching my exposed back. Kimi had her drone feed plus real life rooftops, also diagonal so none of us interfered with the others.

Josh had Bruce and rooflines, including Kimi's.

Bruce stared at his phone though I doubted he was really seeing it, standing painfully straight in the exact spot he occupied when I left. I wished I could gift him a portion of the confidence in my team that was always with me, that hit its peak at times like these. When we were on mission, each person took their role like everyday life was only a costume we wore until now when we could shed it, our true selves coming out.

Minutes ticked by, sweat beading along my scalp and waistband. Josh and Kimi would be sweltering on flat roof tops and catching the sun slanting over them as it descended. Everyone had night vision goggles if needed, Josh with his rifle's scope. We were prepared to wait. It took at least a few hours for the thing to triangulate on stationary pray. Even seeding the area with Bruce's scent probably did less to attract it than to help funnel it to where we wanted it once it arrived.

On the heels of that thought, gooseflesh rippled across my arms, hair standing up despite the temperature. I tensed and scanned the sleepy courtyard.

I tapped my earpiece, using code the way Kimi did. *Report.* Liv and Josh tapped *Negative.*

One click into Kimi's reply, hinges creaked, noise splitting the air like a lightning strike.

The doors to the office building Josh crouched on opened, crime scene tape breaking and fluttering free.

Bruce stumbled a half step, catching himself and stopping as a group of—

"Kids?" Liv's disbelieving voice popped in my ear.

Five kids, none looking old enough to drive much less be out alone walked into the courtyard. They had to belong to an office employee, but we'd swept the place. Thoroughly.

"Are you seeing this?" Liv asked.

"I'm seeing somebody's kids, somehow."

"The fuck—Jace?" Josh's voice echoed, loud enough to make out without the coms.

The gooseflesh sprang up again, hair standing on end. Wrongness washed over me like a cold wind. "Say again?"

"How is—its Jace. He's right the hell *there*." Josh was rattled. Something he'd never been on a mission, not even as a cadet.

"Vee!" Bruce's yell clashed with a river of clicks from Kimi. *Anangoas. My screen is showing cryptids, plural.*

"Take the shots," I barked. "It's the hallucinogen."

I sighted and fired, over Bruce's horrified "Those are kids!"

The kid-cryptid closest to Bruce fell in a meaty *thump* and green tinged blood flew.

The remaining four kids turned to anangoas at the same instant, whatever belief we needed for the hallucinogenic glamour to work gone.

The things weren't ankle height nestlings as we'd assumed. All stood close to shoulder height. Well-muscled, claws bright and deadly.

They split, moving as quicksilver fast as the two adults we'd fought.

One raced my and Liv's way.

The other three streaked for the buildings, defying gravity and flowing up the walls.

My shot took out the one already halfway up Josh's building, the body falling and staying flat. The bark of shots peppered the air, Josh taking out the climber on Kimi's building.

Liv picked off the one aiming our way, its head snapping back at the impact and moving another few feet before its body stopped getting signals from its brain.

The second nestling let out a piercing *skree-hiss* and torqued, abandoning Kimi's wall and throwing itself across the space. Kimi took it out inches from Liv's position.

The splat of it hitting the ground almost covered the squeak of the door to my right inching open.

The dying nestling's squeal had been a call for help and at least one of his brood was responding. Claws skittered across sand and pavers.

The sound way too light for the bulk of an adult. The female hadn't showed yet.

"Staying on Bruce," I whispered, just loud enough for the team to hear me and got a chorus of "Understoods."

Josh would take out whatever came through the door. Either I was right and this was hunting practice, mom setting the brood to take what it saw as easy prey, or the things were the complete opposite of every piece of behavioral intel we'd found, and the mother was throwing her own offspring at us as a distraction.

Whichever was true, she wasn't attacking yet. The feeling of wrongness intensified, settling over me like a suffocating fur coat on a sweltering day.

When she came, it would be after Bruce. That had to be the ploy. The others had ignored the hell out of him, targeting us, despite being closer to him when they spilled out of the office.

Bruce was reserved for Mom-zilla.

"Eyes on Junior," Josh whispered, back to his default cool and collected.

Slowly, I swept the area between the camouflaged manhole cover and the door of the building the other anangoa had used.

Across from me, Liv did the same.

Movement jerked my attention past the manhole to Bruce.

The flash of movement wasn't from an anangoa. My heart bottomed out as Bruce took two long strides toward me, his face frantic. "Vee! Behind you."

"Got it." Liv adjusted her angle, already compensating.

From behind us, the anangoa's claw scratches slowed. Close now, and readying to jump us.

Not done, Bruce waved his arms, either trying to warn us or distract the anangoa.

When that didn't accomplish his goal, he hurled his phone, plastic case bouncing over the ground. Unable to resist the skittish movements from Bruce, the anangoa altered its trajectory. It came into view, streaking for Bruce. Who had moved another step in his effort to alert me, putting himself in Josh's way, and in Liv's.

They couldn't take a shot without hitting Bruce.

Liv swore, then was sprinting from her corner, rifle dropped and favorite blade out. Intercepting the anangoa.

I ground down on the urge to join her. Forcing myself not to give in to the shot of adrenaline. The adult had to be coming.

Liv's blade caught the juvenile. Bit into the edge of its neck. Not severing its head, her aim too far to the side.

It shrieked and spun. A claw nicked Liv, dragging down her arm and fabric splitting. Blood welled up, but Liv whirled. Crouched and blade steady.

The second story window under Josh blew outward in a shower of glass and anangoa.

The adult's roar rattled the wood of my bench. A crack,

and thump of bullet in flesh, was Josh hitting the juvenile as it whirled to grab Liv for a killing bite.

Despite her offspring's cry the mother *hiss-roared* again, slitted eyes fixed on Bruce, still in the no-man's-land between Josh and Kimi. With Bruce feet away from his designated spot, now neither could risk a shot. They had no way to avoid hitting him in the crossfire. Neither did I.

Liv fumbled one-handed for her rifle. Her clawed arm hung temporarily numb and useless.

I let my rifle go, sling pulling it out of my way. I grabbed the longest knife from my thigh, jerking the sheath open in a crackle of Velcro, then squeezed between machines, sprinting out, heart pounding. In fear, not excitement, Bruce's corpse-white face and the anangoa all I could see. Pushing muscles harder than I ever had, the anangoa only feet from Bruce.

I threw myself into a slide, skidding along pavers. Right angled and into the cryptid's path. I slashed and the blade hit tough scales, cutting along the female's thigh.

Claws flashed over my head, a chunk of hair ripped out in a fiery shot of pain as I ducked and rolled. The anangoa's hissing scream climbed higher and my ears rang.

I came up on one knee. Finally between the thing and its target. Kimi's *Go right* clicked a sharp command in my ear.

Right, away from Bruce, leading it so Kimi had a shot. The anangoa spun. Like my thoughts reminded of its purpose, its snarled, green eyes leaving me for Bruce. Its huge thigh muscles bunched, ignoring the line of blood along the leg I'd hit. Still preparing to go for Bruce.

I launched and threw myself at the thing. I swiped for its muzzle. Missed.

Its arm-foreleg slashed at my eyes and I threw myself backward, hard enough things popped. Claws slammed into the ground where I'd been.

It lashed out too fast. The backhand caught me, off center and without claws but hard enough I flew back, no air left, lungs and chest on fire.

A sharp *pop* of displaced air and the thing hissed, clawing at a silver dart protruding from its neck. It swung between the direction the dart came from and Bruce. Then swung back toward Bruce, pushing off.

I jerked a disc out of my pocket. With what little oxygen I had left, tried bellowing "Cover your eyes!" Hoping Bruce heard me. I punched the center of the disc, shoved to stand, and slammed it to the ground.

Lights flared, illuminating the courtyard in blinding, phosphorescent glare. The grenade's shrill, metallic whistle rose over the anangoa's wail, and my grunt as its tail slapped me. Pain flared as my hip hit ground.

I rolled to a crouch, blind and blade weaving a defensive pattern in the direction the anangoa was. Had been. Praying the stunner had worked. That the beast hadn't slipped past me and ripped into Bruce.

I opened my eyes, blinking away after images, searching for anangoa and injured human, choking on sour fear instead of the usual adrenalin rush.

Bruce was—finally—under a concrete table, the second one closest to me, not his. He had his arm crooked across his face to shield his eyes.

I pivoted, trading my blade for a gun, searching the courtyard. Only the bodies of the juvies remained.

Kimi's clicks crackled. *Boundary laser tripped, west side.*

I limped to the table and held my hand out. "Come on."

Eyes streaming, Bruce grabbed my hand and I pulled, hauling him out. Blinking furiously, he tried to adjust his vision. "Is it—"

I made myself let go and held up a silencing hand. "Report."

"No movement," Josh said.

A second later, Kimi reported. *Drones caught it fleeing. It hit a drain a quarter of a mile west. Gone underground.*

"Damn it."

"Could be worse." Liv rose from checking the last anangoa, rolling the headless one over with her toe. She bent enough to hold up the trashed dart casing.

"Is the tracker working?" I asked, hoping the anangoa hadn't knocked the dart out before the rice grain sized tracker head embedded.

*Tracker's a go*, Kimi signaled. *Some interference being subterranean, but I can clean the signal up once we're on base.*

Josh came out of the door of the building, and Bruce jerked. Pulling away before he realized this wasn't an attack.

Josh held up both hands, although the gun in his right probably wasn't as reassuring to a civilian as it was to us. "Easy, man. All-human here." He switched to me. "I swept offices on the way down. Building's clear."

"Kimi?"

She tapped *Coming* and was out her door seconds later. She signed, "All clear."

"Go." I tipped my head at the last building and both agents headed out at a jog. Josh on one side, Kimi on the other. He jerked the door open and she went in, hitting one wall. Josh came after, covering her, guns level as they began their sweep.

I'd have bet anything it was clear. However, I'd been wrong multiple times today.

As Liv checked the courtyard, flipping juvie cryptids and taking photos with her phone for the report, I pulled out my phone and dialed. "Ramirez, code one-one-seven-four-three, Region two. Clean up. Multiple cryptid remains plus cosmetic structural damage."

As Josh and Kimi exited, I pocketed my phone and met them, Liv joining us. "Report."

"All clear. I found where the cryptids hid—the break room closet on the third floor." Josh scowled and flipped his cap forward. "The big one came through another floor."

Kimi signed, "There was evidence of cryptid presence here, in a conference room facing parking, but no bodies. There was nothing here when we swept the buildings."

Yet, we'd walked into an ambush somehow, by predators not known for stealth or finesse. Predators that had somehow also defeated our tech. All I said was, "The Cleaners are en route. We'll have their forensics report and more extensive photos by morning. They've called us in as a contained gas leak in case anyone noticed the flare grenade."

Liv cut her eyes right, brow up. Her code for 'You're dealing with the loud civie.'

"Let's roll. Dibs on the good chair," she said aloud.

As everyone fell in, I nodded and turned to Bruce. I'd felt him at my back ever since he came from under the bench, then scooped up his phone. I could easily see this going furious-Bruce or freaked out-Bruce. Either way it was mine to navigate.

And I finally had a handle on my whatever-it-was. That sucking chest wound feeling we'd discussed, that had nailed me unexpectedly when the anangoa had targeted an exposed Bruce. Once I knew he was unharmed, I'd purposely kept my attention elsewhere, shoving feelings away and concentrating on business.

As surprising as that feeling had been, Bruce's reaction now was even more baffling. His face was still way too pale but he stepped in front of us. "What can I do?"

Kimi cocked her head, the same gesture as when she was

working through a surprise encryption. Josh shot me a questioning look.

I had no clue. Bruce wasn't angry. The danger was past
and nothing left to be afraid of, so that wasn't it.

"We're set. Cleaners will take care of the rest." I tested out
the unknown footing.

Bruce's hands were jammed in his pockets. "I can drive."
Like he just discovered it, he pulled out the truck key fob I'd
given him earlier.

He addressed Liv, the strange expression on his face at
total odds with his calm offer. "I know you're the driver but I
can do this for you."

Oookay. If Bruce needed something to do to help process
leftover nerves, that was a reaction we all understood. This
was also just the Company truck, not Liv's ride so even if he
dented it or scratched paint as the adrenalin rush wore off,
no big.

Against my thigh and out of Bruce's sight, I tapped out
the code for yes.

Liv gave a nearly imperceptible nod, and answered him.
"Sure. Thanks."

I nudged Bruce's elbow to get him moving. "Come on. B-
movie night and pizza wait for no woman."

Kimi signed to Bruce, "Our usual is a Meat Lover's
Dream. Is that okay? It'll be ready for pick up by the time we
hit downtown, no waiting."

Bruce stared at her, apparently lost.

Maybe picky chefs weren't familiar with cheap take-out.
"There's a twenty-four-hour pizza place on the way home. It
works out, since most other places are closed by the time we
finish up a job. Pizza, and not out of our way. Win-win," I
explained.

"I can make you something," Bruce got out, a strangled
quality to his answer.

"Man, it's been *a day*. You don't have to cook on top of playing bait," Josh said.

Bruce closed his eyes for a second before answering. "I'll make pizza."

"Cool." Josh held out knuckles, and Bruce finally tapped them.

As Bruce slid into the truck, I took my usual seat and spent the drive trying to figure out the mystery that was Bruce Kantor.

# CHAPTER 17

## BRUCE

*B*ruce straightened as the team piled into the kitchen, drawn by the scent of the pizza he'd promised Josh.

Monsters. Near death experiences. Pizza. The day was bordering on ridiculously surreal.

None of them had said shit to him about the fucked-up mission. They hadn't discussed it, aside from Kimi handing out antiseptic packets while Liv hacked off her shredded sleeve, and both agreeing stitches were in order instead of the freaky gel. They didn't need to say every one of those stitches was on his tab. He'd run up a bill with a monster but Liv had paid.

Josh, Kimi, and Liv had kept up a lazy commentary on movie choices and the merits of romantic comedies versus action flicks versus binge watching. Meanwhile, Vee had sat silent the entire trip. He felt her attention on him like a verdict. For once in his life, he'd hid. He hadn't taken his eyes off the road. He hadn't had the guts to meet Vee's eyes and see the disappointment and judgment she was keeping under wraps.

Now, he faced the team, ready for the ass reaming he deserved. Whatever they threw at him, he'd take it. Nothing they could say would even come close to him fucking up their mission.

Josh went by Bruce without a word, Kimi right behind him.

Fine. He got it. Vee was leader. She got dibs on chewing Bruce out.

Liv strode in last, no Vee in evidence. His heart jacked against his chest. If Vee was hurt worse than he realized —"Where's Vee?" He stepped in front of Liv.

"Gym. She'll be in by the time the ice cream thaws." Liv kept going, opening the freezer and pulling out a carton.

When she sat it on the sink, the long row of ugly black stitches marring the brown skin of her arm flashed the room like an accusation.

He winced and wished he'd been the one cut up, not Liv. She didn't deserve to be hurt. At least she could use her arm again. He'd been sure it was broken when she kept it tight to her side for the first hour after the fight.

Instead of an apology all that popped out was, "Why is Vee in the gym after a mission like today's? Not even you people need that much of a workout regimen."

"Two words. Hot. Tub," Josh answered in Liv's stead. The guy was loaded down with a blender and limes, the only fresh fruit or vegetable Bruce had seen in the whole place. Kimi trailed after him, carrying tequila, ice, and glasses festooned with cartoon animals.

She arranged liquor, salt, and the mugs on the counter while Josh plugged in his prize, and then mutilated the lime.

Over the whir of the ice being crushed, Josh said, "We can't get well-lit tonight, but celebratory margaritas are an unspoken rule of—"

Kimi elbowed him and signed, "Wrong. We codified that two years ago. It's in the handbook."

"Correction. It's a legit rule that an agent's first job requires a margarita toast." He dumped mixer and tequila in with the ice, hit pulse, then poured the pink mess into the glasses Kimi had dipped in salt, more or less hanging a slice of lime on the side.

He handed Bruce the first cup. Liv and Kimi grabbed theirs. "First mission under your belt, and unofficially, you're one of the team," Josh said and they all fucking tapped glasses.

Bruce stared. There was a decent chance he'd actually gotten beat to hell during the mission, run over by Godzilla, and his head hammered into the stupid picnic table he'd been told to stay at. Meaning this was all a concussion-based hallucination. That, or the monster currently had him and was basting him in anangoa hallucination-juice, because none of this could be real.

He took an experimental sip. Crap tequila drowned in even worse off-the-shelf mixer hit his palate, burning taste buds and definitely not a hallucination.

"Pizza time." Josh slugged the margarita back, leaving a pink-ice mustache, and grabbed one of the plates Bruce had set out.

"Are you for fucking real?" Bruce's voice bounced off kitchen appliances, volume out of his control.

All three agents paused and exchanged glances. Through whatever psychic connection they all had, probably some billion-dollar black ops military invention, Kimi and Josh started on the pizza, leaving Liv to deal.

She sat her glass down.

Good. About time. He straightened for her to finally chew his ass out.

"I understand this looks casual," Liv said. "I promise you,

we are taking the last anangoa seriously though. Vee and I have already debriefed and gone over HQ's preliminary findings—the Cleaners were thorough. Kimi has a program going to isolate the tracker signal even through concrete and tons of dirt."

Kimi raised her glass in acknowledgement, other hand busy folding a pizza slice in half for a bite.

Liv spoke again, pulling his attention back. "We will have a location soon and we will get the cryptid. Within the next forty-eight hours, the United States will once again be anangoa-free."

"Truth," Josh said around a mouth full of mozzarella and mushroom.

Liv rested a hand on Bruce's arm, her expression soft and kind. "Tonight is decompressing, but as soon as our data comes together, we will be ready. Today was violent and had to be stressful for you, but you did great. With the tracker in play, your part is over. You don't have to go out in the field again. Next mission is just us and you'll be completely safe here while we tie this job up."

*She* was reassuring *him.* Liv, who existed for rules, wasn't giving him hell for fucking up a vital mission. She was instead concerned that he was freaked and upset. She was using time she could be relaxing, which she fucking needed after getting clawed up by a hellish beast because of him, to reassure him.

He stared at their hands, both of Liv's elegant but scarred ones now wrapped around his paler, margarita-free hand. She gave him a gentle squeeze and smile, and let go.

"I—yeah. All right." What the hell was he even supposed to say to that?

Kimi handed him a plate, then her hands free, signed, "You are the deciding vote. B-movie night choice—male dancers or fast cars?"

"Choose carefully," Josh intoned, doing a shit movie knight impression.

"Whatever Vee would pick." He turned to Liv. "She's in the gym?"

"Yes. I saved her a slice and her margarita, no worries."

"Better yet, get her started now," Kimi signed, reclaiming his plate and handing him the last glass of shit margarita. "Plus, she hasn't properly toasted your new status."

Liv hesitated in reaching for her plate, but didn't argue when Kimi turned him toward the outer door and gave him a shove.

He took the hint and left, the night air dry and crisp, tiny bats swooping overhead as he traveled to the gym. Lights flared to life as soon as he entered the building.

He hadn't gone further than the section with the heavy punching bags in the past, but checking revealed two doors at the rear of the space. He opened the first, more lights flashing on. They gleamed off of a set of cages, racks of chains, cuffs, and shit he had zero desire to see in use.

When he cracked the second door though, steam wisped out. Off to the far right, an open door showed a smaller version of the main houses' communal bath. The other room held a serious-looking hot tub, but a cheap Ikea-style shelf stood in one corner, packed with fluffy towels in a rainbow of colors, and a matching short table loaded with another of their candles. This one gave off a floral scent, and distinctly non-military bottles of lotions and an inflatable bath neck pillow rested beside it.

Vee had one foot on the table edge, smoothing lotion on her leg. She'd traded utility pants and tee for shorts and matching tank with anime foxes, her hair bundled in a towel.

"Shit, sorry." He started to close the door.

"I was about to head in. Hang on." She wiped her hands on the towel, unwrapping it and tossing it into a basket, then flipped her head upside down and finger combed her hair.

When she turned to him, he got an eye full of her new bruises. One, already turning purple, went from below her collarbone to disappear under her top, emerging again along her upper arm. Another peeked from under her shorts continuing on to her knee, angry red scrapes tracking along her thigh from where she skidded along the pavers.

"Fuck." He sat the sweating glass on the table hard enough half-melted slush splashed out. Then balled his empty hands into fists, stopping himself from reaching for her. He had no right to touch her without asking, and there was no way in hell she'd say yes. Not when he was the one responsible for her injuries, the whole damn reason she'd needed to use an athletic-grade hot tub instead of being inside for dinner in the first place.

"What's wrong?" She cocked her head, hair fluffing around her shoulders.

"That's what the fuck is wrong." He waved at her leg. "The fact that it looks as if someone tried to beat the hell out of you with a concrete block."

She looked down at herself like she hadn't noticed the injury. "This isn't that bad. Some hot tub action, a little arnica, a raspberry margarita, and I'm set." She picked up the disgusting drink.

He took it out of her hands and slammed it back on the table. "Stop. Just fucking stop."

"What are we talking about here, B?"

"We're talking about how all this shit is my damn fault. I fucked up. I got Liv hurt. I got you hurt. Because I screwed up, you and Liv are beat to hell and back, and on top of that, there's a walking nightmare loose out there, doing god knows what." He tried pacing but it only put him in Vee's personal space. "Jesus. Yell at me. Chew my ass out, please."

"Why would I—"

"Because all of this is my fault, and the kindness and the toast and fucking margaritas—I can't take it."

Vee held up her hand, and just like the day in her office, he shut up. "Why would you say that? How is my or Liv's injury your fault?"

He caught himself waiting a beat, making sure she was finished, before answering. "I didn't do the one damn thing you, Josh, and Liv all told me to. All I had to do was not move. Stand in one damn spot. That was it. Instead, I almost —" he had to take a breath to get the words out. "I almost got you killed."

This time, she took a second, braiding her hair into a loose tail and flipping an elastic around the end. Then she leaned her ass against the side of the tub. "Can you listen to what I'm about to say?"

He settled for a nod.

"Good. We always have a plan going into a mission. Sometimes the plan holds. Sometimes it doesn't." She gave a careless shrug. "Adapting on the fly is second nature. So let me tell you what happened today. You, Bruce Kantor, tried to aid a teammate when you thought one was in danger. You drew an attack your way in order to help one of us. Of your own volition you offered to stand in the open, unarmed, to attract a dangerous predator. Then, you went through with it, despite being frightened. You trusted us. Finally, you jumped into danger to save a teammate. Hate it or not, that was a Company thing to do."

She straightened and pushed off the tub. "So if Josh whipped out victory margaritas? You earned it."

"I never wanted you to get hurt and I especially fucking hate that you not only did, but did it on my behalf," he grated out.

"It happens. Agent life—bumps, bruises, and fruity drinks."

"I will never be okay with that."

Tension crinkled the corners of Vee's eyes but she kept the conversation light. "Then make me a better victory cocktail."

He didn't want to fight either, not tonight. "I was wrong."

Vee raised an eyebrow, not quite as accomplished as Liv.

"I was wrong about what you do and how you do it. Standing in the middle of that fight so fucking terrified that I forgot how to breathe was my epiphany moment. You said it —what you do requires flexibility and instant decisions. Neither of which any branch of the government can do for shit. You were right and I was wrong on that. I'll never agree that how the Company structures your life or creates agents is anything other than criminal. Neither is the way our government apparently aids and abets that abuse."

"Bruce—"

"Can we put a pin in this debate? You can call me civilian or soft or what the hell ever teams say about normal people, but I need to be close to someone right now." Honesty compelled him to admit the truth. "I need to be close to you."

"We can do better than a temporary pin. How about friends who don't discuss that one controversial issue? Oh, and who have sex. Definitely that."

He huffed out the ghost of a laugh. "That's called friends with benefits."

"That sounds perfect."

He held out his hand. Friendship was probably more than he deserved. Sure as hell intimacy was. Even as Vee accepted and put her hand in his, part of him disagreed with the claim of perfection.

He shut the voice down ruthlessly and guided Vee in. He tucked loose wisps of hair, curling from the room's humidity, behind her ear. Savoring the softness of her skin. Knuckles skimming along her jaw as he leaned in for a kiss.

Like they were on the same wavelength, Vee's lips parted. They both kept the encounter soft, no teeth and urgency this time. Tonight was about being thankful.

He wasn't giving himself absolution but he could take a page from Vee's book and go with the positives. A litter of murderous monsters would never mature to ruin the lives of people simply going about the business of existing. Nor would they grow up and end the lives of agents who went out every day, without acknowledgement or thanks, and protected all those happily oblivious people. Agents who were trained not to have a life so that others could, at their expense.

He wasn't discounting his culpability either, but he was thankful that Vee and Liv, fuck, the entire team, were here with only injuries Kimi could take care of as opposed to any that would land them in an operating room packed with surgeons.

He was damned well returning some of the comfort and release Vee had given him, and that was cut short the day before. Vee broke the kiss, but ran her hands under his shirt, her body loose and relaxed where she rested against him.

"My room has a decent bed and a door that locks." He traced along her lips.

"Locks are important?"

"Hell, yes. We are taking our sweet time, no performance critiques, no interruptions," he said firmly.

"In that case, my room has all of the above, plus no neighbors next door." She pulled away, backing toward the door and offering him her hand.

He took it and turned her so that she didn't risk tripping on weight benches and adding more bruises. "Sold."

They made it past the crowd yelling favorite lines at the

screen without more than a cheeky wink from Kimi, and through the now-immaculate kitchen. Her well-lit hall was as quiet as Vee had promised.

She closed the door behind them and he made damn sure the lock clicked, sealing them in together.

The room had an ethereal, other-worldly feel, the illumination coming from a couple of neon-filled glass sculptures, one a pink coyote, the other a purple cactus.

Leave it to Vee to employ kitsch-art he'd seen on roadsides, glowing against the desert night and aimed at impulsive tourists, instead of ordinary lamps. There wasn't one damn thing ordinary about Victoria Ramirez.

The neon haloed her like spotlights trained to accent a piece of art.

"Do you remember what I promised you on the rooftop?" His question came out more as a growl.

Vee's eyes widened for a moment then cleared, leaving satisfaction rising to meet his challenge. "You said you would go down on me one day."

He meant to give her another kind of satisfaction. "This is that day."

There was a trunk at the foot of the bed, a twin to the one in his room.

Vee followed his gaze and a naughty smile played around her lips. "I've never seen anything in the Company handbook about employing lockers in the manner you're thinking of trying."

"Flexibility and adapting on the fly are agent hallmarks. That's coming directly from this team's C.O. Besides, you're all about bending rules just shy of their breaking point." He surveyed the shit ton of pillows on her bed. "May I?"

"Go for it. You always have interesting ideas."

"I have fucking brilliant ideas." He sorted and found two flatter pillows. He was damn well ignoring that his niece had the same space princess accessories. He placed both squares on top of the unforgiving metal of the locker for cushioning and the few extra inches of height.

"I get pillows?"

She deserved a hell of a lot more than a crappy pillow, but giving her any of those things wasn't in his power.

His turn to hold his hand out in invitation. Vee accepted and he brought her in for another kiss. "Are you okay with this?" He lifted his lips at her soft exhale.

"Yes." She hooked her thumbs into the waistband of her shorts.

"My job." He lifted her hands away and ran his fingers under the elastic. Teasing along her hot tub warmed skin while sliding her shorts down. Leaving the simple black panties—for now.

He reversed with both palms flat against her hipbones and slid his hands up from her waist to the bottom of her tee, traveling over soft cocoa butter-conditioned skin interspersed with rougher scars. When she made an interested noise, he kept going, bringing the shirt up as he went. She raised her arms and he got the fabric out of their way, tossing it aside.

Her nipples already showed under the cotton of her bra. He bent, catching and sucking, his fingers tugging on the other peak. Vee arched into his hands and he gave himself over to worshipping the breasts he hadn't spent enough time with by half on the roof.

He played along the top of the bra, freeing her nipples. Then pressed her breasts together, taking both nipples in his mouth.

With his unoccupied hand, he cupped between her legs. Fucking loving that she ground against his palm and that she'd already soaked through.

They were doing this his way, and tonight his way was

slow. He let go, and laughed when Vee swore. Then carefully brought the bra over her head and nudged her arm.

Vee took the hint and sat, thighs open for him.

"Fuck, Vee. You are killing me here."

"Good."

He knelt in front of her and kissed the top of her stomach, doing the same along the band of her low-cut briefs. Enjoying the hell out of her twitching and squirming. He kissed the inside of her thigh right above her knee. When he moved to the next spot, trailing kisses along the inside, his beard rasped along her skin and Vee sucked in a breath.

"Too rough?" He paused and checked.

She shook her head. "Beards are new for me."

"Do you like them?"

"I'm going to need first-hand data."

He laughed and with his lips still against skin, the vibration rippled through Vee. She shivered, legs widening. "I definitely like that."

Fuck, but she didn't hold back. Her directness, and the new, throaty purr in her voice, was a sexy as her spread open in front of him. He got back to business, keeping the kisses and contact light. Later, there would be time for teeth and testing limits. He worked along satiny skin, drunk on the perfume of the lotion she'd applied. At the top of her thigh, he switched sides, ignoring the restless way she arched, inviting him in.

This time when he hit the top of her thigh he kept going and caught the last bit, that tiny scrap of fabric between his lips and her sex, and breathed over the spot.

Vee groaned and he gave in, jerking panties down, baring everything to his starving gaze.

"Damn but you are beautiful." He circled her clit, also loving the slick dampness he discovered. Loving it even more when he had to slide his hands up her thighs to hold them open when she clenched.

Switching, he licked over her clit. Plunging in, flicking, then circling again. Vee quivered, muscles in her legs trembling. He dared a look up.

Her head was tipped back, arms braced against the locker's edge and back arched in a taut, graceful arc. Unselfconscious and living in the moment and making it her own in a way few people ever tried.

If his cock wasn't already hard, the look on her face would have sealed his fate. He locked his lips over her sex and devoted himself to pushing her past the brink. He wanted her to lose herself, even if it was only for a few minutes.

"B," she got out, arching off the locker. He caught her hips and she grabbed his shoulders, fingers digging in.

He braced her and she rode the orgasm, head thrown back, one long line of brown skin from her perfect throat to her perfect, flexed toes.

Once the aftershocks wore down, he placed a light kiss on her hipbone and sat back on his heels. He kept a hand resting on her knee, not ready to lose contact.

Vee did a satisfied-as-hell shimmy and opened her eyes. "I like it."

"Care to be more specific? There's a lot going on here."

She smiled and stretched. "I like your ego."

He'd finally realized Vee didn't do sarcasm—when she said something, she meant it. Plenty of online fans enjoyed his attitude and temper. People who dealt with him face to face, less so.

Then there was Vee.

She ran her finger over his lips and jaw. "But this is what I meant—yes to your tattoos and yes to your beard. Who knew they had magical sexual powers?"

He barked out a surprised laugh.

"Speaking of tattoos." She gave his shirt a meaningful look.

"Are you sure you aren't too sore? I don't do that bullshit keeping score thing. I wanted to go down on you, I did, and I enjoyed myself, period."

In answer, she twisted and climbed onto the bed on hands and knees. Watching her ass was almost enough to finish him off. So when she palmed a nightstand drawer and pointed to a box of condoms, he didn't argue further. Vee knew what she was or wasn't up to, and he'd respect that.

She propped on her elbows, not one damn bit shy about being nude and her skin flushed from an orgasm, or watching him and letting him know she was watching him.

He shucked clothes and joined her. "Switch places, please."

She slid over and he laid on his back, then motioned for her. Vee knew her limits but he also wasn't risking hitting anything that might hurt, and that encompassed a good quarter of her body. Naked, there was no disguising that the anangoa had connected hard with her chest, and that most of her left side had made a high-impact meeting with the ground. "This work for you?"

"Yes." She brushed her fingers over his beard again. Even if he'd had his eyes closed he'd have known it was her. His body already recognized her touch.

As she kept going, tracing over his shoulders and down his chest, he rested an arm behind his head and teased along her relatively unbruised leg with his other hand. She could explore as long and as thoroughly as she pleased. If she changed her mind and sex was off the table, that was okay too. He'd meant it when he said he needed the closeness of another person tonight.

He also wasn't surprised when she switched gears and

quit exploring as quickly as she'd begun. She took a condom, rolling it on him expertly and stoking his desire another notch. She caught the base of his cock, positioning herself and sliding over him.

She braced on one hand and set a slow, even rhythm with none of the explosive energy from the rooftop. Maybe she needed this as much as he did.

He shoved a pillow behind him, then cupped her ass, keeping pressure light and off anything bruised.

By some unspoken agreement they maintained eye contact. No sound but their breathing and the hum of the neon lights. It felt as if another connection linked them, more than flesh and sex. It felt like he reached into Vee the same way she reached some virgin spot inside him and woke a nerve he hadn't known he had.

They came within slow heartbeats of each other. As soon as her breathing steadied, she rose enough for him to remove the condom and dispose of it in her freaky cat-shaped wastebasket.

Without him having to ask, she wiggled beside him, and he hitched so they lay on their sides, face to face. He brushed loose waves back, only to watch them curl forward along her ears again.

Vee traced from his wrist, over the lines of the tattoos, not missing a single whorl or bend. A faint frown cut lines across her forehead. This was Vee deep in thought and he craved getting another glimpse at how her mind worked.

"What are you thinking about?" His question came out low and softer than usual, like even his volume respected this moment, the two of them and only a few fantasy lights seeming real. Like they could be the only two people in the compound. The only two people in the world, and nothing outside their sphere existed.

Her response was equally soft. "Thinking about what my

tattoos would be, as a story of my life so far, the way yours are."

It fucking killed him thinking of hers—weapons, fights, loss. Still seeing too deeply into him, she caught his hands, working his fingers out of the fist he hadn't realized he'd made, and twining theirs together. "I meant ours would look so different, like completely separate worlds, but here we are, same time, same place."

He breathed around the lump in his throat, and tugged her hand, asking her to come closer.

Vee snuggled in tight, head on his shoulder. "We could be in the same place, sometimes." The simple statement whispered over his skin. His pulse picked up, excitement beating out after glow.

She continued. "If you're working in our patrol areas, we could see each other. When we had time. If you wanted. It would only require a request form, a couple of interviews, and a waiver. You could sign it when you get your cover story debrief and NDA at HQ."

As casual as she sounded, he felt the real question underneath, and Vee's intensity.

"Friends with benefits." Then and there he decided to delete that fucking phrase from his vocabulary.

"Exactly. You should get some sleep. You can really relax now, since we don't need you this time. Your part is over." She rested her hand on his chest, her breathing slowing. Drifting to sleep and betraying her own exhaustion.

He lay awake staring at a kitsch-stuffed room, the polar-fucking-opposite of his style. This place also the opposite, their life the absolute opposite in every way.

The spot Vee's hand lay over matched the weird, nameless ache he'd felt earlier. The *thing* that had dogged his steps, that he'd tried to evade naming. Fuck, but it wasn't nameless at

all. The spot was right over his heart, which Vee had pene-
trated as expertly as one of Josh's bullets.

For the first time in his life, he wasn't thinking of the next
town, the next opening, his mind already three steps ahead of
his body. Instead, he was present, and content.

The irony of finding the person who met him drive for drive,
ambition for ambition, intensity for intensity—it didn't escape
him that the person he'd fucking fallen for was the one who
embodied his previous no-strings, friends with benefits motto.

*We don't need you anymore.*

Vee had been talking about the mission, but hell. Wasn't
that just the summary of his whole situation?

He'd fallen in love with Vee, and that she was the one who
only did casual had to be the universe's biggest "fuck you" to
Bruce Kantor. Karma was laughing its ass off.

He wasn't capable of half measures. He was either all in,
or all out. No in-between.

The most vibrant, alive person he'd ever encountered also
spent her life speeding toward an ugly, too-early death.
There wasn't a damn thing he could do to change either of
their destinies. He had no more right to ask her to lay down
her weapons than she had to ask him to lay down his knives.

That Vee was going out tomorrow or the next day to
confront a thing that only wanted to slaughter her, and
which possessed the skills to do just that, had every cell in his
body knotted. He instinctively wrapped her tighter, pressing
her against him and her heart beating right over his like they
were synched-up.

The only scenario he could come up with that was worse
than him sitting his ass here, waiting to see if he'd have to call
that number on the phone and give the code that meant the
team was dead, was waiting for a call from Vee that never
came. A date where she never showed up, because she'd gone

after some creature and lost, days or weeks before, and he hadn't even known.

That horrific would-this-be-the-last-time worry always in the back of his mind, shadowing his every step and their every moment together—he couldn't live like that.

At some point, he'd lose his shit with Vee, not able to watch her climb out of his bed and head for another mission. Then they'd have the kind of fight that couldn't be taken back. Possibly the kind that fucked with Vee and threw her that one step off her game with lethal results.

That life wasn't fair to him or to Vee. For once, he wasn't itching to move on. Which meant he had to go, as soon as he could pack his bags.

But for these last, precious hours left in the night, he eased her closer. She murmured in her sleep and snuggled against him, fitting perfectly under his chin. He buried his face in her hair and stared at what he couldn't have.

# CHAPTER 18

VEE

$\mathcal{I}$ fell in with Kimi and Liv, both using the bench to stretch before our morning run. Hooking my heel over the back of the seating, I leaned over my knee, grasping my ankle. Bruised muscles complained, reminding me they had bounced off various hard surfaces recently.

"Did you talk Bruce down?" Liv pulled her heel up to her butt, flexing her always-tight calf muscles. "He was textbook stressed last night."

"Displaced guilt," Kimi corrected, already done with her warm-up.

Liv sighed and switched legs. "Yesterday wasn't on him. The plan went out the window as soon as those hatchlings made an appearance. I tried explaining but I'll give it another shot after breakfast."

Bruce probably had no clue, but Liv was all in on Team Bruce. I checked with Kimi as to her opinion.

"I decided I like him," she signed. "He introduces a fascinatingly chaotic element. I'm pretty sure he falls in the chaotic good alignment."

"I'm not sure gaming character profiles apply to real people," Liv said. "But yeah. He's totally chaotic good."

"Do you think real life friends with benefits correlates to fictional friends with benefits in the same way?" I said.

"Maybe?" Kimi signed, brow crinkled.

Liv straightened fast enough something popped. "You seriously want to apply for Asset status. Why is it suddenly important with this random guy?" Liv frowned and corrected herself. "Okay, not random. He's loud, and demanding, and his attitude is seriously as large as our patrol region, but he is adaptable and comes through in a crisis, and he understands supporting your family."

Kimi signed, "Did you just talk yourself into liking him?"

"Ahh, crud. I did."

They both gave up any pretense of warming up. Kimi glanced over her shoulder, making sure the guys weren't out yet.

"Bruce wants to do this friends and sex thing?" Liv asked.

"I think so?" They weren't the only ones with questions. "He's kind of brought it up both times we had sex."

Except, I'd been the one to initiate the conversation last night. Looking back, he hadn't explicitly said yes. Although we had both been tired and conversation hadn't been a priority.

I couldn't use that as an excuse for this morning. I wasn't sure which of us had woke first with sex on our mind but it had definitely been mutual. Until he'd muttered about showers and disappeared into the communal bath despite my having a private one available.

Liv tapped her fingers against her thigh mindlessly, her thinking tic. "He's seen team life, hardcore."

Meaning that removed one of the two biggest obstacles to having any sort of long-standing personal interaction with a civilian. He knew about cryptids, knew about the

Company, and had been on the frontlines enough to know what agent life meant. There was nothing I'd need to hide from Bruce, no elaborate lies I'd need to attempt to maintain.

The second obstacle wasn't codified. It was impossible to codify something that was the basis of our existences, like breathing. Nothing could come before the team. But Bruce had seen what it took to do our jobs, plus he totally understood investing single-minded intensity in a career.

"Guess I was off about him being one of those civilians who couldn't wait to get away from all things cryptid," Liv said.

"He isn't fascinated by them," I admitted. "And he has this fixation on the Company needing a different structure with cadets or being wrong somehow? I'm not even sure what that means. Like, he is totally behind humans good, cryptids bad, so, kinda hazy on what he's confused over."

Liv and Kimi shrugged, equally baffled by Bruce-logic.

"Asset means he'll have that degree of separation. You'll see each other, but he won't have a front row seat for missions and details, oh, or seeing injuries, because he's a little weird about those," Liv said. "I mean, realistically, he'll only see you a few times a year, which should help, too. Win-win." She bounced, ready to run now that the Bruce issue was settled neatly and within the rules.

The thump of the house door opening drew our attention. Josh hung over the walkway rail long enough to yell, "We've got a tracker signal, and green light from HQ," before disappearing back inside, undoubtedly to exchange shorts for tactical pants.

We all headed for the house to do the same.

Even with the knee-jerk pop of excitement at a mission alert, Liv's win-win stuck like an earworm. I should be pleased that the path to seeing Bruce now and then was clear.

Even a few times a year would be a lot if I was hooking up with another agent.

Somehow though, this felt...not like a win at all. A hollow victory.

I didn't know what to call it, but I wanted what we'd forged the last few weeks—arguing with Bruce, finding out all his chaotic-good sides, what we agreed on and everything we disagreed on, going to sleep with him, and waking up with him spooning me.

He wasn't capable of staying out of trouble, which was equal parts exciting and worrying, and compelled me to be there to help support him when things weren't so great.

I stopped with one foot on the steps. Frozen. Because my emotions regarding Bruce had the same intensity as I felt for my team, my family.

If I used our movies as a guide—I was pretty sure that meant I was in love with Bruce.

Which wasn't possible. That civilian can't-exist-without-you, romantic soul-mate thing was fiction created to make up for not having what we did. The team was it for us, our self-contained unit, filling all of our emotional needs.

Nothing in the rules or codes covered wanting or needing anything outside our unit. The Company handbook also failed to help in figuring out civilian relationships. Like understanding if Bruce felt the same way. If he did, whether he wanted more than the benefits idea we'd tossed at each other.

The rules definitely didn't outline how to be in love with someone who hated the Company that was the rest of my world.

As soon as we completed Mission Make Sure Anangoas Go Extinct, Bruce was to report to HQ, get his cover story, and leave.

Facing off with the anangoa was way less frightening than

figuring how, or if, I could have Bruce and still be me, Victoria Ramirez, Southwest Division Two C. O., and do what I lived for, keeping my team safe.

The anangoa was also far less scary than asking Bruce if he wanted to somehow be part of my life permanently. Because the Company rulebook also failed to address how to deal with a broken heart.

# CHAPTER 19

## BRUCE

*A*s Josh bellowed out the open door, Bruce slammed down the knife he'd been holding. The blade took his displaced anger and regret. He added a heaping measure of cowardice to top off the emotional stew.

He'd been trying to find the words to tell Vee that he was basically balling up her offer and any possible future they might have, and tossing it in the trash.

He really was the world's biggest dick. The opportunity and the privacy had been right there this morning. Instead, he woke reaching for Vee or her reaching for him. He'd given into the almost primal need to touch her. Then he'd bolted like a dine-and-dash jackass when anyone with a shred of decency would have talked to Vee.

Now, Kimi's program had locked on the monster that started this whole chapter of his life. There was no way in hell he'd drop his shitty decision on Vee minutes before she left on a mission.

He kept his back to the hall until the echo of footsteps quit. By the time all four arrived again, he'd hauled out one of Josh's god-awful sports drinks, and coffee for the other three.

He'd originally had a half-assed idea to feed all of them after their morning sweat session, then pull Vee aside. Like an omelet would somehow lessen the impact of his dickishness.

He glared at the tactical pants, knives, and weapons all four were clad in. Hating the symbols of the Company more than he'd hated anything in a spectacularly angry life.

Sliding the bottle down a counter to Josh, Bruce tipped his chin at the mugs lined up on the counter. "Cream, black, cream and sugar."

In return he got a knuckle tap from Josh, and graced with half-hugs from Kimi and Liv, one either side, for remembering their damn coffee preferences.

He put Vee's at the end, closest to him. He couldn't quite meet her eyes. When he nudged the cup her way just as she reached for it, their fingers touched. All he needed to do was lift his hand away. Let Vee enjoy her caffeine fix. Instead, he took his time, rotating the cup around so that the handle was facing her, letting her fingers trail over the back of his hand.

He finally let go, feeling as if her touch had been inked into his skin like a new, invisible tattoo. He cleared his throat. "Finish it. You probably need the energy boost."

As Vee and the team—more team than Vee—went over plans and drive times, he moved around her. Stealing bits and pieces for himself. Memorizing the cadence of her speech and lilt of her voice. The way baby hairs escaped her bun, curling at her temples and forehead. The play of muscles and brown skin as she motioned and talked. Those damn chewed-up cuticles.

Josh and Liv ended up in conversation and Kimi busy tapping at a tablet. He felt Vee's attention on him.

He finally got the balls to look at her. She nursed the untouched coffee, heel hooked over a stool rung. Deceptively casual.

When he nudged the cup her way just as she reached for

it, their fingers touched. All he needed to do was lift his hand away. Let Vee enjoy her caffeine fix. Instead, he took his time, rotating the cup around so that the handle was facing her, letting her fingers trail over the back of his hand.

When he finally let go, it felt as if her touch had been inked into his skin like a new, invisible tattoo. He cleared his throat. "Finish it. You probably need the energy boost."

Hell, maybe she'd rethought her offer to continue seeing each other. Maybe it'd been one of those post-coital, short-lived hormonal impulses that she regretted in the light of day. It was possible she'd be happy to see the last of him as soon as this job was done.

Which would be in the next few hours according to the conversation going on around him.

The possibility of her not really caring, and the reality that the end of the anangoa was the end of their time together sliced through him, more painful than any on-the-job cut he'd ever had. This felt as if it was slicing off part of his soul.

He still had no freaking clue what she was thinking when she sat the cup in the sink and palmed an inlaid metal rosette on the side of the bar. A panel clicked and an electronic screen slid out.

It took Bruce a beat to realize Vee was speaking to him.

"You're in the internal database now. This is the security code." She motioned and he came, watching while she punched a short numeric series in. "It resets every twenty-four-hours, routine. If anything happens and you need in a secure area on base, or even to open gates, press your thumb here." She tapped an oval on the screen. "Then enter the code. The door will engage once you're inside, also routine." She slid the panel back in, the innocuous bit of wood clicking and hiding the tech. "You have the phone and Cleaners' protocol?"

He dug in his pocket and held the phone up, not able to do more than nod. Vee had given him access, which meant she was giving him her trust with no strings and no qualifiers.

A light touch on his elbow turned out to be Kimi. She signed, "You will be safe here, but we all thought you should have full access like any other team member."

Josh shoulder bumped him. "Today is all but a lock. The anangoa is a dead cryptid walking."

"Truth," Liv said.

As the others headed for the truck, Vee paused, close enough he caught the faintest ghost of her cocoa butter. "This is an in-and-out job. The anangoa can't surprise or evade us this time."

His throat ached, with too many words trapped inside. All he allowed to come out was, "Be careful. And thank you. Thank you for everything."

Vee regarded him for a second. Like she really could look inside him. She finally turned to follow the rest of the team. At the doorway, she added, "We'll talk when I get back."

He watched her disappear, the door closing even as the whirr of the garage door rising came through the walls.

He was a coward.

He couldn't watch her walk away again.

With Kimi's tech and the tracker, they'd get the anangoa within the next few hours. He wouldn't be a threat to anyone any longer, no longer a beacon luring danger to those near him.

He made a sweep, tossing his shower kit in his suitcase, and wheeling it into the kitchen. He pulled out the security panel, held his thumb on the pad, then typed in the code.

Digging in his pocket, he pulled out the key fob to his car, and the phone holding all of Vee's information. He left the phone centered on the table.

It would be the first thing she saw when she walked back in. She would know exactly what it meant. If, by some miracle, she hadn't regretted her offer, this would sure as hell kill any feelings she had for him. Except possibly anger. Leaving pissed off people in his wake was his m.o. though.

He told himself a clean break was better. An ache opening his chest that he was going to have to learn to live with, he pointed his car at the gates and a Vee-less existence.

## CHAPTER 20

### VEE

"*A*re you kidding me?" Josh powered the window down like removing a layer of impact-proof glass was going to change the view.

The twenty-foot tall metal cowboy with six guns drawn smiled down at us, rust showing around his edges and the *Wild West Shootout* emblazoned in an arc over his head no longer lighting up and blazing as a beacon to bored tourists. A closed sign hung from a chain locking the front gates. I shut the window, no reason to advertise our presence more than we had to.

"I guess it makes sense," Liv said once we were sealed in, tapping an annoyed beat against the steering wheel. "Plenty of room, minimal chance of discovery, but close enough to a populated hunting ground to be a viable nest."

I frowned at the scanner Kimi had shoved up between our seats as proof, when the signal pulled us toward the desert and the defunct tourist trap. The tracker signal blipped a clear green, further proof that the anangoa was here.

It didn't feel right though. This was out past the city

limits. All of the deaths and attacks had occurred in downtown Scottsdale, around the Arts and Historic District. Even the bar where we had first encountered it was on the cusp of the Art District giving way to local small businesses.

There were a ton of hunting areas between here and downtown. Hotels, outdoor adventure sites, suburbs. Passing those up to hit more crowded areas miles away wasn't typical predator behavior, never mind the restraint required.

There was a chance this was a new bolt hole, and the creature had run in blind panic, ending up here to lick its wounds after our attack.

Maybe.

No matter how it had come about, we had the creature's current location. We also needed to get in and out before we drew any attention. "Universal key time," I said, eyeing the huge lock securing the chain.

Josh hopped out, slid open the under floor compartment, and hauled out a pair of bolt cutters in an efficient, silent motion. He made short work of the lock, motioning for Liv to pull the truck through, then hooked the chain back. To anyone driving or hiking by, the place would still look untouched.

Liv parked the truck behind what had served as the main office as Josh rejoined us.

We had all switched regular blades for the larger machete style we usually reserved for our wilderness call-outs. Josh left his sniper gear in the back, and added a shotgun with saddle and extra rounds, and flare gun modified for incendiary rounds, along with the usual side-arms.

He'd petted the flamethrower and grenades, but grudgingly left them in the armory.

Right now, I almost wished he hadn't. I'd happily burn this site to ash.

There was a slight chance I was riding a frustration and hurt high.

Bruce hadn't looked at me in the kitchen until he had no choice when I demonstrated the security protocol. Even then, there was none of the easy closeness or banked heat we'd had in one degree or another since the market trip. Definitely none of the same-wavelength communication we'd discovered once naked.

Despite asking me to be careful, it felt like there was a new distance between us. Like he was pulling away.

It could either be because I had mentioned continuing to see each other and he wasn't on board, or that we'd blown the last anangoa mission and he had doubts about our ability. He'd sworn he trusted our skills, but that was pre-Bruce-as-bait fiasco.

The first problem, I couldn't do anything about.

The second was my wheelhouse.

Kimi opened the tablet on the truck hood and called up the park's layout and on-file building plans, then a layer with the drones real-time data, then the blip of the anangoa as a final overlay.

The place was lots of open spaces for the shootouts, riders' tricks, and roping demos. The only buildings were the small ticket booth-office unit we stood by, a pole barn that once held the horses, and a dinner theater-auditorium combo that was open on two sides.

The blip was stationary in the open theater. We wouldn't be making the same mistake again, assuming there was only one hostile though. From here on, we'd rely on hand signals and earpiece code in case our target, or targets, was helpfully asleep.

Senses keyed-up, I carefully jimmied the office door. Liv took one side, I took the other, and we eased in as Josh and Kimi positioned themselves on the outside, covering the yard. I slipped inside, back hitting the wall and light on my gun clicking on. Liv mirrored me on the opposite wall, her light flaring.

We swept from the larger closed ticket counter, boards nailed over the windows, down the short hall. Liv took the room on the right while I went left.

My room had been a break and rest room combo. Chairs were turned upside down on a pair of long tables. The counters were covered in dust and grit. A quick check showed the water in the bathrooms turned off, nothing but more grit, all undisturbed and no tracks on the floors or walls.

I tapped *clear* on my earpiece. Liv's echoed a second later. We eased back into the daylight, careful to silently close the office behind us.

Josh stayed focused on the yard, though nothing stirred, only a hawk riding a thermal high overhead, hoping for a careless basking lizard or snake.

Kimi signed, "Target stationary."

I took point, quartering the open area between the office and the pole barn.

Corrals stood empty, the sturdy fences still standing. A wheeled souvenir kiosk sat next to benches and picnic tables, all also in decent shape. Even the bare gift shop, situated to take advantage of resting customers, had held up well to sun and weather. The place felt like it was just waiting to customers to walk in.

Kimi's drone made a silent sweep over the roof of the barn, as all four of us chose corners and jogged through. A bird nesting in the rafter spooked and took off in a flutter of wings.

Barn cleared, we met at the end. The only site left was the theater.

I sent Josh and Kimi for the open ends. Liv and I split up. She took the cutout opening for customers on the right.

I eased left. The larger opening for the actors was covered in blackout theater cloth.

One corner was ripped loose, casting a slanting ray of sun inside. Flies crawled over the torn edge, drawn by blood. Drops dotted the sand in front of me. Back to the hot metal siding, I crept in, rounding the blind corner.

The sun played over an arc of brownish blood, more flies buzzing. Scruffy, wrinkled brown bodies lay in heaps—part of a chupacabra den's population, in various states of chewed up.

Crouched over the largest pile, iridescent scales glittered. The anangoa's back was to me, busy over its meal. The crack of chupacabra bones being methodically crunched covered my approach.

I sighted on the broad back and then tapped out an alert to the team.

In a snap of muscles and scales, the cryptid whipped around. Intestines and tufts of chupacabra hide decorated the thing's muzzle, all the way up to its slitted, reptilian eyes. They glowed with territorial anger, a snarl trickling out from between serrated teeth.

It coiled to leap, powerful leg muscles bunching. Shoved off in a fast leap. Claws stretched and slicing at my face, the stink of rotting carrion hitting me.

My shot took it between the eyes. Brain and blood splattered the sand.

It staggered and plowed muzzle first into the dirt. Head flopping inches from my boots. I got my first good look at the cryptid that had caused so damn much turmoil and grief.

My blood chilled. "Fuck. No, no, no."

The team spilled in, red laser dots clustered and shots pounding into the anangoa. The very dead, very, very male, only three-quarters grown anangoa.

Kimi was on her knees, scanner in one hand, knife out

and slitting through scales with the other. The scanner pinpointed the chip and she dug, coming out with a pink chunk of flesh on the end of her blade. The tiny metal tracker lodged in the center of the meat.

"You hit the adult. I freaking saw the dart. And I *know* what you hit was the adult female." On its own my hand already had the phone out even as Josh and Liv went back-to-back scanning for another ambush.

Every instinct screamed we were alone and in no danger. Because it was after Bruce. It had sacrificed its offspring again. Leaving the juvie as a decoy, making sure it had plenty of food to keep it occupied and easy for us to find.

"He's in the compound. Nothing short of a nuclear strike will get through the security," Liv said, hitting the same conclusion I had.

I knew that.

Every hair on my body stood on end though, and I fought not to break my own rule and call Bruce mid-mission. "Compound security report."

Kimi had a tablet out. "Secure. No breaches detected. No power fluctuations." She flicked to the home drone. "All clear on a visual. Nothing outside the fences. No disturbance inside."

"We'll get it before it ever hits the compound," Josh growled. "Bruce is inside, it's all good." His fingers still tightened on the stock of his gun.

Kimi shoved a tablet in my face. A green blip moved, from a few miles past our road, out toward the main highway. "How is there another tagged—"

She cut off my question. "The tracker is on Bruce's car. I tagged it as soon as the Cleaners dropped it off because he was a flight risk."

Bruce's car, with Bruce in it. Now out of the compound

and undefended. While the anangoa that had marked him, and had distracted us, stalked him.

We sprinted for the truck and I hit the number for Bruce's burner phone. Which only rang and rang, before going to voicemail.

I beat Liv to the driver's seat. The team scrambled in, doors slamming and faces grim. The tires spun, kicking a trail of dust behind us.

I hadn't just failed as a commander and Company agent, failing in our directive of protecting civilians at all costs. I'd failed at protecting *my* civilian, my person. I stood on the gas, wishing I'd learned one of Bruce's prayers.

# CHAPTER 21

## VEE

*I* glanced at the rearview, not sparing attention for what Liv was saying, only to the expression on her face as she called in our route and cleared the way of police and traffic. She gave me a tight nod. She had already called in Cleaners, and our new mission.

Josh methodically checked and reloaded our guns. When Liv hung up and said, "Medical has been notified and a med chopper is on standby," Josh flinched and muttered a curse.

This was too much, too close to his brother's accident. But it was also worry for Bruce.

I wasn't the only one who saw him as more than another civilian, or even an okay acquaintance.

We were close though. A little over a mile from Bruce.

Kimi turned sideways between our seats and flashed the tablet.

The tracker was slowing. Too quickly for a road with no traffic, intersections, or lights. I stomped on the gas, whipping around the last curve, seconds from Bruce's position.

In time to see his car skid, madly trying to avoid the streak of green blasting from a ditch on the side of the road.

Right into his path. Bruce's tires squealed. Protesting the wrenching turn he tried, laying down burning rubber.

Wheels lifted off the road.

The anangoa angled and plowed into the side of the car at full tilt, the crunch of metal carrying even with windows up.

Gravity won and the car rolled down the embankment. Disappearing.

The anangoa leapt after it.

I left skid marks slamming on the brakes. The team bailed, boots hitting asphalt in unison.

Josh dropped to one knee at the top of the embankment, sighting down as we raced past him. A screech of metal tearing propelled us down faster. The car had rolled and stopped on its roof, wheels up.

The cryptid stood on top, claws slashing at the metal. It had torn off the driver's door.

Bruce hung from his seatbelt. My body kept going but everything in me stopped for a heartbeat.

"Fucking fuck," Bruce swore, voice hoarse but very much alive.

My heart started beating again. "Take the shot."

Behind us, Josh's gun barked. The cryptid gave its unearthly hissing roar as a line of greenish blood appeared from the back of its exposed neck to its shoulder.

Another sharp pop from Josh, and the cryptid threw itself off the car.

Glass shattering ruined the hope that Josh made a kill shot. Bruce's swearing ramped-up, fresh fear lacing his voice.

"Flank it."

Kimi and Liv split off. Liv went around the front, Kimi the back.

I dropped to a crouch at the ruined driver's side. Bruce had fumbled one of his chef's knives out, the case on the ceiling by his head now, blades scattered where he'd had the case on the seat as he drove, as usual.

The anangoa shoved a clawed arm in, swiping. Bruce stabbed at it, swearing non-stop.

I grabbed one of the spilled knives and sawed at the seat-belt. "Try to brace."

In a shriek of fury, the anangoa jerked back, car shaking. Liv or Kimi had scored a hit while it was distracted.

The last of the seatbelt split and Bruce's shoulders and back whumped down hard, despite him hanging onto the wheel.

I grabbed and he latched onto my arm. I hauled him free. "Can you stand? Anything feel broken?"

"No. I mean no on broken, yes on standing." He rubbed his forehead, hand coming away with a streak of blood. More dotted his jaw, all probably thanks to the impact.

I steadied him and he used the car to stand.

Another shriek split the air.

"Stay low and behind me." I pressed down on his shoulder, handing him the knife I'd used, and reclaiming my gun. I walked us backward, trusting Bruce to keep us upright, my attention on the car and what it hid. His hand stayed against my hip, light but guiding us.

"Heads up," Liv yelled.

The anangoa hurtled over the upside-down trunk. Landing feet from us. Fury in every line of its poised body.

"I can't get a shot," Josh said in the flat tone he defaulted to when he was in the zone. "Gas tank."

Preparing to go through me to get its real prey, the anangoa's eyes stayed fixed on us, as it shifted its weight from side to side. Still in front of the rear panel and the gas tank. Any shot risked hitting the car, setting off an explosion.

"What's to our right and left, B?" I watched the cryptid's

legs. Watching for the moment it decided we were worth risking exposing itself to Josh.

I had to assume it understood at least voice tone if not language. It had planned and executed an intricate trap, and seemingly not only removed our tracker, but kept it intact and inserted it in a decoy.

"Saguaro cactus on the right, knee height. Bank is steeper on the left, but clear," Bruce said.

A tiny frisson of pride shot through me. Ambushed, hurt, and in the open, he still kept it together and understood what I needed to know.

Going left also meant toward the hood and away from the tank. I altered our painfully slow retreat. Putting space between us and the car.

Giving Josh a clear shot.

"When I hit one, turn and run toward Josh, staying low and left. Get behind him," I ordered. "In three, two—"

The car shifted in a muffled creak-crunch of safety glass despite Kimi's stealth as she climbed on top. Liv materialized at the front.

The cryptid's eyes flicked to Liv, then back. The anangoa's weight shifted.

"One. Go!"

Bruce broke contact, touch disappearing.

The cryptid threw itself to all fours, minimizing itself as a target and streaked at us breath-stealing fast. Understanding what Kimi and Liv were trying for in flanking it.

Shots bit the ground behind it in a steady patter, throwing up puffs of dirt and sand. Kimi and Liv herding it.

The anangoa kept coming. Then pivoted in a sinuous, spine-bending movement, speeding to the right. Still too close to the tank, but going around me in a feint. Still fixated on Bruce.

I jerked a machete free and threw myself in its path. It

lunged left and I met it. Ducking claw swipes, keeping my blade moving. Circling, in a horrible dance, too much intelligence shining from the anangoa's eyes.

"Fall back ASAP," I ordered.

Kimi and Liv didn't hesitate, bolting from their spots. Moving past me. Clear of the car. The anangoa darted again, and my blade blocked its path again. Back and forth.

"B?"

"What?"

"Right. And hustle! Then back to Josh."

Bruce swore, and sand shifted and peppered down behind me, but he ducked and ran, as agile and determined as on the ball court.

The cryptid arrowed at him in a mad rush, bent on getting past me. I scored a superficial cut over a claw. Forced to let go of the machete blade as the cryptid swiped backhanded. The blade went flying.

I turned my back on it, sprinting for the top of the embankment.

Bruce had followed orders perfectly, now disappearing over the rise. The shallow ditch was feet away.

I dug in and spun, bruises and cuts screaming, and faced back the way I'd come. Then aimed over the charging cryptid's head. Fired at the car, the scent of gas already lost under the stink of my sweat.

As I squeezed the trigger, I threw myself backward at the ditch.

The car blew. Heat washed over me, the explosive force knocking me from the lip of the ditch, rolling me deeper in. Pure blue-white light blotted out the world.

The anangoa's agonized wail rose over the thumps and *skree* of flying metal.

A series of sharp pops followed.

The heat lessened even as I patted at my face, exposed

skin worst-sunburn-ever hot. But not on fire. I dug fingers and toes into the hard earth, scrambling up and out of the ditch in a roll. I caught a glimpse of Josh kneeling with his rifle aimed at what was left of the car, then a flash of Liv and Kimi lined up beside him in shooter's stances, Bruce safely behind them.

I kept rolling, pushing to my heels and coming up with my gun out, facing the car and cryptid. The anangoa's charred, clawed hand lay right at the rim of my ditch. Chunks were missing from the body, and what was left was burning merrily away. Enough remained to make out entrance wounds on the side of its head, most of the front pulped and gone.

Josh, Liv, or Kimi's, or maybe all threes', shot had finished it off, saving me from having a burning, pain-crazed cryptid land on top of me in my shelter.

I coughed, throat smoke-scratchy, lungs aching, and gave the command. "Clear. Stand down."

Sand squeaked and I looked over my shoulder for the source. Bruce dodged Liv, who wasn't actually trying to stop him any longer, pelting to me.

He half-slid, banging into me and knocking a grunt out of my bruised chest, almost putting me on my butt. Then I was wrapped in his arms, crushed against him with my face buried in his neck as he repeated versions of "Holy shit Vee, fuck," in a non-stop loop. His heart hammered wildly where we were pressed together, feeling like it should bruise us both.

He was basically unhurt, safe, and the murderous threat to his life gone. The awful barbed knot that had lodged inside me on discovering Bruce was vulnerable, the anangoa was on his trail, and we might not get to him in time disappeared.

A new one took its place, barbs digging deep into my

heart. He'd been vulnerable because he left the compound. I didn't have to glimpse the suitcases in his car or verify that he hadn't answered the cell because he'd ditched it at the base to know he'd left-left. He'd left me at the first opportunity, not even waiting to verify the anangoa was dead. In too much of a hurry to not accidentally have to see me again.

Kimi had shown me his life via social media.

Liv had said he wasn't a joiner.

Bruce had come out and said he couldn't tolerate the same people for any length of time.

I had puzzled over his lifestyle, with no ties to people he cared for or who cared for him. I had argued with him, only a week earlier, over not understanding loyalty. And somehow I'd still closed my eyes to facts, living in such a fairy tale that I'd convinced myself that not only might he care for me, but that he deserved a place in my and the team's life. I'd almost committed the most treasonous, horrific act imaginable, putting my team at risk because of an outsider, a civilian who didn't value me, my purpose, or my family.

"I thought I'd lost you." He finally managed real sentences, his wet whisper brushing across my temple.

I wiggled and he loosened his hold, switching to cup my face, his frantic gaze running over me. "Are you—"

Oh, he did *not* get to ask that question.

I brought both my arms up and out in a hard sweep, breaking his hold. Then shoved him off me, and stood.

He looked up at me from his new position on his butt.

"You are a jerk. The biggest jerk in jerk-landia." I glared down at him, daring him to move even one centimeter.

"Vee—"

"Did you even leave a note?"

His mouth opened. Closed without uttering a sound.

Liv carried on a brief conversation with the Cleaners, then with Medical, cancelling the med flight alert.

The new reminder of what Bruce had done added to the anger-hurt stew. He'd put everyone here in danger. I carried on glaring at him, waiting for an answer.

"Are we seriously having this conversation on the side of a state highway, with a totaled car and a burning monster yards away?"

Wrong answer. "We're having this argument here and now because if I turn my back or wait until a more civilized time, you'll rabbit without a word like the jerk you are. You do not get to ghost and avoid consequences. Again."

My volume might've increased with each word.

Truck doors clicked open then closed, my brother and sisters getting to safer ground.

Bruce's face went from fear-pale to scarlet. Still on his butt, he barked back, "Fine. Yes, I left. No, I didn't leave a damn note, because saying I...that you matter in a letter and *then* bailing is too shitty even for me."

"You may have stood unarmed to lure an anangoa into a trap, and fought one off until we arrived, but you are such a coward."

"I fucking know that!"

"Get in the truck. Kimi will patch up your—whatever. First thing in the morning someone will drive you to HQ for debriefing and discharge."

"Damn it, Vee." He scrambled to his feet. "Let me talk."

I turned my back on him and walked to the truck.

"Vee!"

"In. I won't tell you again." I climbed into my usual spot in front, rummaged through the console until I found sunglasses, and slapped them on. My eyes were burning from the toxic gasoline and roasting cryptid fumes. And from my stupidity, and betrayal of my role as C.O.

The rear door slammed hard enough the truck rocked,

Bruce obeying but showing his temper. He never lied or hid who he was. He couldn't help being himself.

I was the one who hadn't been true to herself and her values.

Lesson learned.

# CHAPTER 22

## VEE

*H*ours later, I massaged my temples, a low-key headache nagging. A combination of minimal sleep, exploding a cryptid, and disappointment more at myself than in Bruce and his decision.

I'd let HQ think Bruce being out of the compound during the incident was simple miscommunication. Not his bailing to evade the debrief process, thus saving his clearly ungrateful butt from reprisal again. HQ was expecting him tomorrow evening, my paperwork filed. We had managed to avoid each other since returning, Liv and I in the office with reports, him in the med bay with Kimi, getting his cuts patched up.

I appropriated one of Josh's drinks, stuffed my phone and Liv's keys in the pocket of the light jacket covering my rarely used shoulder rig, and headed for her truck.

The Cleaners had issued a preliminary report. There had been something the pathology team tentatively labeled "a morphological oddity" in the female's brain, which roughly matched a similar, smaller spot in the adult male's. None of the offspring had the same structure though.

There was also some sort of chip in the female's head. Difficult to say exactly where it had been injected or exactly what type of chip thanks to the fire. The male had one as well —again, damaged catastrophically when we stopped it. The working theory was that the tiny bit of tech was a version of the ID trackers used in pets and some wildlife, placed there by the poachers who bagged the creatures, or by its too wealthy, too naive owner.

Doing whatever magic the Office branch did, a private flight from Malaysia had been uncovered. It landed in Phoenix, with cargo only specified as *cultural artwork*. The timeline fit for the cryptids' appearance.

So did the fact that the person behind the corporation listed on the manifest had been reported as deceased a few weeks earlier. Supposedly in a hunting accident, but more like he'd been the prey, not the hunter. The buyer hadn't understood what he bought or hadn't taken it seriously if he was told, and had ultimately paid with his life.

The deceased owner's place was on the outskirts of town. If he had the anangoas, he might also have more realistic files on his new pets, which could help Liv's report.

Kimi and Liv were busy updating the species profile, convinced the anangoa had been grossly mislabeled on our Company genus chart. Liv thought they were somewhere between a ghoul and a vampire as far as cognition, reasoning, and adaptability.

The previous owner also owned the defunct Wild West Park, a recent acquisition. Coincidences happened—he could have been an eccentric with a taste for cryptids and tourist traps—there were weirder hobbies. Probably. The rest of the team considered the anangoa mystery, and mission, closed.

Something still felt off about the situation, though. I didn't like coincidences or mission reports with so many holes. There were entirely too many of those recently. Thus,

Liv humoring me and allowing me to borrow her very non-Company ride, donning my civi wardrobe, and relying on a concealed carry. And going alone because even if there was more to the anangoa story, this was only recon, not an active mission with a potential for hostiles.

And because the rest of the team didn't deserve to be stuck in a truck with me and on the receiving end of my currently crappy attitude.

When I got close to the estate, my irritation only escalated. The place was one of those closer to the desert, but then the beauty of the land they paid premium for was altered by landscaping that required sprinklers and yard services. I glared and parked out of sight.

The early evening dusk gave me plenty of cover to slip over the estate fence. On the off chance I was caught, my *just a bored civilian* look might get me out faster.

It turned out I didn't need to put in the effort to blend. Aside from the bats flitting around after bugs, and a javalina I startled, I was alone on the property. Without the extra aid of sprinklers and gardeners, the expensive vegetation had crisped under the Arizona sun. I rubbed a tree leaf between my fingers, then dusted the powder off against my jeans. This was way more than a few weeks' worth of neglect.

I went for the back entrance. Two seconds with the lock and I was in. The yard had a discreet home security sticker, but the service hadn't been kept up. I took a beat to orient myself, the door opening into the general washroom-supply room, then flicked my compact flashlight to life.

The only thing in the room was a forgotten broom, tucked in a corner along with the cobwebs and a startled gecko.

I prowled the downstairs, then climbed the ornate staircase to the second story. Every door I opened, on every room, told the same story. The house was bare. No furniture, artwork, or signs of having been lived in. I ran my finger along a marble bathroom counter, leaving a trail, and wiped the thick dust on my jeans to join the macerated leaf.

This had been the owner's only residence.

One that hadn't been inhabited in months and months, at a minimum.

I played with false addresses, and possibly false identities on the drive back. By the time the compound gates closed behind me, I hadn't come up with any logical answers, only another what-if to note on my spreadsheet of unsolved weirdness, which only added to my general life-sucks level.

I parked my sister's baby in its spot in the garage bay off the annex. The yard was empty, the place quiet.

Same for indoors. Where normally the game room would be popping, all of us relaxing after a successful call out, tonight it was a ghost town. Not even because I was hurt and they were respecting my feelings, or at least, not only because of me. Josh, Kimi, and Liv had all let Bruce in, and he had tried ghosting them too. They were in their quarters. As soon as I annotated my report with the new findings, I was also hibernating.

Hibernating, wallowing. Same thing.

This was my issue to deal with and get over, and come back out with my priorities properly aligned.

I stepped into the hall. The last person I wanted to see straightened from where he'd been leaned against my office door.

I really, really hated the stupid, romantic comedy-devoted part of me that flared to life at seeing Bruce. The stupid part that also noticed the circles under his eyes, and the butterfly bandage Kimi had applied to the cut above his brow. The stupid movie heroine part that wanted to check him over, hands-on, despite knowing my sister never would have turned him loose if he had a concussion or other injuries.

Despite my self-lecture about this being my fault much more than his, I so wasn't giving him points for laying in wait, despite my siblings undoubtedly having warned him to steer clear when I was hurt-angry. I also refused to acknowledge the heartbroken label that fit better than a simple *hurt* ever could.

"Yes?" I ignored his hovering, scanning myself in and the door unlocking.

"You were gone."

"You would recognize the phenomenon."

"You didn't let Kimi herd you into medical, but fuck, you guys ignore half the wounds you get, and when I went looking you were MIA, and no one knew where you'd gone. Or at least, they wouldn't tell me." He scrubbed a hand through his hair, as agitated as I'd seen him since he landed here. "I was worried."

"Stop. Do not even go there." Anger flared and I held on to it over the squishier emotions. So much for staying cool and in control.

"Vee, please. Can we talk? Here and now?"

"You left that option on the table when you snuck out. So, no. You made your opinion and desires perfectly clear. We have nothing to talk about."

"Jesus Fucking Christ. I was scared, okay? No, fuck that, I was terrified and I picked a shitty way to try and cope. Watching you walk out that door, and knowing what you were racing toward scared the hell out of me. I should've done better. I should've waited, and had a conversation once you came back."

"Yet you didn't."

"I was scared shitless you *wouldn't* be coming back," he yelled, the last of his control slipping. "Holy hell, I still am. What I saw today was worse than anything I'd imagined. You were a half second and a damn roadside ditch away from blowing yourself up, and ending up in an ICU burn ward. That's if you were lucky."

"What is it that you want?" I spun to face him because angry was preferable to devastated.

He answered before the echo of my question died. "I want to argue with you, make up with you, to discover all the ways we fit together, and marvel at all our differences. I want to fuck on or against every surface in this compound. I want all that, and shit we haven't even thought of yet, and I want it on a daily basis."

Somehow, I'd taken a step closer to him. Everything he said had the ring of truth to it. It also sounded exactly the same as what I'd put on a list for a perfect love story. Our kind of perfect, because neither of us avoided conflict, and sometimes we both went on spur of the moment decisions, and those fell flat as often as they succeeded. Which was part of what made life interesting. Bruce was the first person to totally understand that. He got it.

"But you do more than work a dangerous job, Vee. You throw yourselves on every damn grenade you encounter. You put everyone else first." Bruce squeezed his eyes closed and a muscle in his jaw worked. He opened his eyes, too much sorrow now filling them. "I don't know how to be okay with that."

I stepped back, all the alluring possibilities vanishing. Another fairy tale that didn't belong in the real world. "It's not a job. It's who and what I am. The real problem here isn't cryptids and risks. The problem is that I'm part of something —the team, the region, the Company. Being part of a larger group and calling is a defining aspect of me, Victoria Ramirez, sister, agent, commanding officer. You don't understand how to do that, how it isn't all about you, and about getting what you want every single time. You don't understand that there's a give and take. That there's as much happiness in giving as receiving. That's not who you are."

I'd been willing to change, and make sacrifices, and figure out how to fulfill my role while not taking anything away from my team, but still have a space for something of my own. Bruce wasn't, and wouldn't.

I had no right to try to force him into a mold that didn't fit, and no right to be angry. I opened my door.

Bruce planted his palm on it, keeping it closed. "This can't be…at least answer me this. Do you even love me?"

"Josh will be ready to leave at daybreak. Go get some sleep." Gently, I removed his hand, and entered my office, closing the door on Bruce and the thing I hadn't known I wanted.

# CHAPTER 23

## BRUCE

*B*ruce stared at the closed door until his eyes burned and his vision blurred. He lifted a fist to pound on the door.

His hand never connected. He'd laid out his position. He loved Vee. He despised the limitations her Company raised agents under, and the way they were indoctrinated to see themselves as replaceable cogs.

Vee had laid out her position. She was devoted to her team and mission. She'd also been right when she accused him of sometimes being a selfish bastard.

She'd been wrong about his not understanding family ties and being part of something bigger than his fucking huge ego.

His family irritated the hell out of him. He couldn't be or live the way they wanted him to. Despite the problems he hadn't cut them out of his life. He couldn't make it without his sister and brother, their parents, and his nieces. More importantly, he didn't want to make a life without them. In the space of a few turbulent weeks, Vee was now also on that list of people he treasured.

The soul-sucking pain he'd tried running from swamped him. He wanted Vee in his life. Period.

Pieces began clicking together in his head, the magical alchemy that happened when his subconscious had been marinating an idea, and bam, it came at him fully formed like the myth of Athena emerging from Zeus' forehead.

He retrieved the phone, still on the table where he'd left it, then bolted for his room and his sketchpad.

The plan poured out faster than he could write, and he worked through cramped fingers as the clock on his phone sped closer and closer to dawn. Carpal tunnel was a price he'd gladly pay if it meant he had another shot with Vee.

He made it into the kitchen and got coffee going seconds before the entire team convened, Kimi, Liv, and Vee for their sacred morning run, looking more like sisters than ever. Josh was in a Lakers tee and cargo shorts, ready to haul Bruce's ass out of Vee's life for good.

First in, Kimi scowled at the mugs he'd lined up and signed, "If this is your idea of sucking up, epic fail."

Josh didn't move to grab his drink, and Liv and Vee didn't spare him a single glance.

Fine. He'd earned his way onto their shit list. Now he prayed he could earn forgiveness. He rubbed the Star of David and tucked it back under his shirt.

"Here." He planted himself in front of Vee and Liv and shoved a detailed, five page list at Liv.

Now or never. He loved Vee. Despite his best efforts, he also cared about the whole bunch of them.

Vee still hadn't looked at him, but when she frowned and angled to see the papers, it was with red-rimmed eyes.

He'd done that. He'd hurt her.

This was the last damn time. If she allowed it, he'd never commit that sin again.

"What is this?" Liv held the papers between two fingers. Looking ready to drop it in the nearest trashcan.

"It's what you'll need to requisition or order or whatever you call obtaining supplies for the team." He sucked in a deep breath, and pitched himself and his plan like he'd never advocated for anything in his life.

"We both have careers. Giving them up is a deal breaker. There are parts of your job I have problems with." He looked to each person because he'd already figured out this was as much about the team as it was Vee. She valued them, and so would he. It was a package deal.

"No relationship is always easy and fun. I can run away, and never know if you bunch survive," he turned to Vee, getting as close as he dared, "never knowing if you're hurt, and that not knowing will gnaw at me every hour of every day. I can live like that, or I can be proactive, stay with the person I care about, and do something about the problematic parts."

Vee didn't have her arms crossed. She wasn't glaring at him. Both of which would have been a huge improvement over the flat, weary expression painting her face now. "The fact that you can stand in front of me and say problematic? That's both arrogant and the insurmountable issue."

"We don't have to agree—we have to find a happy compromise. Here's my idea. I don't disagree that cryptids need monitored and eliminated when possible. I was also wrong when I mouthed off about how the Company was structured. Cryptids aren't like anything the government and military have dealt with and neither can pivot quickly for shit. What you do can't be approached conventionally. Trying it would get agents killed and that's not going to happen."

"In a nutshell, man." Josh grabbed the sweating drink and cracked it open, already half-way to joining Bruce's side.

"Forget government rigidity. *You* didn't pivot overnight, B. You admitted that two minutes ago, and I've started actually listening to what you are saying instead of what I think you meant," Vee said.

When he made a move toward her, she gave him a look that froze him in place.

He talked faster, dumping his whole heart into it. "My issue begins and ends with all of you thinking you're replaceable." He stared down each member in turn. "That is bull shit. I don't pretend to understand how you came from the problematic upbringing you did, and I'm never budging on that opinion, but fuck me if you don't all shine like damned stars." He switched to Vee. "You shine the brightest. Like a north star that everyone charts their path by."

He cleared his throat, because every word he said was the truth. "My role here is going to be to remind you of that. You do your jobs. Protect people. Keep families safe so there aren't more crime scene photos like last week's. I will be the voice of reason, though. Every time you go too far and drift into martyrdom when there's even a glimmer of another viable solution, I will be there calling you out."

"B—"

"You are unique. You are important. You're valuable for who you are, not what you are or what you do, and you deserve happiness." He couldn't change anything large scale —children raised in barracks by instructors and indoctrinated with fanatical loyalty, never seeing the limitless possibilities all free people had. He could affect small scale changes though, the way Vee pointed out the micro-shifts in cryptid patterns that led to bigger issues, like the windigo horde right after they met.

He'd introduce Vee and the team to real life, and broaden their horizons by increments every damn chance he got. He'd drag them with him as often as possible. To farmer's

259

markets, to his restaurants, to real food, and real outside connections. Fun for fun's sake, and eventually he'd let them see how real parents—i.e. his—treated their children.

He'd create a subtle layering, like a slow-simmered, all day sauce. It took time to incorporate each ingredient and develop flavors, but the process happened every time.

"How does this fit into your—I'm not even clear on what you think you're doing?" Vee tipped her chin at his list.

He took the fact that she hadn't walked away, or frog marched him to the truck and forcibly placed him inside as a positive sign. "I told you I wanted a real relationship, which means living together. Your career requires you to live here. Since you can't move in with me, I'll move in with you."

Josh choked on a gulp of sports drink. Bruce glared at him as Kimi pounded on her brother's back. Once Josh could breathe again, she hopped onto the bar and got comfortable.

He had no clue if she was fascinated by his proposal and hoped Vee agreed, or was calling dibs on a ringside seat to whatever she thought her sister was about to rain down on him.

Vee only watched him, eyes still unreadable, but an unmistakable tension in the set of her shoulders.

Liv arched a brow and he braced for her twisted streak, now undoubtedly invoked in defense of her sister. "There's no precedent or form for a civilian to essentially join a team, especially as a love interest. Plus, even for the reorganization of a team involving a Company agent, there's an assessment of qualifications and what the agent can bring to the team before approval is granted, and an overall assessment of team performance after."

Unlike Vee's, he read Liv's eyes perfectly. She was fucking with him, her payback for what he'd done to her sister. He deserved it. He also wasn't backing off.

"If there's a fucking form that allows for assets and

dating, they can damn well create one for living together. Tell them I stood in a historic landmark as live bait for a monster. I'm already fucking approved. If they disagree, I'll bring a hiring discrimination lawsuit against their asses."

Getting in on the let's-hold-Bruce's-balls-to-the-fire action, Kimi held up her phone to the group. His social media account was open on the screen, and Kimi flicked, sending a photographic string of different cities and different celebrities scrolling down.

It was Vee who spoke though. "You have a flourishing career, and even if you were willing to leave it, which you aren't, you also have a following. You can't disappear from public view without raising far too many questions. As you were quick to let me know, you have plenty of influential friends who would start some sort of investigation."

He grabbed his sketchbook from where he'd hastily dropped it on the counter when he entered the kitchen. A deep breath, and he held it out to Vee.

The wariness in her expression killed him. After a long minute, she took the pad.

"I can still do what I love." He estimated Vee was about thirty seconds from tossing the book in the trash and leaving him standing, and launched into his hard-sell explanation. "I never stay at one restaurant long. Now, that's my new platform. I'll go in specifically to revamp a stale or floundering restaurant's concept and menu, and consult on the same for new restaurants. I'll also do my own pop-ups. I'm a strong enough draw that other owners will invite me to boost their exposure and audience. I put out feelers last night and already have more offers than I can accommodate in the next year. Since you're based here, I will be too, and schedule my gigs as you rotate, or travel solo for a few weeks when it's somewhere outside your region."

Something dangerous altered Vee's posture from plain

straight to ramrod stiff, and he talked faster. "My fans won't think anything unusual is going on. As for my family, they won't let go of the misconception that I can't hold down a job, so I may as well put that assumption to good use. They'll take my traveling at face value."

Vee slapped his notebook against his chest, hard enough he grunted, and let go. He grabbed in a flutter of pages before it hit the floor and tossed it in the direction of the table. "Shit, Vee—"

"Seriously?" She paced the length of the kitchen, Josh and Liv backing away to give her space. "You told me, in great detail how you can't stand looking at the same people for more than a few months at a time, best case scenario. People bore you."

At the end of a pass, she spun and jabbed a finger in his face. "You couldn't manage to stay for a few lousy extra hours in order to tell me you were—oh, what was it again?" She switched and jabbed him in the breastbone. "Oh, that's right. You couldn't wait long enough to tell me you were leaving."

Taking his life in his owns hands, he caught Vee's and wrapped her fingers in his. "Most people do bore the fuck out of me, because they go through life asleep and complacent. That's never going to be a problem for us. You are life and curiosity distilled into human form. We both are. We take each other's energy and reflect it back, doubled."

She studied him, distrust heartrendingly clear.

He opened himself up, putting it all out there, every bit of himself he kept hidden, the parts he never showed anyone else. Letting Vee read it all, showing her the place she found inside him and unlocked. Betting on that connection they'd had from the first time they met each other's eyes. "Please don't slam the door on us."

"Why should I trust you?" she whispered. "How can I

trust anything you say when your actions are the exact opposite?"

"I want a future with you, both of us living our passions, along with the brand new passion that's us." His heart rate jacked higher. Beating hard enough it felt as if there would be a bruise in the middle of his chest as real as the one the anangoa had left on Vee's.

She pulled her hand away, and his heart went from too fast to a dead stop.

"Stay here." Vee walked out, taking the hall to her office, stride hard and ponytail swinging an angry punctuation to each footfall.

# CHAPTER 24

## VEE

*J* kept my focus on the one task I'd set myself. Tunnel vision was what a past instructor called it, when you narrowed the world to one objective, when it was something awful and you had to get through to the other side anyway.

All of the things Bruce was saying were perfect. I wanted to believe them. Which was precisely why I couldn't.

I'd been wrong once already. An agent might survive making a mistake once, if they were incredibly lucky. Smart agents, meaning those who survived, never made the mistake again. They learned from their fuck up, and incorporated the lesson on a cellular level. They *changed.*

I had made the mistake of wanting something new and non-Company, and of trusting Bruce when he acted like he did too. In return, he'd left without a backward glance.

I felt like a dirty-gray cloud enveloped me now. Insulating me from anything bright and happy.

A shroud.

It felt like a shroud, the thing that was once wrapped around the dead. I was physically okay. That wasn't the problem. I'd sealed off all the heartbreak, pain, and betrayal because I was still the C.O. My role was protecting my team by being the best leader possible. Compartmentalize the dead emotional part, wrap it up so it couldn't contaminate anything else, and keep going.

There was naïve, relationship-sad Vee who would get her team hurt. And there was C.O. Vee, who only let the emotions through that allowed her to do her job. Both parts would function better without Bruce and his tantalizing lies.

I grabbed my laptop, accessing HQ files. I pulled up the pages I needed and stalked back to the kitchen and the charade in progress. Bruce wasn't being cruel on purpose, but the results were the same. He'd proved he didn't understand us.

He didn't understand me.

I'd prove he didn't mean one word of his artistically sculpted speech and drawings, not as more than an impulse he'd regret immediately once reality intruded. It was better for both of us to cut this short. The proof was for him, and me. This would serve as my closure and lesson learned.

He stood exactly where I'd left him, his hands knotted into fists. Face as pale as before the anangoa mission, his frustration and hurt etched along the lines bracketing his lips.

Part of me ached to take his face in my hands and erase the hurt. To feel his lips on mine and the brush of his scratchy-soft beard. To revel in the way we fit together.

All fatal mistakes.

I held the tablet out to him. "Read this. Every paragraph."

The document wasn't lengthy. The Company didn't try covering hard facts in vague language.

Bruce accepted the device. Eyes traveling from line to line, scrolling to the next page and continuing the process before tabbing back to the beginning and re-reading.

Kimi butt-hopped closer to me, and Josh edged in, both lending me support. Liv's weight shifted to her dominant foot, her protective side triggered and ready to lay Bruce out once he refused. They all knew what the contract said.

Liv wouldn't really punch Bruce but only because knowingly injuring a civilian was forbidden. He had a short, uncomfortable escort to the truck in his immediate future though.

Bruce finally redirected his attention from the contract all new inductees signed to me. "Only answer one question, and then I'll sign anything you want me to. Do you love me?"

Maybe Bruce really was being intentionally cruel.

I tapped the screen hard enough Bruce grabbed it with both hands to prevent it from slipping and crashing to the floor. "In order for a civilian to become a member of the Company, you sign on for life. There's no changing your mind, no quitting, and it doesn't matter if your mom is a Supreme Court justice—there are no legal loopholes or outs. This commitment is. For. Life."

"Where do I sign?"

"This isn't a joke." I wouldn't, would not, cry over his pettiness even if I couldn't keep the tears out of my voice. "When I explained the Company's NDA and enforcement policy, it was nothing compared to the commitment joining us requires. They will never allow a civilian to access all that our work entails, then change their mind and leave with that vital information. It doesn't matter how loud and belligerent you get—once you sign? One and done."

"Do I sign a digital copy or do you need a physical signature? Never mind—I'll do both." He thrust the laptop at Liv. "Print off copies. Now, please. Right now."

"Damn it." I jerked the laptop out of his grip and folded it against my chest like a cruddy shield. "This is serious. You don't believe in us and what we do."

"I don't believe in the Company, at least, not in the uncritical, accepting way you do. You? You I believe in with all my heart and soul. I'm signing a commitment to you, and to us. That won't ever change and I won't ever regret it. If you love me, I'm in for life." His voice was ragged, as cut-up as I felt. "Please, Vee. Say the word and we're together. You know once I give my word, I don't go back on it. Not in the kitchen, not in trapping an anangoa, not in us creating a life together."

I shifted the case enough to free up one hand. I worried a hangnail even though it was already shredded. Opening my heart, risking what was left of it, scared me. Something told me it wouldn't be as simple as sectioning it off and continuing on if Bruce left again.

He stepped closer, a plea written in the slope of his shoulders and the hope on his face. He reached for the computer, gently prying it out of my grip. He propped it on the bar, opening it, and scrolling to the end of the contract. Then signed it with his finger, not even waiting to pop the stylus free. He held it out to Liv, only looking at me though. "Print copies, file this, whatever it is that happens next. If you don't reciprocate my feelings, fine. I'm not walking away though. I'll be here every damn time you get ready to roll out of that front gate, reminding you that you're more than a soldier."

I'd done lots of things that frightened me, because there was something worth the risk at the end. Becoming an agent was worth the risk. Becoming a C.O. was worth the work and risk.

"I love you." I didn't have the safety net of trainers or team for this one, but Bruce was worth the risk. "I love there being an *us*, and adding happy cheese and really expensive cleaning supplies to this compound."

I had to ask my family though, since this impacted us all. I checked with Liv, who nodded. Kimi signed a simple, "I called this from the first day he was here." Josh was too busy to answer, sniffling the way he did when the couple ended up together in *Pretty Woman.*

Liv plucked the computer and contract away and I faced Bruce. "It's unanimous."

"Fucking hell." Half exasperated, half tearing up, Bruce closed the last few inches between us. We still fit together like we were the last two pieces completing a puzzle.

His arms locked around me, heart beating fast against me, mine doing the same against his chest. Soft lips met mine. This kiss held every bit of Bruce's promise and hope and commitment, the real contract between us.

He lifted away enough to say, "I love you, Victoria Ramirez, Commanding Officer of Region Two, and I always fucking will."

When we finally came out of our bubble, Josh had the blender and tequila out. I was pretty sure Kimi was attempting to cut the limes into heart shapes. Liv perched on the stool at the bar, laptop open and typing away. I bet my signed *To All The Boys I've Loved Before* box set that she was drafting a letter to Legal, outlining our case for accepting Bruce, with pertinent data, dates, and a sample form she'd created on the fly.

Bruce tried glaring at Josh as the whir of the blender rose, but his lips quirked up, happy winning over grump. He nuzzled against my cheek. "This is what you want? Us, for always. This is another time when you have to be clear, and say it, no misunderstandings. If this was me bullying you..." His hand clenched mine like he couldn't help it, then loosened. "Be honest about that too. I'll deal."

I twined his fingers in mine. I so owed our friend Ridge a huge apology for doubting that civis could fill a hole in an agent's heart. "I love you, and yes, I want you in my life every day. I'd also like to get right on that list you mentioned last night, the one with the entry about having sex on every hori-zontal surface."

Bruce tightened his grip and pulled me toward the hall and the rooftop ladder. He bellowed over his shoulder "Liv! Add a decent queen size bed and a fucking expensive mattress to that list."

# EPILOGUE

## BRUCE

"*M*an, aren't you ready yet? You take longer than my brother, and he has seven different moisturizers," Josh whined.

"What the fuck did I tell you about privacy?" Bruce growled from his seat behind Vee's desk, concentrating on the files more than his new housemate. "Do I need to write the rules on your forehead in Sharpie this time?"

One of his first home improvement projects was a list of house rules, and yes, he damned well had made Josh sign them.

"I got it already. You aren't our cleaning service. When you're at a pop-up and we have a mission, I call as soon as we hit the truck seat afterward, or else my Kobe jersey is toast. Closed doors are closed for a reason," Josh quoted back to him.

"What else?"

"No shit junk food," Josh muttered, as sulky as one of Bruce's nieces. "That's still not cool. Sports drinks should get a pass. It says sports, right in the name."

"You'll survive, I promise," Liv said as she and Kimi joined

Josh. Both women were in short skirts, the opposite of their regulation uniforms, and both were crackling with party energy.

Kimi shoved at her brother from behind, propelling him down the hallway with hands on his shoulder blades like a medium-sized human bulldozer.

"B, come on. We're going to be late." Vee poked her head in the doorway, loose waves swinging and lights catching the streaks of mahogany in her hair. He'd never get his fill of looking up and seeing Vee and her energy shining back at him.

"You can't fucking be late for karaoke. Two more seconds while I finalize this pop-up schedule." Hastily, he closed out the last of the cryptid report files, copies now joining as many graphic mission photos, lab analyses, and internal office reports as he'd been able to locate and access.

He popped his thumb drive out and tucked it inside his idea sketchbook, the one place everyone in the compound respected his privacy, thanks to a couple of top-of-his lungs discussions on boundaries.

The drive was the beginning of his vow to protect Vee and the team. They believed, blindly, that the Company took the best possible care of its agents, as far as their hazardous vocation permitted. They couldn't imagine a scenario where the Company would sacrifice teams needlessly or for political agendas.

If that loyalty proved true, fine. If it didn't, he'd save Vee and her family by any means necessary.

The Company's motto was humanity first.

His motto was this team and humanity first. He dropped pad and digital insurance in the drawer Vee had allotted him, giving up a bit of her precious desk space, another example of her not thinking twice before sacrificing for others. He loved that selflessness as much as it terrified him.

He packed his worries away with the pad. Tonight was about a successful mission and celebrating because they could.

He skirted the desk and caught Vee's hand, twirling her in a graceful step and dip, then pulling her against him. "Let's go live a little."

* * *

READY FOR MORE REGION TWO?

If you enjoyed Vee and Bruce's story and want more of Region Two's cryptids, snark, found family, and steam, check out **Agent Down: The Region Two Series, Book 2 HERE. Or drop by my website at www.janetwaldenwest.com**

# ALSO BY JANET WALDEN-WEST

If you enjoyed Vee and Bruce's story and want more of Region Two's cryptids, snark, and steam, check out Book 2, **Agent Down: Region Two Series.**

## THE REGION TWO SERIES

Agent Alone: Region Two Series Prequel Novella .5

Agent Zero: Region Two Series Book One

Agent Down: Region Two Series Book Two

Agent of Chaos: Region Two Series Book Three

Visit and sign up for my newsletter to be the first to hear about giveaways, bonus content, and new releases!

Janet Walden-West Home

**Urban Fantasy Short Stories**

Road Trip in Chasing the Light Anthology

Stalking Horse in Witches, Warriors, and Wise Women

Glass Ceilings in Predators in Petticoats Anthology

**Contemporary Romance**

SALT+STILETTOS

# ACKNOWLEDGMENTS

As always, thanks to the best critique partners around—Jes, Kat, Mud, Cynthia, Gia, and Cath. None of whom have killed me despite my dropping last minute manuscripts in their laps, and begging them to do their magic ASAP.

All my gratitude to the amazing Anne Raven of Black Bird Book Covers, as well as to fabulous editor Jenny Lane, and the incredible PR teams at Psst Promotions and Let's Talk! Promotions.

To the GH group, especially the Omegas and our monthly Zoom accountability/cheerleading/problem-solving, you all helped make this series happen. And for Marty Mayberry and Tracy Brody, a thousand good karma points for your generosity.

Thanks to my sis, Amy, and other-sis Deb, for listening to endless rambling monologues concerning book plots and publishing world details, and to Cathy for creating a published-by-my-daughter-in-law bookcase display.

Finally, all my love to Mr. WW for his support, eye for details, and enthusiasm.

# ABOUT THE AUTHOR

Janet Walden-West lives in the Southeast with a pack of show dogs, a couple of kids, and a husband who didn't read the fine print. A Weird Dog Show Chick in her downtime, she's also a Pitch Wars Mentee/Mentor alum, and a Golden Heart finalist. She writes intersectional sexy-times romance, and boss-girl fantasy heroines.

She is represented by Eva Scalzo of Speilburg Literary Agency.

Visit and sign up for her newsletter to be the first to hear about giveaways, bonus content, and new releases!

www.janetwaldenwest.com

f  facebook.com/janetwaldenwestauthor
🐦  twitter.com/JanetWaldenWest
📷  instagram.com/janetwaldenwest
♪  tiktok.com/@janetwaldenwest

CPSIA information can be obtained
at www.ICGtesting.com
Printed in the USA
BVHW030128100123
655814BV00001B/3